I0645437

Age of Saints

Book Seven in The Druid's Brooch Series

Christy Nicholas

Green Dragon Publishing

Table of Contents

Chapter One

Cnoc an Dúin, Mide, Éire, 520 BCE

Conall let out a grunt as he struggled to lift the heavy stone block onto the wall. As he pushed it into the precisely cut space, he scraped his fingers, swallowing a yelp of pain. Once it fit flush against the edge, he panted in relief. His legs ached and he shifted his posture to stand at a different angle, alleviating the pain. He wiped sweat and his curly, black hair from his eyes with an already-soaked rag, glancing at his stepfather, Sétna, for approval.

The blond, burly man chuckled as he traced the thin line between the blocks, the dappled sunlight shining through the trees in a shifting pattern. "Not bad, boy. Not bad. Now, cut five more like that, place them along the wall, and we'll be done for the day."

Sétna whistled for his deerhound. When the gangly, gray dog bounded to his master, the man played with the dog for a few moments before settling on the wall to observe Conall prepare the next stone.

With a cough to clear the stone dust from his parched throat, Conall sat on the low stool in front of several rough-dressed blocks. He marked the edges to be cut with his chalk, whistling a spritely tune as he worked. The scent of stone dust tickled his nose, and he rubbed furiously to keep from sneezing.

Both Sétna and his hound, Grár, watched intently as Conall chiseled the sides of the stone block, sanded them smooth, and wrestled the heavy thing to the half-built wall.

As Conall dug his fingers beneath the block, lifting one edge, the dog scampered around him. He wished Sétna would call the hound away, but he daren't spend attention on the beast. With only a few scraped knuckles, he managed to lift the block high enough from the ground, inching it toward the next spot on the wall.

A sudden bark startled him, and his grip slipped. Despite scrambling to catch hold, the block slid away. He had no strength to stop the stone from falling, and Grár's sharp yelp made him wince.

The dog sprinted away, whining as he ran. At least the dog could run, which salved Conall's worst fears. Sétna thundered over him and boxed his ears. "Pay attention, you dolt! You could have killed Grár! I'm off to check his leg and you'd better finish before supper!"

Conall welcomed the pain to assuage his guilt. As his stepfather stalked off, Conall sat on the offending stone, head in his hands, worried about the dog. He saw no blood on the ground. Conall hoped the poor thing wasn't hurt too much. With a deep sigh and a glance toward where the hound ran off with his master, he stood to finish this stone.

While he greatly appreciated his stepfather's instruction and knowledge, Conall preferred to work alone, away from scrutiny. He worked much more quickly when no one was watching.

He carved the next stone to his stepfather's specifications, and now he needed to lift the errant block into its place. His eyes flicked around the clearing to ensure no one watched.

While closing his eyes, he drew upon the power of a magical brooch gifted to him by his real father. While the artifact was well-hidden in his sleeping alcove, Conall only needed to concentrate his will upon the magical object to draw on its strength. He willed the magic to flow through the ground, into his feet, up his legs, his body, and out through his hands.

The surge made his fingers tingle and he grew dizzy, but he braced himself against the power, directing it to the newly cut stone.

With the gentle touch of practiced magic, the stone rose to knee level, drifted to the wall, and settled into its place with a scrape. Conall opened his eyes and a grin spread across his face. Practice made perfect and, when his stepfather didn't lurk about, he could wield his magic with impunity.

A rustle behind him made Conall whirl, frightened that his power had been discovered, but the chittering of a squirrel made him sigh with relief. The squirrel darted away.

His father had warned him to always keep their secret close.

Conall swallowed a sudden surge of melancholy at the memory of his father. While Sétna cared for him, his sister, and their mother, Conall wished his father hadn't disappeared. That had been two years before, and he missed him with all his heart.

He shoved away the recollection of those heart-breaking days and wiped the sweat from his forehead as he bent to work the next stone. A few dry, lonely leaves drifted from the autumn trees. One landed on his stone, and he brushed it away irritably. He crouched next to the next stone and picked up his chalk. He had three more stones to carve and place before he could collect Lainn and return home for supper.

Conall's hand trembled as he marked out the lines. He growled with dissatisfaction, rubbed out the chalk and drew them again. Three times he drew the lines before they looked as straight as he could make them. Finally, he let out an exasperated breath, rolled his eyes, and reached for the mason's pouch of tools Sétna had lent him. He'd almost forgotten the string.

He rubbed the chalk along the thin jute rope, then held it taut against the side of the stone. With the lower end secured by his foot, he snapped the rope against the stone surface, causing the chalk to leave a faint line, straight as an arrow's flight.

Conall grinned at the clever trick, as he did every time he used it. In short order, he'd marked the rest of the stone's sides and carefully returned the string to the mason's pouch.

His freshly sharpened chisel and small hammer offered no tricks or shortcuts, so he spent the next hour carving the stone and refining the edge to fit into the wall. His sweat was coated with stone dust, making his skin gritty and itchy.

Once he'd dressed the stone, he brushed away the dust and surveyed his work. Then, after a quick glance around, he used his magic to lift it into place, taking a moment to wipe down his face and hands. With a long-suffering sigh, he sat beside the fourth stone.

Before he finished the fifth stone, the sun had dipped considerably lower in the sky, behind the dappled canopy of autumn trees. He ran his fingers along the straight cracks as Sétna had, marveling at the fine work he'd finally achieved. For two years, he'd practiced under his stepfather's exacting tutelage. While Sétna was a tough taskmaster, he gave clear instructions. Conall brushed away another coating of dust and smiled with pride.

With a sudden glance at the lowering sun, he hurriedly gathered his mason tools and wrapped them in the leather strapped bag. He'd better hurry if he wanted to meet Lainn at the crossroads.

The half-hour walk along the edge of the bog offered him little novelty, as he'd been exploring this area for many years. They hadn't been born here, but had moved when his father found the great fishing in *An Bhóinn*, the river skirting the ancient bogland. Conall didn't remember why they'd left his previous home, as he'd been too young to know much beyond their move. Lainn had only been a baby.

While she'd been a merry, laughing child, his little sister was growing more annoying with each year. He'd been heartily grateful when the druids had accorded her the signal honor of studying with them. Every day, she spent time in their oak grove, learning histories, songs, and chants. She'd used this new knowledge to torment him often, though he wouldn't let on how interesting he found the tales. If she realized he actually enjoyed them, she'd instantly stop and find another way to bother him.

He spied her dark auburn curls bouncing as she jumped, trying to reach a yellow apple hanging from a low branch. He chuckled and reached above her head, calmly plucking the prize and taking a big bite. In the last two years, he'd grown a full foot over his younger sister. He'd seen seventeen winters, but she'd only had sixteen.

"That's my apple, Conall! You've no right!"

He shrugged. "T-t-taller people get the better apples, Mouse. Height is right!"

"You know I hate that name! Give it!"

When she kicked at his shin, he skipped back, holding the apple above his head and out of her reach. "You can't catch me!"

She growled and charged him, but he laughed and ran. He spied another apple and picked it as he skipped by, so she'd have a treat when she tired of chasing him.

Lainn came close to grabbing his *léine*, so he put on a burst of speed. He couldn't let her win. He wove through the trees, zigzagging until he was panting. When he finally stopped near a small stream, she limped up, her freckled face red and sweating.

Conall offered the second apple as a peace offering with a wide grin. His sister snarled at him before snatching it from his hand. They crunched the sweet fruit in silence as the trickling brook sang. Bees buzzed around them, making Conall swat one away from his face.

"Don't hurt him!"

He blinked at his sister. "Him? Blood and bones. It's a bee, not a p-p-person."

"You should be kind to bees. Adhna says so."

Conall rolled his eyes. "Adhna's madder than a drunken hare."

She shrugged and took a final bite of her apple. "That doesn't mean he's wrong. Are you done yet?"

He tossed his core into the stream. "Sure. Ready to go home?"

She gave him a sly smile. "Not yet. I made a promise. Follow me!"

As she ran off to the north, the opposite direction from home, he let out a sigh and ran after her. He'd worked hard all day and had little energy or patience for his sister's antics. Her training with the druids must be less physically demanding than his own training as a mason, and she still had the endless energy of youth.

With a groan and a protest from his aching leg muscles, he felt every one of his seventeen winters as she led him on a merry chase through the glades.

Through several clusters of trees, along the edge of the bog, and through two clearings, Lainn led her brother. He knew exactly where she must be headed, so he slowed as the stitch in his side ached. She darted through a line of bushes into the shaded grove where bees buzzed in the slanted late afternoon sunbeams.

As a crumbling turf cottage came into view, another bee buzzed in his face, followed by three more, but he didn't swat these away. These were Adhna's bees and Adhna's home. To offer such an insult would be dangerous. The old man might act batty and scattered, but Conall sensed his hidden power. His father had often warned against angering those with power, be it mortal power or otherwise. Conall didn't dare to ignore any of his father's precious lessons.

When one bee landed on his nose, Conall froze, crossing his eyes to look at the creature. Lainn glanced back to see what had halted her brother and then let out a delighted laugh. She danced around him, chanting a nonsense song about bees, flowers, and honey. He glared at her and tried to swat her, but she skipped out of range and stuck out her tongue.

6

These antics caused the cottage door to creak open. Out stepped a spry man with dark hair and a few streaks of silver, using his elaborately carved oaken walking stick to help him down the rickety steps. Conall doubted he actually needed it, as he'd caught the man in some rather acrobatic acts in the past.

Adhna's long, intricately braided beard had several ornaments of silver and gold glinting in the light. His bright blue eyes laughed at their antics. "I see you've found Barnabus. He seems to have taken a shine to you, lad. Off now, Barnabus. Shoo! You've work to do before the sun sets."

The bee obeyed, and Conall's eyes ached from being crossed. He gave the old man a sheepish smile. "Good afternoon, Adhna. I hope our intrusion isn't too disruptive? I didn't know you named them all. Don't you run out of names?"

With an earnest chuckle, Adhna shook his head. "Not all, by the stones! No, never all. They won't stay still long enough for me to name them, mostly. But a few deserve our regard and respect. Barnabus, here, has helped me on several occasions. Would you like to hear one of his stories? Lainn, my dear child, do stop flitting about like a butterfly so I can see you."

Lainn nodded so hard, Conall feared her head would snap. The old man sat in the gnarled tree trunk he'd carved into a comfortable chair. The wood gleamed where his hands rested, showing many years of loving use. Lainn crouched next to a small circle of autumn flowers, playing with the petals as three more bees buzzed around her head.

Conall chose a mossy stone next to Adhna's cottage, noting the length of the shadows. They'd only have time for a short tale before they had to be home for supper. He didn't relish disappointing Sétna twice in one day, especially as he'd already felt his stepfather's heavy hand. Worse, their stepfather might decide Lainn needed a lesson.

Adhna cleared his throat and glanced around several times, searching for something. With a grunt of surprise, he stood, leaning on his staff, and climbed back into the cottage. Several moments later, he re-emerged with a full waterskin and three mugs.

"Today is a warm day for the late season. Would you two like some cool buttermilk? Here, child, hold the mugs while I pour."

Once all three had cool mugs in their hands, Adhna drank half of his down, wiped his mustache and lip with the back of his hand, and let out a sigh.

"Now, then. Now, then. Which story would most delight and amaze my young friends this day?" He tapped a gnarled finger against his lips and narrowed his eyes. Barnabus—or some other bee, as Conall had no way of telling them apart—flew into his long locks and buzzed in his ear. Cocking his head, Adhna nodded a few times. "Yes, that might be the best one, at least for now. It's a blessedly short tale, to be certain. Our dear Conall is in a hurry this evening, Barnabus. We must be cognizant of his eagerness to be home."

Conall regarded the bee with renewed interest. Did the bee really speak to the old man? Not that Conall believed Adhna to be a man in the strictest sense. Many anomalies hinted at some supernatural blood, if not a full blood Fae.

Long ago, maybe three or four years past, Conall's father, Fíngin, had given him many lessons on how to spot Fae. While Adhna didn't have the most common sign, the cat's eye pupils, other signs were apparent. Fíngin had spoken of an affinity for living things, be they creatures or plants. Still, while Adhna constantly spoke to both, a mad human might do the same thing.

Conall thought back to the day he'd offered to help the old man repair his apparently crumbling and decrepit cottage, to sand the moss from the stones and re-thatch the roof. Adhna had laughed, and lights danced around his head like fireflies. He drew the boy into the dim space.

"Come here, lad. Put your hand on your wall, just there. Hit it. Harder, boy, harder! You won't knock it down. It's as solid as they come. Now, see up there, in the thatch?"

8

Conall had to admit the stones felt solid beneath his hands. The thatch was full of growing things and drying herbs. Insects and birds crawled in the straw, but none of this bothered Adhna. No cobwebs or mold grew within the straw, only healthy plants and vibrant creatures.

While the cottage looked decrepit, it had more living strength than many. This alone made him think Adhna must have some Fae blood. He'd only known the man for a few years, since his father disappeared. In that time, Conall had witnessed more magic and unexplained things than in his entire lifetime, short as that had been.

The only other magic he'd seen had been his father's.

Memories came crashing through despite Conall's resolve, flooding him with emotion and pain.

One spring morning several years ago, Fíngin had brought Conall to an empty glade on the edge of the bog. Several faerie stones stood in a circle, which Conall recognized as dangerous. No one wished to be caught in their spell. And yet, his father sought them out.

As the bright morning sun struggled to pierce through thick fog, beams of gray-gold mist caressed them in the center of the circle. No birds yet stirred in the damp air as his father sat cross-legged and gestured for his son to sit.

His father removed a wrapped piece of white linen from his pocket with extreme care. One by one, he opened the folds to reveal an exquisitely carved brooch inlaid with blood-red gems. Dancing animal forms entwined in gold and silver. A sunbeam broke through the mist to highlight the brooch, making it glow like magic. Fingin's heart raced at the wonder of it all.

"We have a legacy, my son, that dates back to your great-great-grandmother. She helped a creature of the Fae escape from a fate worse than destruction, and for that aid, he gifted her this brooch."

Impelled by the shining treasure, Conall reached out to touch the prize. However, his father pulled it away. "Not yet, my son. I must give it to you soon, as my health is failing, but I must prepare you first. Rise."

As they scrambled to their feet, the sun cleared only the center of the circle. The glade remained shrouded in silence.

His father led Conall around the outside of the stones, sunwise, slowly marching and trailing his hand across each stone in a loving caress. Conall did the same, amazed at how warm and dry the stones felt, despite the lingering fog and the chilly air.

When they'd completed three circuits, the center of the stones glowed like embers in a sullen fire. His father beckoned him inside the circle.

Conall didn't want to enter, but his father pulled him in. "Don't worry, son. The magic is attuned to us now. It won't harm you."

With a swallow, the boy straightened his shoulders and walked within, not daring to breathe. The brooch burned bright. Shafts of blood-red light pulsed from the scarlet stones like a living heart.

His father held out the sanguine jewel, and with only a moment's terrified hesitation, Conall took it.

A visceral pulse pushed from the ground, up through his bones and into his mind. The heartbeat of the world echoed through Conall's head, and grew into a painful, silent scream, like a sharp edge upon raw nerves.

Just as he thought he'd go mad from the pain and the sound, the entire world screeched to a stop. Conall collapsed into a pile on the ground, letting out a whimper, and everything went gray.

When he finally regained his wits, he cracked his eyes open and glanced at the brooch in his palm. It no longer shone with preternatural light, and the gemstones had turned to an ominous black.

His father patted him on the shoulder. "That means the brooch has accepted our transfer, son. The magic and the jewelry belong to you. There are several rules you must abide as a holder of the brooch."

"Wh-what rules?" Before he touched the brooch, he'd never stuttered. Now, he attributed that habit to the magic he'd received. Some days, he wished he had neither.

His father gave him a fierce hug. "Good lad. First, keep it secret. Christians are gaining much power in the land, and they get violent against anything that smacks of old magic. They've committed horrible deeds on the continent. Secret is safer."

Conall gulped but nodded. "What else?"

"Second, the brooch gifts each holder a particular magical power."

Conall glanced at the jewel in his hand with renewed apprehension. "What sort of p-power?"

With a shrug, his father said, "I don't know, lad. My talent is the ability to communicate with animals. You'll have to experiment to find your own talent."

Conall's mind swam with the possibilities, but his father's words brought him back to task. "Third . . ." His father stared off into the distance where the mists swirled and thinned before the rising sun. "Third, when you see your own death approaching, you must pass the brooch and the magic to someone of our own blood, lest it be lost to this world forever."

Coldness gripped Conall's heart, and in the following weeks, his father had wasted to a thin copy of his former self, pale and wan as a changeling. He no longer had the strength to cast heavy fishing nets into *An Bhóinn*, and finally refused to eat or drink.

Several moons after the brooch gift, on a dismal, rainy morning, his sister Lainn ran to his bed in tears, burying her face in his chest. Conall held her tight, but couldn't understand her words, she sobbed so hard. Finally, she sniffed in and swallowed. "He's gone! Da is gone!"

"G-g-gone? What do you mean, gone? He's just at the river, checking his nets."

"No! I looked at the river. I searched each bank, all the way up and down."

Conall scowled at his little sister. "Lainn! Don't do that alone! You could have slipped in the mud!"

She shoved at his chest but had no power behind the angry gesture. "It doesn't matter! He's gone! He left us!"

When the import of her words finally penetrated, Conall's heart broke. He hugged his sister tight as they both bawled.

When their mother woke, she refused to speak about their father. For her to be so silent on the issue, he must have left with her knowledge. No matter how many times Conall tried to talk to her, she pressed her lips together and ignored him.

Less than a season later, she'd married Sétna, and the entire family moved upriver to a larger roundhouse near the quarry.

Tears brimmed behind Conall's eyes, and his throat grew tight. He drank a sip of the now-warm buttermilk to ease the blockage, but it hurt when he swallowed. He blinked several times to disperse drops on his eyelashes.

Adhna clapped his hands as part of his story, bringing Conall's attention back to the present. This time, he successfully pushed the pain away. "And then the raven swooped down to catch the bees, but Barnabus, here, he let loose with his trap! Let me tell you, that raven never bothered Barnabus's hive again."

The young man grinned at the old man's storytelling theatrics. His sister clapped her hands in delight and turned to Conall, her face glowing with joy. She loved tales, any tales, and devoured them like a starveling. He would have thought she'd get her fill of stories and histories at druidic training, but evidently, her desire was endless.

Conall sighed and glanced toward their home, worrying about getting a beating for being late.

The old man scratched his beard, eyeing Conall's expression. "Ah, I see your brother staring at the shadows again, child. It seems you must be off to the mundane humdrum again. Off, then, shoo!"

Feeling like Barnabus the bee, Conall grabbed his tool bag and tied it back onto his belt. He didn't remember when he'd taken it off, but he mustn't lose it. The fine tools had been an expensive gift from Sétna, necessary for his apprenticeship in the mason trade.

He took his sister's hand and led them both away, as Adhna spoke intently into his beard. Conall thought something had moved within.

Lainn bounced as she walked, her arms swinging. "Let's not go home right away, Conall. Let's find something for Ma! She loves blackberries. Can we bring her some blackberries?"

Despite their tardiness, Conall nodded. "They should b-b-be ripe and juicy. Do you think the p-patch down near the bend will be untouched?"

In answer, she yanked his hand until he laughed and ran after her. They pelted across the hilly grass, dodging random boulders and leaping over low walls. When he found the bare bramble patch, he let out a grunt. Birds had denuded most of the berries, but then he spied a cluster still hanging within the thorny bush.

They made a small pouch of the sweet berries, and by the time they'd finished, his hands were sticky and stained purple.

He glanced at the sun and spat a word he knew his stepfather would smack him for using. "Time to run!"

They turned right into the solid barrel chest of Tomas, a boy several seasons older than Conall. "Going somewhere, C-C-C-Conall?"

Conall backed up several steps, shoving Lainn behind him. Tomas grinned and Conall envied him the even white teeth as one of his own front teeth grew crooked.

He clenched his fists and scanned the area for an easy escape. One of Tomas' cronies had blocked the best route from the clearing. He glanced back the way they'd come, but Tomas laughed. "Little C-C-Conall's going to run! Be sure you don't trip over your feet as often as you trip your tongue, little stutterer!"

The larger boy shoved Conall's chest, and he stumbled back, but Lainn caught him. Quick as a fox, she ducked under Conall's flailing arm and punched Tomas square between the legs.

"Oof!" The brute doubled over, and Lainn scooted off the way they'd come. Conall hurried after her with just one backward glance.

Tomas's friend helped him to the ground, yelling nasty names after them, but at least they'd escaped. For now.

"You shouldn't have hit him, Lainn. He'll make you pay for that, you know it."

She skipped backward, her head cocked, and sang, "He has to catch me first!"

With another turn, she darted faster, curving around the edge of the wood, so they curved back toward their home. They'd be very late, and Conall dreaded their arrival.

The sun had set by the time the forest opened to reveal their home. Their thatched-roof roundhouse had several outbuildings attached, with stacks of quarried stone piled to one side. A kitchen garden and an animal pen stood around the back. The tall limestone hill next to them had supplied the stone, the mason's reason for moving to this spot.

Conall halted, suddenly fearful of his stepfather's wrath, but Lainn cast him a half-smile and skipped right in. "Ma! We brought you blackberries, see?"

With a deep breath, Conall squared his shoulders and ducked through the doorway. He'd grown in the last few years, almost a head taller than Sétna, but he weighed half as much. He stumbled on the step and gripped the doorframe, adjusting his eyes to the dim interior.

Sétna sat at the head of the huge wooden-block table, scowling into a mug of small ale. He glanced up when Lainn opened her bundle of blackberries, but his eyes then slid to Conall. With a duck of his head, Conall avoided his stepfather's glare.

Their mother echoed Sétna's scowl and began her evening chatter. "You should have been here ages ago. Look at the state of you! Purple stains all over your hands. Lainn, you've torn your *léine*. What have you been doing, diving into the brambles? You are well old enough to know better than this. You aren't a child any longer. With sixteen winters and our status, you must take better care for your appearance! You aren't a lowly fisherman's daughter any longer. You're a young woman with good standing of almost marriageable age and worth a considerable bride price. Off to the well to clean up. And you, Conall! Still covered in stone dust? I swear, between you and Sétna, I'll be breathing that dust the rest of my days. Go clean yourself as well! Your stew is cold."

With a wry smile at their mother's fussing, Conall led his sister to the well. The cold water made him gasp, but they made certain to clean their faces, hands, and the worst of the berry stains.

Cold stew would be better than being sent out a second time, a result completely within their mother's custom if they didn't wash well enough. Not that their mother's stew would ever be tasty, even hot.

As they sat on their stools and shared a rye loaf, Sétna still said nothing. The heaviness of his stepfather's regard grew leaden on Conall's shoulders as he concentrated on chewing and swallowing a piece of roast turnip. The lamb had a piece of bone, but he surreptitiously removed it before he cracked a tooth.

Their mother had always provided plenty of food, even as a lowly fisherman's wife, but she had no skill at cooking. He'd had much better meals at Adhna's house, and the old man barely cooked, preferring fruit and cheese to meat.

His mother cleared her throat, and Conall peered up to see her staring pointedly at him. At a loss, he glanced toward his sister, but she stared at him. He covertly wiped his face in case he'd dribbled stew on his chin.

His stepfather's voice fell flat upon the silence. "Conall."

With his heart racing, Conall lifted his gaze to Sétna. The older man's jaw twitched with tension, and Conall suspected he'd done something wrong.

"Yes, Father?"

"I must travel to *Maelblatha* tomorrow. The blacksmith here is a feckless idiot, so I'm going to my uncle for some new iron tools. Teaching you has worn my chisels down twice as quickly as normal."

Conall waited. Sétna hadn't asked a question and therefore wouldn't appreciate a response.

His face warmed with embarrassment as his stepfather stared at him for several moments before continuing. "Normally, I'd take an apprentice with me on such a mission. However, I've no interest in making a several-day journey with a thankless child. Therefore, you'll remain here."

Conall nodded and shifted his gaze to his plate. He had to resist the urge to smile. Not only had he anticipated something far worse, but his stepfather's news came as more of a relief than a punishment.

Lainn kicked him under the table, and he gritted his teeth to keep from yelping. He glared at her, but she simply ate her stew as if nothing had happened.

After they ate, Conall helped his mother with the cleaning while Sétna took Lainn out to the stable to help him check the horse for the trip.

His mother used one finger to lift his chin, though he'd grown taller than her. "Conall, my child, are you upset about not going tomorrow?"

He shook his head and gently batted her hand away. "No, not really. I mean yes, I'd love to travel, but I'd rather do so with someone—" He swallowed and glanced at the door, unwilling to speak of his dislike of his stepfather.

"Conall, be cautious. You're smarter than that."

"Yes, Mother."

In painful silence, they washed the bowls.

Lainn still hadn't returned by the time he finished helping Mother. Conall's body ached from crouching and chiseling all day, followed by running, Tomas's shove, and the tension at supper.

When Lainn finally tiptoed into the darkened roundhouse and crawled into her alcove, he whispered, "What kept you, Mouse?"

In the gloom, he only saw her form as a deeper black against the edges of the night. "Nothing. I'm tired."

"Why did Sétna keep you so long? Did you find something wrong with the horse? Has his fetlock healed enough for the journey?"

"Go to sleep, Conall."

Her tone brooked no argument. She sounded very like their mother when she was upset and tried to hide it. He didn't like that, nor what it might mean, one bit.

Conall glanced back out of the alcove and across the murky darkness to where his mother and stepfather shared an alcove. Murmured voices with undercurrents of annoyance drifted across the silent space, but he couldn't make out the words.

Anger and fear bubbled inside Conall, crowding out his sense of place and propriety. He clenched his fists and thanked the gods his stepfather would leave in the morning. Sétna was double his mass, but if he hurt Lainn, the older man would feel Conall's retribution.

Chapter Two

By the time Conall woke the next morning, Sétna had left on his mission. Their mother had prepared their morning meal and was working in the garden. Lainn's cot was empty, blankets in habitual disarray.

He dressed and grabbed a bowl of porridge, pouring more honey than he'd normally be allowed. Without Sétna to glare at him, he felt wild and free.

Female voices in the garden lured him outside, and he found his mother arguing with a boy. No, not a boy—Lainn, dressed in Conall's old clothing.

"I will not have you traipsing around like a vagabond, young lady! Get back into that roundhouse and change into a proper woman's *léine*. I should have burned Conall's old things as soon as he grew too tall for them. You look ridiculous!"

Conall chuckled and their mother spun to glare at him. "Conall, don't you think she looks ridiculous?"

He scraped the last glop of his porridge and ate it, taking time to circle his sister. Conall inspected her from each angle, the corner of his mouth screwed up in concentration and evaluation. "I think she looks natural as a young lad, Mother. Without a beard, it's difficult, but give her warrior's braids and a proper belt, she could just pass. Maybe rub some dirt on her chin to make it like stubble."

His mother sighed with exasperation and threw up her hands. "You're worse than she is. I will not allow our family to be open to mockery for. . . this. . . deviance. March right back into your cot and change your clothes, Lainn. I'll not hear another word about this."

Lainn sighed and rolled her eyes. "Yes, Mother." She didn't seem as contrite as she sounded, and Conall noticed a twinkle in his sister's eyes, so he followed her back into the roundhouse.

He cleaned his bowl and found her in her alcove, dressed in her own clothes and calmly folding his old *léine* into her carry-sack. She glanced up as he watched and winked at him.

He rolled his eyes. "Are you ready? We're running late already."

"I'm just about ready."

"Lainn? About last night—"

She stood up and threw her bag over her shoulder. "Let's go." She affixed a steely gaze on him, forbidding further inquiry. He really wished she didn't seem so much like Mother when she did that.

The walk to the oak grove was short on words but rich in birdsong. The autumn sun had burned through the morning haze already, and flickering puddles of sunlight dappled the leafy path. Lainn skipped from sunlit spot to sunlit spot, laughing as she hopped.

Conall followed in a more dignified manner, hiding a smile at her antics. Whatever had bothered her the night before didn't affect her now. Lainn whistled at a dove, which warbled back to her, and they held an incomprehensible conversation while he caught up to her.

"C'mon, Lainn. I thought you wanted to get to the grove on time?"

"Time is fluid in the grove. I told you that."

She'd never told him any such thing, as far as he recalled. But arguing with his sister when she got inscrutable never resulted in clarity, so he grunted and walked in the right direction, trusting her to follow when her whimsy allowed.

He'd only gone a few steps before she raced past him, jumped a fallen log, did a somersault in the middle of the path, and ran forward, arms up and head back. Just as Conall thought she'd run smack into a tree, she wove to the left, then to the right, twisting through the obstacles like a fish in a stream.

"Catch me if you can, Turtle!"

With a roll of his eyes and a long-suffering sigh, Conall concentrated on his measured steps. His legs ached from yesterday, and he had no wish to chase her this morning, no matter how fine the weather.

"Aren't you going to run after her, Conall?"

He whirled at the coy feminine voice to spy Aoife leaning against a tree, her arms crossed. She looked at him from under lowered lashes, and her bright red *léine* and white-blonde hair shone so brightly in the morning sun, he couldn't understand why he hadn't seen her from leagues away.

After pushing off against the tree, she sauntered toward him, her hips swaying. "I rarely see you wandering the woods at this time of day, Conall. What brings you so close to our farm? Could you have been hoping to spend time with me?"

Now barely an arm-span away, she lifted one finger and traced his cheek down to his chin.

He swallowed as his skin pebbled. "No, I'm j-just walking Lainn to the grove. In f-fact, I've lost sight of her, and best c-c-catch up."

Conall turned away, but Aoife's hand caught his arm. "Surely, you can tarry a few moments? I won't bite, you know."

He shook his head hastily. "No, no, we're already much t-too late. I'm so sorry, Aoife."

"Ah, another time, then." She kissed him on the cheek, a butterfly touch.

He hurried off, trying to make sense of the tingling in his nether region, at odds with his distaste of the encounter. He found Lainn picking wildflowers of purple and yellow in a small glade.

She glanced up with a puzzled frown. "What *have* you been doing, brother? You're red as the setting sun."

He let out a growl and grabbed her arm. "We need to go, Lainn."

Finally, the grove entrance came into view. While the druids never built a structure to study or worship within, they had encouraged trees to grow into an arched tunnel, and that led to their meeting place.

He'd only come this far a few times since Lainn had begun her lessons last spring, yet the archway never failed to impress him. Even in the autumn, with leaves fading from their summer glory into crunch brown, the tunnel loomed to cut off the bright sunlight. He shivered, thinking of the frightening mysteries that might lie through that darkened path.

Lainn tugged at his arm. "Aren't you coming in? I want you to hear me sing today."

He yanked his hand from her grip, taking several steps back. "Come in? Lainn, I can't go in there! I'm no druid acolyte!"

She pursed her lips. "The proper term is *fochlac*. After several winters studying the basics, I'll move to the next rank. That's the—"

He held up his hand. "I didn't ask for a lesson, Lainn, and I'm not going in there." He eyed the darkened entrance and shivered.

"*Scared*, are you? Conall is scared of trees! Trees!" She bounced around him, grabbing his hand again and turning him in a circle.

Conall's heat rose in mortified embarrassment. "I am not!"

With an over-sweet smile, she clapped her hands once. "Then you *will* come! Wonderful!"

He didn't resist when she pulled him in this time, but he closed his eyes as they went through the tunnel. With relief, when they emerged on the other side, the welcome warmth of the morning sun shone on his face. He was glad no one else had witnessed his cowardice.

Despite his fears, he peered around the clearing with great interest. A circle of ancient oaks surrounded an empty glade, perfectly groomed and precisely maintained.

Each massive tree grew gnarled and twisted, like old men curled with bone-ache, leaning heavily on their walking staves. Faces glared at him from within the knotted bark, and he glanced back at the tunnel, wondering how long it would take him to run back through it.

Lainn laughed. "Those are just the guardians. They won't hurt you, not if you don't insult them."

What would insult a tree? A non-druid coming into the glade? His desire for flight grew stronger.

"Come *on*, Conall. The beehives are this way."

Conall kept glancing back at the formidable sentries with trepidation until they were no longer in sight.

They wended through the woods on a path invisible to Conall. Lainn seemed to know exactly where to go, though, and led him through several twists and turns until the trees opened to another clearing. This one stood full in the mid-morning sun, buzzing with bees and late summer wildflowers. The entire area dripped with white, purple, and yellow flowers, and he daren't step lest he tread on the busy insects.

He wondered vaguely if any of these bees knew Barnabus.

"Walk around the edge, Conall. See that man over there? He's my mentor. His name is Gemmán. Haven't you met him before?"

Conall glanced at the tall druid, wearing a threadbare brown *léine* and a frown. His long black hair hung in a dozen braids, each one decorated with flowers and amber beads. Entwined markings of blues and greens circled his arms, legs, and up around one side of his face. He didn't seem particularly old but had an air of confidence and gravitas around him. Conall wondered how the sprightly and silly Lainn got along with such a serious teacher.

His sister bounced toward him. "Gemmán! Gemmán, look who I brought!"

The druid looked up, giving the impression of a very hooked nose and a long face. The saturnine lines of the man's face broke into a joyful smile at the sight of Conall's sister.

With the help of an elaborately carved rowan staff, esoteric symbols limned in blue and disappearing in a spiral, he got to his feet. Two other young men sat with him, one with white-blond flyaway hair and a scowl, and the other with curly black hair like himself.

Gemmán opened his arms wide. "Lainn! My precious flower. I despaired of seeing you this fine morning. What a shame that would have been, as the gods have smiled on us this day. Come, come, sit in your spot. This must be your esteemed sibling, Conall?"

The man held out his hands in greeting, palms up. Flustered, Conall covered them in the appropriate manner. "I greet you, Druid Gemmán."

"Just Gemmán, my lad. We stand on no ceremony with outsiders within our grove. These promising young lads are Ernán and Laisrén. Have you come to see your sister take her final test as a *fochlac*?"

Conall turned to stare at his sister, who perched daintily on a moss-covered rock and blinked at him in pretended innocence. "Final test? You never told me that, Lainn!"

She gave him a shrug. "You never asked."

He glowered but found a grassy spot to sit next to the blond, Ernán, and wrapped his arms around his knees. Both boys nodded in greeting and promptly ignored him.

Gemmán cleared his throat and turned to Lainn. "In your own time, child."

At first, Conall heard nothing but the faint hum of bees and water trickling somewhere out of sight. Then the overall buzz of the glade fell to complete silence—a silence so heavy, his ears ached.

The faint whisper of a tune drifted from Lainn. Calling it a tune might have given it too much credit. He didn't recognize his sister's voice. The tune seemed like birdsong, but no avian he'd ever heard.

He closed his eyes as her delicate voice drifted up and down, gently like a lazy river wending through the rolling hills. The sound tickled his ears and caressed his soul. His chest tingled with the desire to fly into the hazy air and ride the dust motes until the sun set.

When he opened his eyes again, every bee in the glade surrounded his sister. His heart leapt in panic, but a glance at Gemmán calmed him. The druid sat in tranquil approval, nodding his head. Conall couldn't see one inch of his sister under the blanket of buzzing yellow and black.

When the song drifted into silence once again, Conall felt an intense longing for the sound to return. His heart felt empty, forever bereft of the joy of her voice, her music, and the freedom it urged upon him.

Tears ran unchecked down his cheeks.

Gemmán clapped, startling the bees away from Lainn. "Well done, child, well done! You've learned this stage even more quickly than I'd imagined, even more quickly than my husband did. As much as I love him dearly, Olchobar made a reckless mistake the first time and got stung right on the nose!"

That elicited a chuckle from the brown-haired lad, Laisrén. "You've demonstrated your ability to recite the first thirty histories with the added talent of singing to the bees. Despite what the others say, I'm thrilled to confer upon you the title of *iníon fuirmedh*. Congratulations on graduation to the second tier! We must celebrate."

Her cheeks grew flushed at his praise.

Ernán scowled but his companion shot an elbow into his ribs, and both boys congratulated Lainn with mostly sincere smiles and claps on her shoulders.

Conall didn't know what to say to his sister. She'd only been with the druids for two seasons. He thought each stage of the druid education took several years. He'd never really considered Lainn to be particularly smart, but perhaps she'd been hiding her talent all along.

A surge of sudden envy shot through Conall at his sister's singing talent and the obvious approval of her mentor. He'd ached for that sort of praise from his stepfather since the first time he'd picked up the mason tools.

He shoved that envy down as an ungrateful and ungracious notion and hugged Lainn tight. She trembled in his embrace, and only then did he realize how nervous she must have been.

Conall held her at arm's length and stared into her eyes, suddenly glad she'd insisted on his coming to witness her trial. "You make me proud, little sister. Da would be proud, too."

He choked back any more words and hugged her tight again as the bees buzzed merrily around their heads. Sunlight faded as a cloud covered the light, dipping them into cool shadows.

Gemmán clapped a hand on his shoulder. When he turned, the older man grinned fit to crack his face. "And you, young man? Have you a voice akin to your sister's, to charm the creatures of the forest?"

With a nervous laugh, Conall shook his head. "N-n-no, not at all. I c-croak more like a frog."

Both boys twittered until a glare from Gemmán quieted their mockery. "Ah, well, I'm certain you've your own talents. Everyone has something they can do. What's your specialty, then?"

With the man's intense green eyes staring through him, Conall could only remember his father's insistence to keep the brooch's magic safe and secret. Could the druid see his secret? His heart raced as he stammered, "St-stone-working. My stepfather is t-t-teaching me."

Gemmán narrowed his eyes and continued to stare at him. "Intriguing. Intriguing indeed. Well, I'll not press you to speak of it. Come, it's time to celebrate your sister's success. Will you join us for mead? It's the least we can offer as your sister's trial involved bees."

Ernán begged off. "Our father is expecting us for supper, honored teacher."

"Go then, lads. I'll see you on the morrow. Your test is next, remember! See if you can do as well as our dear girl here."

As the boys left, the blond shot a glare of pure hatred at Lainn, but she remained oblivious. The obvious threat made Conall clench his fists and stare at the young man as he disappeared among the trees.

Gemmán placed a hand on his shoulder. "A druid should never seek a violent solution, lad."

"Good thing I'm not a druid then, isn't it?" Conall ducked his head and glanced at Lainn, but she had a butterfly on her finger and brought it up to her face. The insect alighted on the bridge of her nose, and she crossed her eyes, trying to keep it in sight.

When it flitted away, she giggled and twirled in place, her arms flung out for balance. Conall had to smile at the sight of his sister back to her cheerful, silly self once again.

The three of them strolled out of the bee-loud glade and to a series of small fountains. Each one fell into the next one down a hill, through a ladder of several decorative stone cataracts. The trickling water drowned out the buzzing bees and the air cooled under the canopy of trees. A faint breeze rustled leaves as a few yellow ones drifted down into the fountains.

Gemmán opened a small cupboard cleverly built into the side of the fountain stones and pulled out three stone mugs. "Normally, I'd put the waterskin in the fountain for a while, to cool off the drink. However, I think we should celebrate while we can. Does anyone object?"

Hearing no protests, the druid untied the waterskin from his belt and poured them each a mug of sweet, warm mead.

Conall had only tried mead twice before. First, at his mother's wedding to Sétna, a day so fraught with stress and celebration, he couldn't remember exactly what happened during the ceremony.

The second time had been just a month before, when Aoife snuck some from her father's supply, daring him to quaff the entire cup in one gulp. After much cajoling, he'd given in, though he'd coughed with the syrupy heat of the alcohol. After he'd won his dare, she'd grown uncomfortably friendly, rubbing her hand along his hip and caressing his upper leg.

Conall had grown flushed, whether from the drink or from her attentions. When her hand inched toward his nether regions, he'd stuttered some poor excuse and run away.

His cheeks flushed again, either at the embarrassing memory or the alcohol. Either way, he no longer felt the chill of the shaded fountain glade. Gemmán and Lainn chatted about her next steps in her education, so he stood and wandered, studying the fountain construction.

The stones appeared to be rough hewn and poorly set, covered in moss and yellow and white lichen. However, when Conall traced his finger along the spaces between the stones, he realized how precisely they fit together. Someone had cut each one to the shape of the next stone, irregular as they were rather than uniform blocks. Conall appreciated the planned chaotic beauty.

The stone puzzle construction fascinated him, and he studied how the pieces fit together and how they balanced physical space and visual beauty. Conall ached to try such a construction, but he knew without a doubt Sétna would never agree to such an artistic variation on the basic mason's work. He didn't seem to appreciate unusual beauty.

A splash of cool water in his face made him shake it off and glare at Lainn, who stood on the other side of the fountain, a mischievous grin on her face. Instead of reacting, Conall wiped his face calmly and gave her a half-smile. "Thank you, kind sister. The mead made my f-face too warm. The chill is a welcome respite."

Judging from her frown, his unwillingness to answer her mock attack displeased her. Still, when she glanced back at Gemmán, cleaning out his mead mug, she nodded with calculated patience. Conall knew exactly what that meant.

She'd get him back, but not now, not yet. He'd have to watch his back for the next few days. Her revenge would be creative and unexpected.

Better to give her as little opportunity as possible. "I should get back, Lainn. Mother'll need my help on the farm, since I've no duties with Sétna today. Will you need me to come to fetch you at the usual hour?"

She gave him a nod as Conall turned to Gemmán. "Thank you, D-d-druid Gemmán, for allowing me to be part of my sister's trial today. I greatly appreciate the honor."

He gave a small bow and turned, uncertain how to exit the grove to an area he knew. With a sheepish grin, he turned back. "Uh. . . how do I find my way out?"

Gemmán gave a low chuckle. "See the river? Just follow that, lad. It meets up with *An Bhóinn* about a league north of here. You should find your way home from there."

Resisting the urge to knock himself on the forehead for his own idiocy, Conall nodded in formal thanks and walked along the riverbank.

More clouds chased the first, and soon the sun hid behind a solid bank of gray. By the time he reached familiar ground, the day had cooled enough to make his skin pebble, and he rubbed his arms.

He'd been foolish to wander around the countryside in early autumn without something warm to wear. More clouds gathered and he glanced up several times, waiting for the first drops of rain.

The anticipated downpour never come, but when he approached his house, someone stood in the front yard, staring at the door. From the back, Conall recognized Adhna, his ragged brat dangling with several pine needles and a tiny pinecone.

Conall came up behind the old man, asking, "Adhna? Were you looking for me or for Lainn? She's at her lessons."

The man didn't turn but continued to stare at the door. "There's something amiss here, lad. Not yet, but soon."

Confused, Conall stood next to him. "Not yet? I don't understand. If something's wrong, isn't it wrong now?"

The old man shook his head. "Time isn't so straight, my boy. Not in the slightest. Still, you should be strong enough to cope with the change."

Just as Conall turned to ask for clarification, his mother emerged from the barn, her hair pulled up in a messy bun and two full milk pails in her hand. "And just where have you been, Conall? I've been looking for you. I need your help, now. Your father's due back soon, and I've only half the chores done. Oh, I suppose you've been dallying with. . . with this."

She flicked her hand at Adhna as if trying to shoo away a horsefly. The old man grinned, showing a few ragged brown teeth. "Ah, Ligach, you're looking well."

She looked him up and down, her lip curling. "I realize you had dealings with my husband before he died, old man, but in case you haven't noticed, I've remarried. My new husband is much higher status. It wouldn't do to cater to vagabonds and miscreants, and I'll not have my household sullied by such as you."

Adhna raised his eyebrows while Conall's mouth dropped open, horrified at his mother's rude words.

The old man cleared his throat and his tone was kind. "Ligach, I'd never cause you grief. You enjoy your new husband, but I've a duty of care for the lad here, as well as his sister. I vowed to Fíngin that I'd watch over them both, and I do not break my vows. You should be well aware of this."

She put both her pails down and crossed her arms, glaring at Conall until he dropped his gaze and shuffled his foot on the path.

His mother's scowl deepened. "Fine. You can watch after them from afar. I'll not have you in my house, you filthy thing. Now go."

"As you wish, good lady." Adhna nodded, and before Conall could look up, he'd vanished. Was the old man really that quick? Or had Conall lost time? This wouldn't be the first time he'd missed a few minutes of memory, but it didn't happen often.

"You, young man, need to muck out the stables and feed the pigs. Now."

With a quiet voice, Conall answered. "Yes, Ma."

"I told you before to call me Mother now. Ma is for peasants and fisherfolk."

"Yes, Mother."

While he swept out horse manure and old straw from the stable, Conall tried to make sense of the confrontation. His mother cared a great deal for appearances and status, even more so now that she'd married well. A fisherman wasn't exactly low status, but lower than a mason. What had Adhna meant about a vow to his father?

And why did he say his father had *left* instead of *died*? Could his father be alive somewhere?

Conall shivered, possibilities rushing through his mind as he finished the mindless tasks of feeding the pigs and chickens. He swept out the chicken pen, absent-mindedly petted the nanny goat, and drifted into the roundhouse, his thoughts still in a crazed dance.

The thunk of stone on wood jerked him out of his ruminations. He hurried to the front door and peered into the eating area. His mother's head was down on the table, a stone jar in her hand.

"Ma? Are you alright?"

A soft snore greeted him.

With a practiced hand, Conall extracted the stone jar from his mother's now-lax fingers and peered inside. Empty. It had been full just two nights before.

Conall let out a heavy sigh and wrinkled his nose at the odor of strong, raw cider. He sat on the bench next to his mother to see how drunk she was.

She wouldn't open her eyes, even when he called her name or shook her shoulder. Very drunk indeed, then. He sincerely hoped she'd sober before Sétna returned. In the meantime, her back would hurt less if he could move her to her cot.

With a mighty grunt, he pulled her right arm over his shoulders and lifted, pulling her limp body with him as he inched toward her sleeping alcove. When he was close enough, he gently lowered her into her cot and covered her with a woolen blanket. He laid her on her side in case she vomited.

Once his mother was settled, he studied the rest of the roundhouse. It appeared in good order, but a few dishes needed cleaning. He straightened the cooking area and set dried beans to soak for the evening meal. Then he went out to finish feeding the horses.

By the time he'd completed his chores, Lainn needed collecting. Conall glanced at the sky, but the sun still hid behind dark clouds. He tapped his lip before grabbing both his brat and his sister's. The rain might let loose before they made it home.

As he trudged down the path toward the oak grove, wind whipped up, lashing dried leaves into a swirling maelstrom. Conall shivered and drew his brat more tightly around his shoulders, his steps quickening. He kept his head down into the wind and, as a result, didn't notice the figure in his path until he ran into him.

"G-g-g-g-g-going somewhere, stone-b-b-b-boy?"

"I don't have t-time for you right now, Tomas." Conall tried to shoulder past the solid lad, but the bully moved too quick and stepped back in his path.

With a quick peek around him, Conall realized Tomas was alone. His normal pack didn't appear to be in attendance. That made his decision easier. "Out of my way, T-Tomas."

Tomas crossed his arms. "M-m-m-m-make me. Maybe if you ask really nice, I'll let you go, but when you come back with your sister… well, I won't be so generous. She's growing up to be rather pretty. A bit fat for my tastes, but her breasts are big enough."

Conall's ears roared as his blood grew warm, and he balled his fists. How dare Tomas talk about Lainn that way? Before he thought better of it, he called upon the brooch's power.

He didn't dare perform visible magic, but his father said nothing about using the power subtly. He concentrated on the arc of his fist toward Tomas' face, and just as flesh met startled flesh, he threw his magic behind the punch, making his adversary fly into the thorny bushes to one side of the path.

Proud of the seamless illusion, Conall allowed himself a private smile as Tomas spluttered and flailed, trying to drag himself out of the bracken. Conall strode away, his head held high.

The wind rose again, blowing strong against his back. He picked up his pace as Tomas' curses faded into the crackling leaves.

Lainn perched on a low stone wall next to the oak grove arch, drawing pictures into the dirt with a stick. When he walked into the clearing, she jumped up. "Conall! I've been here forever waiting for you. What took you so long? It's going to rain soon."

He held out her brat with a silent smile, which she returned, flinging the small cape around her shoulders. "I ran into Tomas but escaped unscathed. We'd best hurry."

Rain sprinkled on them as they hurried home, but the promised storm never came. Their hair was barely damp by the time they arrived. The roundhouse was silent and still as they entered, shook off their brats, and hung them on hooks by the door.

Conall glanced into their mother's alcove, but she still lay on her side, one arm flung up over her head. He checked to make sure she still breathed before he walked into the cooking area.

He cut up several turnips and herbs before remembering to ask Lainn to build the hearth fire.

His sister added kindling to the banked and smoldering peat, coaxing a cheerful blaze into the central hearth. She swung the heavy iron pot into place on a tripod stand. Conall dumped water into the pot, and they both sat, waiting for it to boil.

Lainn poked the peat bricks with a stick, making them glow more brightly. "Is Father due back today, do you think? Or will he stay overnight?"

Sullenly, Conall stared at the glowing embers. "He's not our father, Lainn. He'll never be our father."

"Fine. Our stepfather. You know he'd cuff us if he heard that."

"I know. It doesn't change the fact."

They stared at the smoldering peat for a few more moments before he answered. "I think he'll stay overnight. It sounded like he meant to."

"Good."

Their mother let out a moan. Conall glanced up but, when nothing else happened, he shifted his gaze back to the peat glow.

Lainn shoved the stick into the fire, causing sparks to flutter. "Are all the animals cared for?"

"All but the horses' evening feed. I usually do that after we eat."

Once the water bubbled in the iron pot, he fetched the turnips, rosemary, and garlic. He carefully poured these into the boiling water, along with the soaked beans. With their stepfather out of town, they'd eat no meat. That would have warranted a harder blow than Conall wished to earn for a bite of chicken.

He glanced at his sister's pensive profile. In a low voice, he asked, "D-do you ever wonder what happened to Da?"

She shrugged, her gaze still fixed forward. "Da got sick and died. I wish he hadn't, and I miss him terribly. What else should I wonder?"

"Adhna said something that made me think maybe Da didn't d-die."

She gave him a sidelong glance. "Conall, have you been eating mushrooms from the faerie rings?"

"No, Lainn, I'm serious. This isn't a jape. Adhna argued with Mother earlier. He told Mother that Da had 'left,' not that he'd died."

She rolled her eyes. "Wishful thinking. You're just trying to twist his words into what you want to be true."

Conall pressed his lips thin. Lainn was right. He hadn't wanted to believe his father had died and grasped at any slight hope.

But Adhna's words haunted him, and he still couldn't shake the idea that Adhna's words had hidden clues. Perhaps the old man spoke in allegories? Lainn had explained the term to him last month, and now he saw them in everything. Then again, maybe Adhna was simply batty, forgetful, or both.

With a grunt, Conall tested the stew and decided it was fit to eat, if not delicious. Delicious would need several hours of simmering, hours they didn't really have. He filled a bowl for each of them and ate. Thanks to time spent with Adhna, Conall had some knowledge of herbs, and his food ended up tastier than their mother's efforts. Despite that, he didn't relish his meal.

It tasted of ashes and false hopes.

Chapter Three

A crash echoed through the wood of the roundhouse. Conall jerked out of a sound sleep. His cot, attached to the wall, resounded with fading vibrations from a slammed door.

The banked peat fire lit the house with a sullen glimmer. Within this limited view, Conall watched his stepfather stomp into the roundhouse, shake the rain from his travel brat, and fling his boots off. "Ligach! Ligach, wake up!"

A painful moan from his mother made Conall sit up with sudden concern. She might still be drunk from the night before, and his stepfather was rarely in a tolerant mood.

With a silent prayer, Conall urged his mother to respond coherently. He slipped his *léine* on quietly in the near darkness. He poked Lainn awake, but her eyes already glittered out of the gloom.

Another crash made him jump. "Ligach! Get up, lazy slut! Get up!"

His mother's voice slurred in the darkness. "Go 'way, Sétna. Not tonight. My head hurts."

Sparks scattered as Sétna kicked the peat fire. Grár whined as they flew toward him, and he scuttled away. Sétna swore and stalked to the alcove he shared with their mother.

While Conall could only make out vague shapes in the firelight, his mother's screams made him cover his ears. His stepfather yanked her out of her cot by her hair. The pleading, mixed with screeching, angry curses and whining, cut through his meager attempts.

Shapes came more clearly now. Perhaps dawn finally arrived. He clenched his fists, aching to defend his mother, but knowing Sétna would only beat them both. Instead, he pulled on his brooch's power. With a small push of his will, he stirred the peat as if a breeze caressed it, making it flicker.

Now that he could see better, he watched Sétna relinquish his grip on his mother's hair and yank up her sleeping tunic. Conall concentrated on his stepfather's feet and, with a silent regret for the need, made him step on Grár's tail.

The resulting yip of pain shifted Sétna's rage into concern for his beloved hound. Conall's mother scuttled away from Sétna's reach, crawling into Conall's alcove. Lainn joined him and they stood together in front of her while she retched in the corner. The stench made Conall's own stomach roil.

But Sétna was full of solicitude for his wounded dog. His rage at his wife had evidently been forgotten, for now.

Conall listened for Grár's whine, but the dog made no noise. He hoped the poor creature hadn't been badly hurt. His stepfather went into his alcove and soon, snores filled the roundhouse.

Conall and Lainn got no more rest that night. They both sat vigil over their comatose mother.

As the sun rose, Lainn nursed their mother to a semblance of competent sobriety while Conall served breakfast and kept their stepfather occupied by asking about his trip.

Sétna waved his hand in a contemptuous gesture. "You'd think a well-known blacksmith would have a wide selection of implements. He carried barely any quality chisels at all! The price he wanted for each item was ridiculous. What with the added cost of no work for the day and feed for the horse, it was a wasted trip. I might as well have bought from the local idiot for all the good my trip did."

He paused to shove a slice of bread in his mouth, speaking around the crumbs. "I'd just started the trip home when the horse, out of sheer spite, threw a shoe. I had to turn back to get him re-shod, which of course, the thief charged another premium for."

By the time he finished, their mother looked tired and wan, but presentable. "Sétna, would you like more food to break your fast? Or would you prefer to rest after your long journey home?"

Sétna's brow furrowed, and he clenched his fists, but Lainn broke in. "I picked blackberries. They would be lovely in some fresh cream. Shall I go fetch them?"

He gave her a curt nod, and she dashed off with a smile of forced cheer. Conall wanted nothing more than to escape and sit beside the river to collect his thoughts, but he must be a shield in case Sétna's anger roused once again.

Sétna frowned at Ligach, tapping his finger on the wooden table. "I'll rest after eating. Conall made bread, but I'm still hungry. Just some porridge, nothing fancy. Berries will be a nice addition. She'd better have enough."

The silent moments grew long as the three waited for Lainn to return with her sweet bounty. When she arrived, the skip to her step had sunk to a shamed shuffle. She held a purple-stained cloth in her hand, her eyes glistening with unshed tears. "A raven ate them all! I told him to leave the berries alone, but he stole them anyway!"

Conall cringed inside. He'd warned her many times never to mention her abilities with animals. Normal people didn't sing with bees or talk to ravens. He glanced at his stepfather, waiting for the explosion.

Grár whined and nudged his master's hand, making the older man smile. Conall wondered if the hound had distracted Sétna on purpose or if he was just reacting to the tension.

Either way, Conall sighed with gratitude as Sétna ignored Lainn and her sorrowful face. He turned to their mother. "Just add honey to the porridge. I'm exhausted and should sleep through the day."

Conall helped his mother clean after Sétna went to his alcove. They took care to be as quiet as possible. When he and Lainn finally escaped at mid-morning, mist still clung to mossy tree trunks.

He walked Lainn to her lessons and took the long way home, along the riverbank. He needed time to himself, without mumbling mothers and raging stepfathers.

Rocks and fallen trees littered the shore, but Conall treated it as a puzzle, something to solve as he made his way along the edge. Taking the path would be the easy way. Figuring out the more difficult way occupied his mind.

His stepfather's temper had never been even but seemed worse lately. He didn't want to think about his mother and the danger she might be in. And he felt like a base coward for not wanting to be there to protect her.

Conall found a warm spot on a flat rock jutting into a curve in the river's path. He sat and shredded a fallen branch, tossing the crumbled bits of red leaves into the swirling water while he thought.

His mother suffered Sétna's heavy hand often enough, as did Conall and Lainn. But lately the blows came harder, more often, and his mother's bruises showed darker on her fair skin. The old ones hadn't healed before new ones came.

While Conall was tall, Sétna outweighed him at least twice over, maybe three times. He'd never win in a physical fight with his stepfather.

Unless he used his magic.

Such an idea occurred to him, of course. He railed against the injustice of using magic to hurt someone, despite their physical disadvantages. He'd only used his powers in small ways before, but the incidents were growing more frequent. First Tomas and now Sétna. Could he harm an attacker with his power? Could he bring himself to harm anyone at all? He couldn't even rid himself of the guilt of hurting a dog.

His branch ran out of leaves, and he whipped it into the water, watching it fly, end over end. He nudged it with his power, and it spun more quickly, slicing the surface of the water like a watermill before he let it fall.

"You really shouldn't demonstrate your power where others can witness it, lad."

Conall almost leapt off the rock at Adhna's voice. Where had the old man come from? He'd heard no one walk on the crackling leaves.

After trying to calm his heart, Conall shrugged. "What power? I just flung a stick into the river."

"Where it danced like a Faerie on midsummer eve before you let it go. Don't deny it, Conall. I can see the power as clear as a sunrise. It glowed around both you and the stick. I've noticed it before but kept my silence. A warning seems to be in order. Does your stepfather know?"

Conall clenched his jaw, unable to think of a way to persuade Adhna he possessed no power.

"Come now, don't be reticent. Your father spoke to the creatures in the forest. Who do you think introduced me to Barnabus? Your father asked me to look after you and your talent when he left."

At first, Conall wanted to ask if that's where Lainn got her ability to sing to the bees, but Adhna's last word distracted him. Eager at a chance to clear up his doubts, Conall turned to face him. "Left? You mean *d-died,* right?"

The man shook his head, a few stray leaves falling from the many braids in his dark hair. The beads in his beard rattled. "I didn't come to speak to you of your father's fate. I came because I heard your anguish. Tell me of your pain."

Which pain should he begin with? The pain of being unable to protect his mother? Or of missing his father so much it felt like he'd lost an arm? The pain of knowing his sister might be in danger? The pain of being bullied by Tomas? Even the pain of Aoife and her constant push for affection tormented him.

His father once told him pain meant you lived. Conall had just shrugged, but now he understood. Did he really want to live with all this pain? He bowed his head, resting his forehead on his knees, trying hard not to sob in front of Adhna.

"Lad, lad. There's always a way. Your father taught you that, didn't he? There comes a time when every person must make their own life, make their own choices, for the good of their heart. This may be when they choose a trade or marry a loved one. It may be when you have children of your own."

Conall shook his head, unwilling to even consider a future like that. How could he be happy with all this on his soul?

"Some don't find their true soul until they are aged like me. Some few never find it and drift through life hating the world and everyone in it. These souls are the cruel ones, those who inflict pain with no thought of how their actions affect others."

Adhna settled next to him on the rock. "Conall, you will never be one of these. You can already see you must take a different path from the one you're on. It's quite apparent to any that care to look that you won't be what others expect you to become. You're over-young yet to take such responsibility, but it should be soon."

Conall stared at the water, watching the swirls of leaves eddy and flow across the rippled surface. The motion made his head reel, and if he hadn't been firmly sitting upon the rock, he might have lost his balance. Adhna placed his hand on Conall's back. He drew strange comfort from the older man's proffered help.

With pleading eyes, he turned to Adhna. "I don't understand what I'm t-t-to do. What would Father have done?"

The older man waggled his finger. "We can never know what another might do in any situation, young man. We can only listen to our heart and soul to decide what is best for us. What does your heart say?"

Conall stared at the rushing river and spoke in a low voice, for once, not stuttering. "We need to leave. Mother, Lainn and me. We need to escape and never return."

"And how would you engineer such an escape? Would Lainn come with you? Would your mother leave?"

Anger and pain gripped Conall's heart as he considered each question. He owned nothing of value to trade for supplies, other than his father's brooch. Lainn would go anywhere he took her.

His mother, however, hated change. She hated insecurity and the dangers of not knowing what her future might be. They'd heard her rage often enough of such things after their father. . . left.

Well, she'd found her security, and at a terrible price. They did live much better now than they had with their father. As the family of a poor fisherman, they'd lived in a much smaller hut. While he'd be thrilled to never eat fish again, they'd never gone hungry.

Kindness was food for the soul, and they'd always been well fed with love.

Now, they ate meat almost every day. Sétna had replaced their threadbare *léinte* with finer cloth, despite his sneer of thinly disguised repugnance at the old garments. He allowed Lainn to pursue her dreams of studying at the oak grove and taught Conall the mason's trade. Still, Sétna starved them of affection.

Mother might have chosen worse, he supposed.

Her bruises still haunted him like physical blows. Conall squeezed his eyes shut, trying to erase the images from his mind. "Mother will never leave him."

Adhna nodded as if he knew what the answer would be. "And your sister?"

"She'll c-c-come. Lainn is tied to no place for long. She's m-more of a free spirit in the world than anyone I've ever met."

With a knowing half-smile, Adhna nodded again. "You're wise to recognize such a thing so young, Conall of the Druid's Brooch. When will you leave, then?"

Adhna said that like Conall had already made his decision. And he supposed he had done so, at that. However, the timing was a much more difficult decision.

Conall gave a sullen shrug. "I have no provisions or food for a journey. I have no place we can go to find safety."

"You are always welcome to my care, of course, but I'm too close to your stepfather's house. My cottage would be the first place he searched. However, I can supply bread and cheese, though it pains me to give away such delicious treats."

Conall laughed, his heart suddenly lighter. Adhna's penchant for cheese was a standing joke.

His mirth faded as reality pressed in. "But where would we g-go?"

"With Lainn's connections with the Druid grove, she could search for others. There's a large conclave to the northwest, on *Cnoc Uisneach*, two days' travel west, though the way is difficult through the hills."

Conall twisted his fingers, his discomfort at the idea of leaving everything he knew, his mother, his home, unsettling his stomach and mind. "I've never traveled alone. I've never even traveled farther than the oak grove by myself."

Adhna patted him on the shoulder again. "You'll do well. You have your talent, and with Lainn's ability to charm animals, you'll survive well enough. Just remember to keep watch in the evenings."

He couldn't leave today. Maybe tomorrow. Or next week. Lainn had just passed to the next level of her lessons. She might not be willing to leave and ruin everything she'd worked for.

"You'll know when it's time to leave, lad. Trust your heart, remember?"

Conall nodded, but when he turned to ask Adhna a question, the old man had disappeared.

"Blood and bones! I wish he wouldn't do that."

Several weeks later, Conall woke from a nightmare, and his heart seized in his chest. He tore through his belongings with increasing terror, certain someone had found his father's brooch and stolen it. The brooch his father gave him in sacred trust, the family heirloom full of magic that must, before all else, be kept secret and safe.

He'd hidden it in the sack he kept under his bed, packed and ready to leave at a moment's notice. He'd slowly filled the sack with preserved food, a few iron utensils, a bowl, a few left-over, old masonry tools Sétna no longer wanted. At the bottom of the sack, wrapped in the old bit of white linen, should be the brooch.

But it wasn't there.

In desperation, Conall searched under his cot, under Lainn's cot, through her clothing and growing collection of pinecones, colorful autumn leaves, and dead butterfly wings.

What if his mother found it? Would she recognize it as something of Father's, or had he kept that secret even from her?

What if Sétna found the brooch and sold the precious jewelry to some tinker, passing through town and traveling far away, never to be seen again?

Reason asserted itself. If Sétna had found a brooch that valuable within Conall's things, his stepfather would have confronted him and accused him of thievery. With no accusation, Sétna must not have found it.

But his mother might not bother with finding out why he had it. She'd just sell it for strong wine and enjoy her spoils until she passed out.

With shaking hands and a mental kick, Conall left Lainn's cot and reached under his own pillow. As soon as the sharp point of the pin pricked his finger, he let out a sigh of relief. He'd forgotten he'd placed it under his pillow the week before, worried that heavy rains would flood the roundhouse and get the sack wet.

Conall hugged the tiny treasure close to his chest, ignoring where the filigree metal bit into his tender skin. He closed his eyes and carefully placed it back into the bottom of his sack, safe and sound and ready to flee.

Chapter Four

Several moons later, Conall still fretted over when they should leave. Lainn came home each day, ebullient with tales of her new lessons, eagerly describing all the wondrous things she learned. She practiced on him, telling him stories she'd memorized.

Conall didn't mind, even though he'd heard many of the tales before. Watching her search for the right detail, an obscure name, or a list of three magical items as part of her recitation was a bit distracting, but her enthusiasm was delightful.

Lainn always grew quiet in the evenings. She usually helped Sétna with the horses after supper, while Conall helped their mother clean. During this time, he didn't envy Lainn her talent with animals. He had to keep an iron grip on his temper with Sétna all day in their masonry lessons. The evening respite was cherished time with his mother.

As he helped her clean after supper, he forced himself to ask in a casual voice, "Do you ever think of moving away from here, Mother?"

Conall held his breath and silently urged her to say *all the time.*

She shook her head. "Why should I leave? My husband and children are here."

"No, I mean when Lainn and I are grown, with families of our own. And if you weren't married."

She let out a snort. "If I weren't married, how would I live? I'd have no house, no food, no cattle. You aren't making sense, Conall."

He glanced at the door to be sure his stepfather hadn't overheard and wished he had the courage to ask her outright.

Run away with us, Mother. A thousand times, he rehearsed the words in his mind. Every day, he vowed to ask her, but each time, something stopped his question.

Perhaps he read the look in her eyes, a flinch, a whispered warning in the evening air. Whatever the reason, he never found the courage to ask. Without asking his mother, he didn't dare take Lainn away. And so they stayed in the same old patterns.

The winds now grew cold as night fell on the shorter days of winter. Ice formed among the cruel bare branches and the path to the druid grove grew slippery. Still, he insisted on walking Lainn to her lessons every day.

He hadn't asked his sister about leaving, either. But he knew they must leave. His decision weighed on his shoulders more heavily each day. Every new bruise upon his mother's cheek made him clench his fists in simmering rage, and yet he couldn't act.

His family's lives relied on a fragile peace. What would Sétna do to their mother if Conall and Lainn disappeared in the night? He couldn't be the cause of that. Or shatter their dreams with his lumbering half-baked solution.

Would running away even solve anything? What if they starved in the woods? Winter punished those who lived without shelter, especially spoiled children like themselves, children who'd never lived rough in their short lives.

He considered asking Adhna to teach him more woodcraft as he hurried to the grove to pick Lainn up from the day's lesson. A rustling in the brush made him turn, and a bright flash of red caught his eye. The blonde girl's artful smile made his blood run cold. Aoife.

Running along the muddy, icy path wasn't an option. She blocked his way and, from her sly smile, she knew she'd trapped him.

"I'm late, Aoife. P-please, let me by."

"You needn't rush off so quickly." She stepped close to him, her warm breath misting on his mouth, her hand caressing his upper arm. He licked his lips and swallowed. He wanted to back away, but he was rooted to the path.

Aoife ran a hand down the front of his chest, pulling the wool of his *léine* as it traveled down. His legs finally obeyed him, and he backed away, almost slipping on the mud.

She pouted and stepped toward him again, but this time, he pulled on his power and made the mud shift beneath her feet. Aoife fell in the icy slush and cried out in pain and indignation.

Conall scurried away while he had the chance. He yelled back, "Sorry!" and dashed toward the oak grove, slipping twice but not falling. He used feather-touches of his power to keep himself from falling.

Her voice chased him, haranguing him for not helping her up. As her words faded, he slowed, gasping for breath as the icy wind seared his throat and lungs.

The oak grove entrance came into view, and he pushed thoughts of Aoife away, searching the clearing for his sister. She wasn't waiting for him, so he must not be as late as he thought.

Conall perched on the stone wall along the edge of the clearing, after sweeping off dead leaves and slushy ice. The stones chilled his butt, but his legs were trembling after his escape from Aoife. He needed time to think.

Aoife used to be mean to him. Like everyone else, she used to tease him for his stutter, pull his braids, and throw cow pats at him.

Only in the last couple of months had her attentions shifted from disdainful cruelty to aggressively amorous. He wished she'd return to the cruelty. He knew how to handle bullies.

Why did she terrify him so much? She was attractive, interested, and certainly a decent match, as far as his stepfather would say. Her family was wealthy with a large stake of land and forty head of cattle.

The thought of wedding and bedding Aoife made him shiver and shrink inside.

He didn't hate her, but he simply had no interest in bedding her. Conall imagined himself lying with Aoife in their marriage bed, and he might as well have considered laying with his sister. He had absolutely no desire to touch her, to share intimate moments together, despite her attractive curves and sweet smile.

He'd had such thoughts in the past. Any young man had dreams. His fantasies were nebulous, and he'd never been able to bring the face of his imagined lover into focus. He just knew it wasn't Aoife.

Freezing wind blew dust and debris into his face. He sputtered and wiped his eyes, and when he glanced at the sky, he realized he'd been waiting for Lainn for a long time. *Was she still in the grove? Should I go find her?* Maybe he had been as late as he first thought, and she'd left before he arrived?

A raven cawed behind him, making him jump off the wall and spin around, almost slipping in the mud. The enormous bird cawed again and hopped down the path toward home. It glanced back at Conall and skipped forward several steps. It looked back at him again.

Conall shrugged and followed. One didn't question a raven with such clear signals.

Once Conall began following, the raven barely stopped, causing Conall to rush after the creature. Past the spot where he'd evaded Aoife, past the ruined roundhouse where rumor said air-daemons lived, past the bend in the river which ate more of the bank each year. Only when they neared his home did the raven slow.

A shudder which had nothing to do with the winter air spread through Conall's bones as he studied the silent roundhouse. The farm was never silent, but nothing stirred now.

Conall straightened his shoulders and went to the barn, as Mother or Lainn should be there, feeding the animals. One mare nickered and pawed the ground. The other let out a huff of air and shook her head. The rest of the stable stood empty.

A stricture in his throat made it difficult to swallow, but he took a drink of cold, clear water from the well before venturing into the roundhouse.

The interior seemed darker than usual. A glance at the center hearth showed the fire had burned down to glowing embers. The dim light of the early evening barely seeped through the windows.

No one was in the main room, but a shuffle and a whimper came from his stepfather's alcove. Had it been Grár? No, the whine sounded human, not animal. With growing dread, he crept to the alcove and pulled aside the curtain.

At first, he couldn't tell what was happening. His stepfather's back blocked most of his view. But Lainn's coppery curls sprawled out on the cot and she cried out. "Conall!"

Anguish and entreaty in her voice spurred him to shove their stepfather aside with all the might and magic he could muster. The older man crashed into the wicker wall, landing with a grunt and a thump. His *léine* had been rucked up to his waist as had Lainn's, and her legs lay naked on the cot. She shot up like a rabbit and dashed out of the roundhouse, a look of pure terror on her face.

With an enraged glance at Sétna, who lay still on the ground, Conall ran to his own alcove and grabbed his shoulder-sack. He'd kept it packed since he spoke to Adhna months before, adding preserved food, a discarded tool, and clean *léinte*. Conall spent a few precious moments making certain the brooch was still inside and yanking some of Lainn's clothing from her alcove. He stuffed them into the top of the sack before he darted outside.

Lainn stood at the well, splashing water all over her lower body, despite the freezing wind. Either tears or wash water streaked her face. Conall couldn't bring himself to ask.

He hefted the sack over his shoulder. "I've packed clothes and food. Where's Mother?" No further explanation seemed necessary. He knew what they must do.

Lain glanced at his sack and raised her eyebrows. "She went to visit our aunt. As soon as she left… he… I should have waited for you! I wanted to hurry home, but I should have waited!"

His sister dissolved from the strong, sweet, flighty girl he'd always known in his heart to a fragile, shaking creature full of pain and fear. Conall hugged her tight, reaching into his sack to draw her brat around her shoulders. When her shivering eased, he held her at arms-length and stared into her eyes. "D-d-did he… succeed?"

She shook her head. "He would have. He would have if you hadn't come right then. How did you make him stop? I didn't even see you swing your fist, you struck so fast."

"Later. We have to leave. He may wake up at any moment. Can you walk?"

She took a deep breath and stared at the roundhouse. "I never want to see this place again in my entire life. This I swear."

A shimmer passed through the clearing, shifting the monotonous grays and browns to an instant flash of intense color. As soon as the wave flashed, the light disappeared.

He grasped her shoulder. "Adhna. We must get to Adhna's first. He'll give us food and help us on our way."

As the falling dusk gripped them in chilly arms, they trudged along the river path to the old man's roundhouse, praying Sétna remained passed out long enough for them to escape. Conall wished he could fetch their mother, but he didn't know where their aunt lived now. She'd just moved to a new *túath* last month, and he didn't even know the name of the village.

Full darkness fell before they reached the bee glade. None buzzed in greeting. Lainn placed a hand on the hive, her eyes closed as if giving a blessing. "They know we're here. They'll help us."

"How can bees help us, Lainn? You're making no sense."

He heard the sad smile in her voice. "Sense is over-rated."

The door to the roundhouse creaked open, and a dark shape stood in the doorway, silhouetted by sullen firelight. "You've come. I suspected it wouldn't be long. Come in, then, children. Come in from the cold."

The dark danger of winter gave way to cozy warmth in Adhna's cottage. His peat fire glowed like a beacon of heat and comfort in the center of the roundhouse. While the older man's home was too small for multiple alcoves around the outside edge, it held a riot of objects which made Conall turn and twist his head in the low light, trying to see and identify every item, but with little success.

Carvings with writhing figures of birds, bees, and other creatures of the forest covered the house pole in the center. They danced in the flickering light, almost as if their eyes watched Conall as he sat on the floor. He'd expected icy ground, but Adhna had placed several thick wool carpets around the hearth.

Lainn hugged the old man with fierce abandon before she sat next to her brother. Holding her chin up, Adhna searched her eyes for several moments. "You should have left 'ere this, children. No matter, you're here now. Let me get your supplies, and we'll discuss your plans."

He walked to one curved wall where a series of stone shelves held wooden drawers and boxes. Each one he drew open, rifled through, and sometimes pulled out an object. These findings he placed in a pile, but the peat glowed too dim for Conall to make them out.

His eyes drooped from panic and fatigue, but he must stay awake. If Sétna came to find them and got to Lainn again…

He glanced at his sister, but she seemed engrossed in picking the fringe of her brat free of twigs and dried leaves from their flight through the woods. Adhna shoved one of his wooden drawers onto the shelf with force, which caused Lainn to jump. Her eyes darted around, looking like a frightened rabbit, wary of a cat.

Conall's anger bubbled up, and he wanted to hit something. Preferably his stepfather's disgusting face, but without his ideal target, he'd take another option. Adhna had an exquisite chair carved from a living tree stump, rooted to the ground. On this chair lay several decorative cushions. Conall used one of these to vent his rage and frustration in silent violence, but it didn't do much to ease his mind.

Adhna hummed to himself while he added to his odd pile. As he hummed, Lainn's agitation eased. When she finally closed her eyes and let out a deep sigh, a raven cawed from the shadows. A mad flutter of wings revealed an enormous raven.

This might be the same bird that led him home that evening. The raven watched him and blinked three times before settling in Lainn's lap. She cooed and petted him, which made the bird trill. At the very least, the corvid calmed her. For this, Conall felt grateful, regardless of whether it was the same bird.

Adhna returned with a large linen bag and stuffed the eclectic pile of objects in with no care for delicacy or order. "This should keep you for at least a week, barring disaster. Maybe even with disaster, depending on its form. Disaster sometimes swoops in unexpected. Well, often, to be fair. Still, it has much to do and might miss you completely."

Conall swallowed his fear, forcing himself to nod as if the man made any sense whatsoever. What had Lainn said? *Sense is over-rated.* Though perhaps a whimsical philosophy, its application to survival in the wilds of winter was slight.

"Now, children, I wish I could invite you to rest before your journey, but Sétna is awake and furious. He's on his way, so I must get you gone."

Lainn's eyes darted around again as she dove under Adhna's cot. Conall stooped down to speak to her face to face. Her dark eyes glittered with unborn tears in the blackness. "Lainn, come out! We have to go."

The raven cawed, and Lainn slowly crawled from her shelter. When she emerged, dust clung to her cheeks and hair. Conall wanted to wipe away dust, wiping away her wariness.

She'd never before feared the world. He already missed the carefree sister of last year, skipping and running through the woods. This new sister broke his heart, and he didn't know how to help the old one return.

Conall hefted Adhna's heavy linen bag over one shoulder. Things inside clanked and clicked, so he shifted it until it settled more comfortably. He took Lainn's hand and squeezed hard. This earned him a sad, quick smile before she turned her solemn gaze to Adhna. The raven hopped to Adhna's shoulder and cawed so loudly that it echoed through the cottage.

As Adhna flung open the door, a blast of winter wind made Conall stagger off-balance. He gritted his teeth and pushed through the wind out into the ink-black night. Skeletal branches twisted in the gale, reaching for their clothes and hair.

Adhna had to raise his voice over the howling wind. "Keep west until you find Loch Ainninn. Two hours west of the loch. Uisneach is a massive hill above the landscape. If you wish to apply to the druids there, they will shelter you."

Conall furrowed his brow and hugged Lainn tight, away from the biting wind. "Apply?"

Adhna picked at his mustache and nodded. "There's no guarantee that they'll take you in, even with my recommendation, you understand. With Lainn having some schooling, it's a high possibility, but they're a law unto themselves, and will take whom they want."

That didn't sound certain at all to Conall, but the alternative was impossible. He shivered and pulled his brat closer around his neck, hugging Lainn more tightly.

Adhna whirled to the door and then back to them. "Quickly, now! He comes. Take Rawninn with you. He'll show you the way to the druids."

The enormous black bird cawed again and hopped onto Lainn's shoulder. Her face brightened and they dashed off in the icy darkness. Behind them, the bee glade faded into the murky mystery of the night.

Conall hoped Sétna wouldn't be in such a rage that he hurt the old man. Still, he suspected anyone who threatened Adhna would get more than a sharp rap of his walking stick. Certainly, Conall would never dare cross him, Fae or not. He almost wished he could stay here, invisible, to watch the confrontation. But not enough to actually stay.

Angry darts of sleet savaged his face. He pulled his brat over his sister's head and then covered his lower face with the other part. Seeing their way had been difficult before. Now it was nigh impossible. The slush underfoot grew more treacherous, and without the raven guiding them, they might have merrily walked into a raging river and never noticed.

Each step was a trial of momentum and determination. Every muddy slip, slash of icy rain, every caw of the raven turned Conall's journey into a tunnel of forward momentum. Even slight nudges with his magic didn't help, and he had no strength left to try.

Lainn's warm form next to him was his only comfort, someone to protect, someone to keep him going on through the pain and fatigue.

When she slipped, he pulled her up, and they moved forward together. Always together. He'd never leave her to be hurt again, he vowed. This whole situation was his own fault, his own failure to leave when Adhna first urged him to go. *Why did I wait?*

A loud caw in his ear brought him back to reality, and he halted before he stepped into an icy pond. The path disappeared into the black water, glinting with ripples in the dim scattered moonlight.

"Conall…"

"It's not big, Lainn. We'll find a way around."

"Conall, I'm sorry."

"Sorry? For what?"

She bowed her head. "I'm sorry we had to leave. This is all my fault."

"What? No!" He bent over so he might make out her eyes in the dark. "None of this is your fault, Lainn. I knew we must leave ages ago, but I put it off. If anything, this is my fault."

The raven cawed several times impatiently, and Conall glanced up with a half-smile. "He just told us to shut up, didn't he?"

With a sudden giggle, Lainn nodded. "That's pretty much exactly what he said. Also, that there was a time and a place for regrets, and this was neither."

"All that in a few caws?"

"Ravens get to the point more quickly than humans do."

He stared at the black water and examined the edges of the puddle. Thorny bracken lined the left side of the barrier, but the right side looked clear. Squishy with rain-sodden moss, but at least spiny daggers wouldn't rip them to shreds. Carefully, he led Lainn around the left bank.

When they regained the path, he wiped rain from his eyes. They only got wet again an instant later, but it made him feel slightly better for trying. He stepped over another puddle, but the solid ground beyond it was a lie.

This fake puddle sunk deep into the path, water spilling over the tops of his boots. He cursed under his breath and shook his foot, trying to lessen the sopping mess, again to no avail.

He slipped, falling hard into the mud, his going in two directions. The hip bone on his left side found a sharp rock. "Blood and bones! That *hurt!*"

With Lainn's help, he got back to his feet, his entire side covered with mud. Even the torrential rain did little to wash it away. He took three steps and winced at the pain in his side. His entire lower body ached.

"Come on, Conall. Rawninn's almost disappeared."

He pressed his hand into his hip, trying to alleviate the pain. "That bird needs to remember humans have to walk. Flying's all well and good, but the path is dangerous in this weather."

She crossed her arms and glared at him through the rain. "That bird hates flying in this, too. Most birds do. He's helping us. We should be kinder."

"We're far enough away for tonight. I have to stop. We'll hurt ourselves if we go further. Let's find a place off the path to rest."

Lainn pursed her lips but didn't gainsay him. A glance in the direction the raven had gone was her only reply.

Conall hunted for a few minutes and found a dry spot under a rocky overhang. He shoved out most of the wet, dead leaves and they huddled beneath, hugging each other for warmth. Conall hoped Rawninn would find them again. He just couldn't walk any further tonight. His side ached horribly, a sharp pain twisting through his hip every time he moved.

Hours of freezing, dripping misery passed and Conall couldn't sleep. Lainn snored in his arms, snuggled up against his side. He didn't dare move lest he disturb her.

At least one of them got rest. Booming thunder moved farther away as his breath froze into misty crystals on his chin. Several times he wiped it away, yet it always reformed.

Once, he thought he heard the familiar caw of the raven, but no black bird intruded on their hidden shelter. The one thought which kept him from complete despair was that Sétna would never come looking for them in this weather. They were safe from him. For now.

Conall shoved away the haze of sleep and dreams. The sweet call of a lone songbird pierced his brain and forced him out of his languor. *Birds shouldn't sing so loudly on a freezing winter morning.*

White-fleece dreams of dying a peaceful death beneath an icy lake shattered into shards of glass, glittering in the winter sunlight. He tried to fall back into the blessed comfort of sleep, but a bee buzzed in his ear. It flew off when he tried to smack it.

Lainn remained in his arms, a warm lump of sighing slumber. Her breath kept his shoulder warm, but the rest of his body had gone numb. He didn't feel his feet, his hands, not even his buttocks. His hip, however, ached in full force and reminded him pointedly of his fall the night before. In fact, if he didn't stand now and shake off the pain, he might just scream.

Gently, he extracted himself from his sister's somnolent embrace and stretched his long, lanky body until the muscles in his arms and legs popped. He cried out in pain and pleasure at this unkinking of his limbs.

Lainn sat up, rubbing her eyes and brushing ice from her clothing. "What? Are you hurt?"

"No." He rubbed his hip and winced. He pulled up his *léine* to examine the spot and traced a deep, purple bruise with his finger. "Well, maybe a little bit."

She chewed her lower lip. "Gemmán could help with that. Maybe we should head back to the grove."

He shook his head. "That'll be the second place Sétna check, after Adhna's c-c-cottage. The druids would have to give you up since you're still Sétna's ward. Me, they'd have no call to hold anyhow, even if they deigned to shelter me to begin with. In fact, I doubt the druids Adhna wants us to find will be any different."

The enormity of their situation crept into Conall's mind. They had food for a week, maybe. They had two sets of clothes each and their brats. His feet were soaked to the bone despite his boots, and Lainn's were just as bad.

They had no shelter from the harsh winter. No tools or weapons to hunt food, even if the forest yielded any game. The raven had abandoned them.

Conall sat back down into the muddy pile of freezing dead leaves, drew up his knees, and cradled his chin on his crossed arms.

Lainn paused in shaking the leaves from her cloak. "Conall?"

"What are we even thinking of, Lainn? We'll never survive out here on our own. In summer, maybe we'd have a chance, but solstice is a fortnight away. We don't have a prayer."

His sister set her lips into a thin line. "I hope you aren't suggesting we go back home?"

He shook his head. "No, I'll never ask that of you. You vowed never to go back, and I mean to honor that vow. I just don't know where to go from here."

Lainn sat next to him and put her arm around his shoulder. "We'll figure something out. We're both smart, resourceful, and talented." She glanced around as something moved in the brush, but when a mouse skittered across the clearing, she let out her held breath.

"We know what we can't do. We can't go back home, and we can't go to the oak grove. We can't go to Adhna's cottage, and we can't find our mother at her sister's house. These are all places Sétna could bring us back home from."

"He'll put out a call for us. People may see us."

She shrugged. "Then it's a good thing you've brought clothes for yourself. I'll wear yours, and we'll be two boys, rather than a boy and a girl. I'm more comfortable in your clothes, anyhow. The shorter *léine* is more practical for everyday work."

He frowned. A change of clothes wouldn't make Lainn into a boy. She was slender but some curves showed. "Maybe I can plait your hair into warrior's braids. I have beads to attach. You can't grow a beard, but you're obviously young."

"My brat should hide any other clues. Now watch me and see if I walk right." She strutted around in a circle, her gait shifting to a stronger, wider stride.

If he blurred his eyes, he just might imagine her to be a boy rather than his own beloved sister. "Well enough. When did you learn that?"

In a comically low voice, she said, "I've been watching you and Tomas. He walks with more swagger. Easier to copy."

He chuckled, despite the despair of their situation. "You aren't actually going to t-talk like that, right? You sound hilarious."

With a scowl, she batted at him, her voice still low but closer to normal. "Always the critic. Is that better?"

He grinned and nodded. "Right. Let's work on your hair. Then we should g-get going. Rain might return, and once the sun comes up, the slush will be everywhere."

The act of brushing out her hair, braiding strands into twenty long, thin plaits, and tying them off with twine was oddly comforting. The rhythm of the braid, the silky smoothness of her hair, and the low tune she hummed transported him to another time, another place.

When he finished, this wandering sense snapped back into his soul as if resentful of the return.

Chapter Five

After an endless day of rough travel, Conall eyed the far side of the river, focusing on the dark mouth of a cave. While it looked difficult to approach, he spied several places along the riverbank that he might fashion into steps. He nudged Lainn and pointed to the spot. She made her own assessment and nodded.

While the river flowed low in winter, the water grew wide at this point. Further upstream might offer a better spot to ford, so they hiked along the bank.

By dusk, they found a tree fallen most of the way across the river. With careful steps, they balanced on it, walking to the crown. They had to jump into the freezing river for the last few steps, but the prospect of starting a fire to dry their freezing, water-logged clothing and boots worked as motivation.

They made it back to the cave they'd spied earlier. The mouth looked low but deep. In the back, the ceiling rose high enough that Conall could stand. No sign of animal or human inhabitants littered the ground, so they gathered sticks and started a small fire on the outside ledge.

As the wood was well-soaked from yesterday's rain, they'd produce billows of smoke. If they started it inside the cave itself, they'd be driven from the space.

Therefore, once the fire had started, they laid more kindling around it to dry them out. They could shift the fire inside after the new wood had dried. Conall hoped the smoke wouldn't be a beacon for anyone to find them.

For the first time since they'd left, Conall allowed himself to relax. Once they'd changed into fresh clothing, with their soaked garments and boots laid out to dry, they opened Adhna's linen sack to look at the objects he'd gifted to them.

Conall gently poured the contents onto the cave floor, peering at each item in the firelight. Conall picked up a small wooden box, about as big as his fist, sealed in wax. He felt carvings on each side, but it was too dim for him to make out shapes. He placed it to one side and picked up the next object.

One long white peacock feather, broken in four places. Several long strips of white silk which had seen better days. A ball of twine. A single yellow onion. Two carved wooden bowls. One red bean. A candle stub. Six apples. Thirteen turnips. Three bits of colored wool fluff. A small leather bag with flint and pyrite inside. Two spoons carved from bone. A wineskin filled with strong-smelling mead. A stoppered stone jar of honey and comb.

Some honey had seeped out and coated the candle, flint bag, and the onion. Conall set these aside and continued. Several small packages of food, including a hunk of cheese, some mushrooms, three loaves of rye bread, dried venison, and hazelnuts.

Two objects remained, wrapped in ancient gray linen. Lainn picked one up and unwound the cloth, revealing a bronze leaf-shaped dagger, elaborately carved with a primal, triple spiral design. The blade glinted in the slanting sunlight, throwing reflections on the cave walls.

Conall selected the last item, unrolling the cloth to reveal a Brigid's Cross. Several rushes wrapped an even-armed cross, bound in the center in a time-honored tradition. The rushes crackled in his hands, well dried and ready to burn in the Imbolc fires.

Tradition held a Brigid's Cross prevented home fires and should be made on the day midway between midwinter and *Alban Eilir,* in the spring. Then the cross from the prior winter should burn on the Imbolc fire.

With the sincere hope Adhna hadn't relinquished this precious protection for them only to suffer a house fire until he could make a new one, Conall hugged the charm to his chest. He closed his eyes in prayer to Brigid, the goddess of fire, healing, and blacksmithing. If she heard them, perhaps she could guide them to safety. His nostrils filled with the dusty scent of dry straw.

His stomach rumbled with alarming volume, and Lainn giggled. "Here, eat some of the dried venison. I'll boil water and cook a turnip."

He raised his eyebrows. "You will? With what pot?"

She looked at the items before them, her lips pressed together.

"Luckily," Conall rummaged through his own sack, "I p-packed one before we left. It's not a large pot, but it should suffice for the two of us."

He pulled out the small iron pot, stuffed with a spare brat and a few older tools. He'd kept these as Sétna replaced his own tools with better chisels and hammers. They weren't in good repair, but he might earn food with his masonry efforts, once they settled somewhere.

Lainn gave him a long-suffering look but took the pot and filled it with river water. When she returned and placed it in the coals, it sizzled and popped until the water dried.

For a long time, Conall stared at the water, waiting for it to boil. Belatedly, he recalled the venison and chewed on a few bites to quiet his angry stomach. He offered some to his sister, but she shook her head. "I'll wait for soup."

They had no herbs, no salt, no flavoring. Still, the turnip, onion, and dried venison soup tasted like the finest meal they'd ever had. Granted, their mother had been a horrible cook, but Adhna had fed them, as had their aunt on occasion. When Conall made dinner, they ate better. This time, hunger and desperation seasoned their meal.

As he chewed a tough piece of venison, he turned to Lainn, who had just refilled her wooden bowl. "Do you think we should try to find the druids Adhna told us about? Are they likely to take us in?"

She narrowed her eyes. "I think so, but you don't? Why?"

He shrugged and took another spoonful. "You, certainly. They'd sure take you in. But why would they be interested in taking care of me? Other than my relation to you, I have no value to them. I'm no student of the arts, nor of history. While you can sing to the bees, I have no talent for singing or the law."

He stared at the burning wood, poking it with a stick until sparks flew. "I'm happy to take you to the druids, so they'll care for you. It might be easier for me to survive on my own."

Lainn put her now empty bowl on the ground with a hollow thump. "Take me to the druids and leave me? You're going to dump me with a group of strange men and go traipsing across the countryside on your own? You will do no such thing!"

He blinked several times. "I don't mean t-to abandon you. I only meant—"

"You only meant to leave me *safe* with men. Men we don't know, have never met, and cannot understand. Men, I might add, that might do what Sétna tried."

"But Adhna said—"

"Adhna can go soak his head in honey! I won' surrender myself to the whims of any man ever again. I thought you understood that?"

He swallowed his half-chewed bite of jerky as he thought about her position. "It's no less dangerous to be living rough in the winter. Especially for a girl."

She gave a shrug. "Then I'll be a boy. I feel more like one, anyhow. I don't do the girly things Aoife or the others do. *They* only think of attracting husbands. I want to learn new things and explore places. Besides," she patted her head, "I adore these warrior braids. So much more practical than loose hair."

Conall realized the conversation had been closed. No more argument mattered once Lainn made a decision. "Then we need to find a place for both of us to stay. This place isn't good enough. It's too close to Sétna."

She picked at the end of her brat. "Even if we can't stay with the druids at Uisneach, let's travel in that direction. We can follow the river west. We might find a *túath* or abandoned roundhouse."

He could see nothing wrong with her idea so, after they ate, they curled up in the back of the cave for a much-needed sleep.

In the morning, they re-packed their bags. Conall took care in placing each object in the linen sack, and as a result, it sat more comfortably on his shoulder, each object in its place. He shifted a few times to make sure everything was secure.

In a panic, he unpacked his own bag again, sighing in relief when he found the small package containing his father's brooch. For a horrible moment, he thought he'd left it behind.

Lainn peered over his shoulder. "What's that, Conall? Something else from Adhna?"

His father's admonition for secrecy in mind, he shoved the package back into the bag with a shake of his head. "Just something f- father gave me long ago. A sentimental keepsake."

She narrowed her eyes but didn't push. Instead, she belted her *léine* around her hips like a boy rather than around her waist. She'd added more beads to her braids, and they clicked as she walked.

As they left the cave, Conall watched her with a critical eye. Lainn moved more like a boy now. Her swagger wasn't as exaggerated, but she walked differently from the girl he'd known. She kept her shoulders squared and her back straight, which helped the illusion of confidence. Her face was delicate, but a fixed scowl made it less sweet.

Conall shifted the sacks on his back and followed her. He scanned the treeline in hopes Rawninn the raven had found them in the night. While birds rustled in the branches, no enormous black raven cawed for their attention. He felt both panicked and relieved at the bird's disappearance. If Rawninn found them, Conall would feel guilty for not seeking out the druids, as Adhna had urged. However, if he didn't find them, they might wander the forest all winter until they died of starvation or exposure.

The day dawned bright and relatively warm. Icicles melted as they walked, dripping and sparkling in the wintry sun. They followed the river as it wound through the valley, clambered over piles of bracken, stone outcroppings, and skirting around the few *túatha*.

Conall wanted to get at least a day's travel from Sétna before they met anyone who might tell him. And longer before they even considered a place to stay.

Glinting ice-strewn water blinded Conall, making him blink against the glare. Even then, images of shining spots burned in his vision. He stumbled on the rough rocks and landed on one knee, letting out a yelp of pain, setting his hip to ache again.

Lainn, who'd trudged ahead of him, glanced back. Seeing him already picking himself up, she continued. Her previously confidant stride degenerated into a tired slog. His own energy had long since left, as a night sleeping in a cold cave didn't give him a good night's sleep, but still they plodded on.

Conall pushed himself to walk more quickly to catch up to her, his knee aching with every step. His hip protested, shooting in pain. He hoped they found a place soon. His body complained more painfully with each passing minute.

The tree next to them exploded in a furious cacophony of black feathers and harsh birdcalls. Conall and Lainn both covered their heads from the onslaught, waiting until the last crow flew into the sky. The branches looked half as full as they had before. Watching the birds fly into the distance, they looked like an arrowhead pointing to a long, low hill on the horizon. Conall tried to see if Rawninn had been among the flock, but all the birds had been smaller.

Were they trying to point the way?

Trees on the side of this hill grew in a straight line, like a procession way. Perhaps it was a trick of the light, but Conall thought he spied stones on the hilltop. Conall wondered if it was the same hill where the druids lived, the hill Adhna had sent them to. If so, those stones must be faery stones, portals into the land of the Fae.

A dangerous place, druids or not.

He shivered and tore his gaze away from the beckoning hill. As he glanced down to the riverbank, he noticed a thatched roof just beyond a large rock. He poked Lainn and pointed.

The roundhouse had seen better days. Part of the thatch had fallen in. Gaps in the wicker and daub walls had allowed wind and wildlife pick away at the structure. Still, the rest of it looked sound, and the base stones seemed solid.

They approached with due caution, Conall listening for any human or animal. No one had lived here in many years, judging from the tangled dead weeds and rough ground.

With measured steps, he inched around one side of the cottage while Lainn explored the other side. Without words, they agreed to examine the inside together, but Conall entered first.

Dim light filtered through breaks in the wattle walls, forming broken shadows, masking amorphous forms with mystery and danger. Conall held perfectly still, listening for shuffles or creaks of an animal or human hiding within the shelter.

Nothing stirred, so he took three more steps as Lainn came in behind him. He touched one lump, discovering an overgrown hearth filled with ancient stones. A broken wooden cot lay along one wall, while a cracked stone water basin sat nearby. He found nothing else inside but layers of dust and dirt, leaves and twigs from countless abandoned winters.

Lainn put her hands on her hips. "Well, if no one claims this place, it might do for the winter, at least. Better than a freezing cave, at any rate." She surveyed the dusty corners, and her mouth curled up. "It could certainly use a thorough cleaning."

"See if you can find a d-decent branch with some leaves still clinging. That might work like a broom and should get the worst of it. I'll see if I can repair the cot frame."

They spent the remainder of the afternoon clearing out the roundhouse, weaving rough branches into the largest holes, and daubing mud into the cracks. The thatch would have to wait for another day. Exhaustion crept into his bones, and his hip screamed at him.

As evening fell, Lainn gathered sticks, but Conall stopped her. "We shouldn't light a fire tonight. We're both too tired to stay up, and we can't risk the place going up in flames. Tomorrow, during the day, we'll test the hearth and watch it carefully."

"Why didn't we do that today, then?"

"The walls needed fixing first."

His sister muttered under her breath, something about being able to do both, and then bit into one of Adhna's apples. "We should also find the closest *túath*. Soon we'll need more food than what Adhna gave us."

"We have nothing to trade. I might offer my services to do stonework, but it will take a while for the local people to trust us. If there even *are* any local people."

"I could sing or tell stories, just like a real bard."

"Won't that get you in t-trouble? You're barely one season trained."

She shrugged. "They never told me not to. I've memorized the fifteen stories from the first year and most of the second fifteen. Even if people are familiar with the stories, the storyteller's job is to bring them to life, to coax nuance out of the tale itself, and bring the characters awake. Gemmán always said I was particularly talented at that aspect. That must be worth something to a small *túath*."

Remembering the hill in the distance, Conall wasn't certain that would be the case. If an enclave of true druids lived so close, a trainee wouldn't be in much demand. Many of the locals might already know the first fifteen stories just by sheer exposure. Still, he didn't know for certain, and he didn't wish to crush Lainn's idea out of hand. She may end up being their savior.

They curled up next to each other for warmth, draping all their brats and furs over them both. Exhausted as he was, it took Conall a long time to sleep, staring into the inky black winter night.

An owl's hoot roused him from half-remembered dreams of being chased through a raging river, not being able to move his feet fast enough to escape the angry river monster. He jerked awake but held still until the owl hooted again. He detected no alarm in the call, only a statement of existence. The owl wanted all to know he watched the night.

Conall shivered, his back and left side frozen from the cold earth. Where he curled around Lainn, his body warmed. He promised himself he would always protect her from danger, no matter what befell them.

Even if he hadn't promised his father as much, he would always protect her.

He slept more soundly after that.

Chapter Six

A *túath* stood a half hour's walk south of their found home, consisting of ten roundhouses around a gathering circle for festivals and bonfires. The bonfire was stacked high with sticks, probably in preparation for mid-winter celebrations. The farmers had likely been stacking deadwood on the pile for weeks, and it rose even taller than the houses.

Farmland radiated from the center like a wheel. While each resident eyed Conall with suspicion at first, Lainn was his saving grace. She still wore boys clothing and kept her voice low. But where doors were shut in his face, people smiled at his sister. When she offered to sing them a song, they listened, rapt at her perfect voice.

Bright red cardinals alighted on her shoulders when she sang, making children gasp in wonder. Folks offered them food and drink for the entertainment, even inviting them in for a meal now and then.

After several days of gathering supplies, they returned to their cottage with riches of meat, cheese, and bread. They smiled and joked with each other on the journey back, their spirits and outlook lifted considerably.

The hearth needed work, but by moving the old stones to the edge of the cottage, they blocked the worst floor drafts. Plenty of dried branches and twigs lie around them in the forest.

Conall wove a serviceable basket from dried reeds. With this creation, he concentrated on remembering all his father had taught him about fishing. While his father had fished every day, he'd seldom brought his son until the last year or so.

Conall had been barely twelve winters old when their father had fallen ill. Even then, his father had not deliberately taught him, not like Sétna taught the mason's trade. He simply fished and let Conall watch.

Sétna explained each step, the reason behind each step, and hints on how to avoid making mistakes. For all his faults, Sétna was a much more effective teacher than Fingin had been.

The comparison rocked Conall. His father held a special place in his heart, almost a god-like status. He could do no wrong in Conall's eyes. The honesty in this assessment, showing Fingin as less than perfect, especially as compared to Sétna, shattered that illusion of perfection.

Shaking away the disturbing revelation, Conall picked up his basket and tools and stalked down to the riverbank. After several tiring hours in the slushy water, he returned with three scrawny trout. While their size muted his success, he still felt proud of his catch. They roasted the fish on a stone near the hearth that evening.

A large bubble formed on the skin of one fish and Lainn pushed it down with her finger, instantly putting the finger in her mouth to soothe the burn.

Conall laughed. "So, did that grant you all the knowledge of the world?"

She grimaced around her finger. "It's not a salmon, silly, much less the Salmon of Knowledge. And you're no wizard."

"No, but we still have to figure out how to get enough food for the winter. I hope you gained some wisdom."

She poked the fish again, this time being clever enough to use a stick rather than her tender flesh. "We'll figure something out. My singing went well today, don't you think?"

He nodded. "More b-b-beautifully than when you sang for the bees. But we can only count on that for a while. Soon the local people will grow weary of even that beauty. Would you dance, perhaps?"

She shook her head. "Not while singing. I have to concentrate on one or the other. Besides, that would ruin my disguise. What about you? You used to juggle."

When he'd been younger, juggling, manipulation, and all sorts of tricks fascinated him. But his mother hated them, berating him for foolish pursuits, so he gave it up. Now they might be useful skills to hone again. Especially now that the brooch's magic gave him the power to move objects. In fact, juggling might be the perfect thing. He smiled. "I'll find good, round stones tomorrow and practice. I'll be rusty, I'm sure."

"Your body will remember how." Lainn spoke with such certainty, Conall couldn't argue.

As he pried the roasted fish from the stone, Lainn poured the last of the mead into their mugs. "At least we've plenty of fresh water with the river nearby."

His sister shook the wineskin several times, trying to coax the final drop out. She peered in to ensure it was empty and a drop fell in her eye. Conall laughed as she squinted and shook her head, trying to wipe the honey alcohol out.

He snorted as he served her a portion. "And we only need to freeze to death to get it. The cliff is steep here. I wish we'd found a gentler shore to access the water in a safer place."

His sister stared at him, not touching her fish, for several moments. "I do believe you would complain if a god sat next to you and offered you the crown of the world."

Conall took a sip of water and when he put his cup down, pursed his lips. "Well, you'd invite the goddess of d-death in for a d-drink and a nice chat."

She scowled and poked at her fish. "I see nothing wrong with that. Everyone deserves kindness."

"Except Sétna."

Silence fell as they ate their fish in sullen contemplation. Conall regretted his words, his reminder to Lainn of what she'd almost suffered at their stepfather's hands. He wished his magical talent allowed him to wrestle time backwards, just long enough to erase his thoughtless words.

Instead, he stared at the thatch. The one big spot would take a lot of work to fix. Even just covering it with branches and bracken would take a lot of effort, securing it in place with twine. Such a temporary repair wouldn't stand up to the fierce wind of a winter storm, much less a heavy layer of snow.

To truly fix it would require dried hay, which they'd have to trade for from a farmer. This late in the season, no farmer would want to part with their livestock's fodder. Maybe some sedge grass or cattails would do for this season?

Lainn hummed low, a sad melody with poignance and pathos. Though she sang no words, the tune distracted him from his plans, making him long for his father with an aching need. Was his father still alive somewhere in the world? If so, why hadn't he come back for them? Why had he left?

He swallowed against the tears and wondered how their mother fared. She must have realized they'd disappeared by now. What story had Sétna spun about their flight from home? Conall knew the truth wouldn't have been any part of it.

His sister's voice wrapped around his body, the melancholy music making him close his eyes and fall asleep in untroubled slumber. When he woke, the morning sun shone strongly on his face, but he felt more rested than he had in weeks.

Had Lainn sung him to sleep? Had she used druidic magic to soothe his troubled soul? He glanced at her, peacefully snoring under her brat, close to the banked peat fire. She must have more magic than even her druid tutor had realized.

Had their father given her a magic brooch as well?

No, her magic seemed more primal, more visceral. Hers must be an innate talent, not one granted by a magical artifact. Conall didn't know why he knew this, but when he said the words in his mind, he realized their truth. As he had many times in the past, Conall considered telling her about the brooch. His father's words, urging him to keep the magic safe and secret, kept him from sharing.

Despite his resolve to keep his secret, if she'd given him a decent night's rest with her magic, he'd be grateful. It felt like years since he had slept through the night.

He stirred the peat to rekindle the fire, adding several pieces of kindling and branches. Fetching water from the river, which involved a treacherous climb down a slippery cliff, he heated it in the pot. Some warm fruit would be a welcome morning meal.

Lainn still hadn't woken by the time the fruit stewed. With a resentful glance at her sleeping form, he ate his portion and wandered outside, intent on gathering materials to repair the roof. He found several thin, dry branches that spread flat rather than round. Those might work for the framework if he could secure them to the existing eaves.

Once he gathered that pile, he clambered down to the water's edge to search for dried sedge and grass. The trick to thatch being waterproof was layer upon layer of thin straw. It took so long for water to work its way through the layers, it coated the straw rather than drip down. While he found no true straw, reeds would do. He found cattail roots, flat grass, and several stands of winter-dried sedge. After cutting them with Lainn's knife, he made another pile.

As he reached for another clump of cattails, the ancient bronze knife held ready to saw at their base, the mud below him shifted, and he slid down into the icy river. He tried to use his magic to save himself from the water, but the bank gave way too quickly, and soon he stood waste-deep in the freezing river.

"Blood and bones! That's cold!" With chattering teeth, he dragged himself to a rocky outcropping and dragged his sodden self to dry land. Conall lay on the rocks, panting from his effort and wishing for a hot, crackling fire to warm his icy skin.

After cursing himself roundly, he forced himself to rise. If he gave in to rest now, he might never get up again. He could die from a chill easily here next to the water, half-frozen from his spill. With renewed determination and clenched teeth, he attacked another tuft of sedge grass, working his way toward firmer ground along the riverbank.

By the time he had sorted, stripped, cleaned, and bundled the grasses, he sat on a log outside the roundhouse and wiped his brow. Despite his dunking, he was sweating. While his boots were squishy and his toes were numb, his *léine* had almost completely dried, and his stomach growled with startling volume. Lainn should be up by now.

The sullen glow of the fire didn't illuminate the interior well, especially after the brightness outside. When Conall's eyes adjusted, he saw Lainn still curled up next to the fire.

With a frown, he shook her shoulder. "Lainn? Lainn, wake up, lazybones."

She grunted and waved her hand in dismissal, turning away from him.

Exhaling deeply, he stared at his sister. If she needed sleep so badly, he should let her. He left the rest of the stewed fruit in a bowl next to her. He grabbed a stick of dried venison and some bread and cheese from yesterday's barter and went outside.

Clouds had chased the bright sunshine away, and the air grew considerably colder. Conall shivered and pulled his brat back around his shoulders. He should get the roof repair started before those dark clouds brought a storm. He didn't want to wake Lainn from her sleep, but he could prepare the frames.

First, he tied all the frame branches into a bundle and tossed it onto the good part of the roof. Then he did the same with the grasses. He missed the first time and kicked himself for stupidity, using his talent to ensure it worked the second time.

Next, he used the doorway to haul himself up, at the expense of a few scraped knuckles. He held his magic ready in case he fell. He'd never tried to lift himself and he didn't want to try unless he had no other choice.

Conall used twine to secure the branches in place, so they stayed parallel with the edge of the roof. However, he needed at least three more to complete the job. He scampered back down but, before he jumped the last few feet, he tried to lower himself to the ground with his magic. It worked, but a strong wave of nausea hit him. If that happened each time, he should only use such a trick in extreme need.

After he dry-heaved a few times, he scoured the nearby brush for three more stout, flat branches. He only found two. A rustling in the bracken startled him, and he took a few steps back, only to get a face full of black feathers and raucous screeches. He covered his head with his hands and cried out, falling on his backside as he tried to escape the attack. His hip cracked on a rock.

When he opened his eyes, a huge black raven sat on a branch, cocking his head several times in curious regard. "Rawninn, is that you? Did you find us?"

The raven cawed once, flapped his wings, and then flew into the roundhouse. With a sigh, Conall gathered his two good branches and followed with a limp. While relieved the raven had found them again, the annoying bird had best let Lainn sleep.

Inside the chilly roundhouse, the raven picked at the stewed fruit and Lainn still slept. Conall whispered, "Leave that, Rawninn! That's for her. Here, have some fish." He tossed the bits of bone left from last night's dinner, still with some flesh on them, toward the bird. Rawninn caught the bones in his beak and fluttered off to a stone along the wall to enjoy his treat.

The sky grew dimmer with more clouds, despite being only mid-afternoon, and Conall rushed back up to the roof to finish his repairs. He bridged the gap with only two branches as best he could.

Once he secured the frame, he placed a layer of grass crosswise, so they pointed from the center of the roof to the edge. After the first layer covered the frame, he tied it down with twine and set a second layer, and then a third and a fourth. He wished he had enough grass to do a fifth or even a sixth, but the first drops of freezing rain convinced him his efforts had to do for now.

Conall slithered down the doorway, almost slipping at the last moment. His hip felt better now, but he didn't need to injure himself again. He'd had horrible luck so far, and he didn't wish to make it worse.

Rawninn still picked at his bones and Lainn still slept. The first glimmer of concern washed over Conall, but he shrugged it off. The last few days had been full of trauma and uncertainty, pain and physical exertion. If Lainn needed time to recover, he'd make certain she got it.

Conall sat inside the roundhouse and stoked the fire up to a comfortable level. Rain pounded on the thatch, but not through it. His patch job had held so far, and he smiled in satisfaction. Despite his stepfather's complaints, he *could* do something well.

Anger shoved aside for survival's sake boiled inside him now. That Sétna should try to molest Lainn felt so wrong, so evil, Conall couldn't breathe when he considered it. The attack seemed a dream, something too horrible to be real. Yet it had been real. Sétna had tried to bed his own stepdaughter.

Maybe people did such things elsewhere. Perhaps this would be normal to someone else. Where Conall grew up, this wasn't normal, and he wouldn't allow it to be, not with Lainn. He'd promised their father he'd care for her, and no matter what happened, he meant to keep that vow.

Conall swallowed back unexpected tears and glanced at his sister, still slumbering beside the fire. Darkness had fallen outside, the glowing fire casting strange shapes on the walls. Shadows danced and writhed, forming demonic shapes in the strange roundhouse. These dancing shapes lulled Conall into a fitful sleep.

Sliding ice shifted beneath his feet, and he couldn't find balance in the world. Around him, screeching creatures reached for him, tugging and pulling at his ragged clothing. Frozen wind whipped against his face, numbing his skin and stealing his breath. Everywhere he looked, terror awaited him.

Conall sat up with a scream, his heart pounding within his chest. All was quiet within the roundhouse. Lainn lay in her spot and Rawninn slept with one wing tucked over his beak.

His blood raced as his nightmare echoed in the waking world. Knowing he was too tense to sleep again, he flung the blanket off and rubbed his face. He glanced at the door, but no light seeped through the wattle cracks. It might be near midnight or near dawn; he had no way of knowing. Still, the fire had burned down considerably since he last noticed, so it must have been a few hours.

He glanced at the plate with stewed fruit, still untouched since the day before. Lainn needed to eat, and soon this would be more important than sleep. Didn't she need to relieve herself? She might have done so while he repaired the roof. She might also have eaten then.

Reassured, he kept himself busy by unpacking the food onto the stone shelf along one wall, forming a pantry. He took stock of their supplies.

Their food might last most of one moon if they ate carefully. Fishing would help, and they could set snares for rabbits. Midwinter was barely a half-moon away, but three more moons of winter remained before the spring growth would provide any food. Even then, animals would be lean from winter and wily.

Lainn could sing and tell stories. He could do repairs to stones, even roofs or doorways. Conall remembered Lainn's suggestion about juggling and cursed himself for forgetting to find suitable stones. They both might entertain surrounding *túatha*.

Only two apples remained, so Conall grabbed three turnips. They weren't round, but they'd do for practice. He cut off the greens and the pointed tips and hefted each one, testing their weight. One was lighter than the others, so he'd have to compensate.

He stood near the glowing fire and drew in his will, gathering his magic. While a bouncing turnip on the ground wouldn't make a lot of noise, Lainn still slept, and he wasn't sure how much bouncing the vegetables would take. Better to have his magic primed and ready for immediate use.

Since he'd gotten the brooch, Conall had learned he needed to concentrate on the brooch, pull his power in through the earth and into his body, and then direct it from his body to whatever object he wanted to lift. All this took time and practice.

Perhaps that explained why he'd been so nauseous trying to move his own body. If he didn't prepare the power ahead of time, he might get a trickle, but never the full effect. And afterward, he paid the price.

Even if he prepared, his strength drained easily using the magic. As a result, he'd learned to use the power sparingly.

While re-learning to juggle wasn't a life-or-death skill, it might mean the difference between eating and starving over the course of the bitter winter months. The price might be worth it.

Thinking back to when he first learned the skill, he took just one turnip and practiced tossing it up in a perfect arc, then passing it low between his hands. Over and over, he made a perfect oval with the single turnip until he grew dizzy from focusing on the heavy vegetable in the near darkness.

Once he grew more comfortable with that action, Conall turned in place, keeping the oval perfect even as his body spun. Careful step by careful step, he turned once, twice, three times, all while concentrating on his oval.

His body remembered what to do, even though it had been at least four years since he'd tried to juggle. He didn't yet need his magic to assist his dexterity. Conall smiled in the dim light, proud of his ability.

The raucous caw of the raven shattered his concentration, and the turnip thumped onto the ground, rolling across to tap the sleeping Lainn on her head. She mumbled but didn't wake.

"Rawninn! Shush. You made me mess up."

The annoying bird ruffled his wings and opened his beak but remained silent. He settled back down on his perch and glared at him with glittering black eyes.

Conall stared at his sister, his brow wrinkling in bitter confusion. "Really? Even *that* didn't wake you? You must really be away with the faeries to sleep through that racket."

Light seeped in through the door and walls, so the dawn must be approaching. Conall stretched his back and made it crack before replacing the turnips on the shelf. His muscles already ached from the unusual activity, and he knew better than to hurt himself with over-weaning effort.

He considered their supplies and decided to hunt for herbs to season their meals. Not much grew in winter, but he might find a few stalks of sage or rosemary in the bracken.

Glancing at the roof, he remembered the cattails. The roots were edible. Maybe he should cut some down? No, they needed the roof. He'd just have to find more.

He might find parsley or coltsfoot for a touch of saltiness. Pine nuts would add some flavor, and he could make pine needle tea. Turnips tasted much better with butter and salt, but they'd been unable to buy butter in the *túath*. Wood ash would give it a salty flavor, but Lainn hated the charred aftertaste.

He grabbed his travel sack, now almost empty of clothes, tools, and supplies, put on his almost-dried boots, and walked outside into the crisp pre-dawn air. Crystalline dew and mist covered every object, making the landscape ethereal and wondrous.

Not a creature moved in the stillness, and his breath created puffs of steam. Conall almost didn't dare to breathe on the spider's web sparkling with frozen dewdrops. The beauty and delicacy required that he stop and admire the artistry.

A lone bee few across his line of sight, buzzing lazily around the web. Conall shooed it away lest it got caught in the gossamer creation. Lainn would be pleased to find bees nearby, though it seemed much too cold for them. It flew around the back of the roundhouse in a wobbly spiral.

Conall flung his empty sack over his shoulder and walked to the river's edge. Most plants grew better near the water in the winter months. He walked to where he'd found the cattails the day before, searching for the tall sprigs of rosemary and the ground cover for coltsfoot or parsley.

A roe deer lifted her head from the opposite riverbank as he approached, her dappled coat betraying her youth. Conall stopped, allowing her to get used to his presence. "Don't worry, doe. I'm no hunter."

She flicked an ear several times before she bowed her head, took one more drink, and then bounded off into the brush. Her graceful leaps made almost no noise.

The grace of such creatures never failed to amaze Conall, no matter how many times he witnessed it. The freedom to run as far and as long as he liked seemed like the ultimate joy. And while he knew he ought to hunt her for meat, the notion disgusted him at the moment. Not that he was much of a hunter. He didn't even have a bow.

His nose tingled with a tangy scent, and he smiled in delight at shoots of wild garlic at his feet. He dug one up, disappointed to find no bulbs yet. He'd have to wait for spring.

Wrinkling his nose, Conall scanned the ground for other herbs, but nothing green grew nearby. Almost by accident, he noticed rosemary behind him. With a grin, he harvested several woody stalks, bundling them together. He sat up, despite a twinge in his hip, and brushed off his hands, ready to find more winter bounty.

A fat hare flicked across his path, its gray-brown fur blending into the forest floor so well, he almost missed it. He made a note to set snares, as the meat would be a welcome respite to dried venison.

A raven cawed in the distance, making Conall rush back to the roundhouse. He cursed himself for leaving Lainn sleeping alone. What if someone came and found her asleep and alone? He scrambled up the bank, slipping several times until he abandoned all caution and used his magic to push himself up the bank. The wave of sickness made him bend over and cough, spitting up as he ran the rest of the distance.

The bird perched on the corner of the repaired thatch, wings spread, but Conall saw no one else. A quick check inside proved Lainn still slept. Conall frowned and checked the night basket. Only his own waste was there. The stewed fruit looked untouched.

Conall knelt next to his sister, apprehension growing within his heart. He put his hand in front of her mouth, and her breath warmed it, which reassured him. Next, he shook her shoulder. Gently at first, he increased his efforts when he elicited no response. "Lainn? Lainn, you need to wake up. Wake up, now. Wake! Lainn! Please, wake up."

Rawninn cawed several times, flying into the roundhouse and swooping in circles. Conall flung his arms over his head. "Stop that! Go away!"

A moan from Lainn distracted him from the bird, but she didn't rouse.

The raven landed on the shelf, picking at a turnip. A single bee buzzed into the roundhouse. Conall watched as it circled the interior of the roundhouse, flew near the raven, and then came toward him and Lainn. He didn't understand why the raven didn't eat the bee but the bird just cocked its head as if listening.

The bee circled above Lainn's head several times before landing on her ear. Worried about the bee stinging his sister, Conall leaned closer to watch the insect. It moved its legs several times, but he couldn't make out much more without better light.

Lainn gasped, her eyes flying wide open. Conall's forehead almost collided with Lainn's as she shot up. Her eyes darted around, flickering to each dark shape in the roundhouse, to Rawninn, to Conall, and to the still-open door.

A cold breeze brought in the scent of rotting leaves and fresh rain.

Lainn's eyes grew wide as she turned to Conall. Her voice came in a hoarse whisper, almost unrecognizable. "He's coming. He'll find us."

"Shh, we're safe here, Lainn. He wouldn't c-come this far."

She shook her head, her braid beads clacking discordantly. "He'll be here soon. We must leave! The bee told me."

Belatedly, Conall glanced around for the insect but saw no trace of it. "You had a bad dream, Lainn. Here, let me help you to the night basket. You must be bursting."

She allowed him to help her to her feet, but her eyes flicked at every movement, nervous as a cat. When she finished, he made her sit and eat.

His sister shoved fruit in her mouth, but mumbled as she chewed. "Pack the food, Conall. We don't want to lose what we've gathered."

He rolled his eyes, but it would do less harm to humor her. Packing the food wouldn't hurt it. Wasted effort, but it kept her calm.

Everything fit into both sacks and her small bag. They'd only been in the roundhouse for a few days, after all. Time melded together as he tried to remember. Without the daily routines he'd lived with all his life, he'd lost track.

A loud crack outside made him jump. Suddenly, Lainn's dream-fueled fears didn't seem so ridiculous. He scrambled to grab both sacks, flinging the larger one over his shoulder. He threw his brat on and tugged on his boots. Lainn did the same, and then scattered the remains of the peat fire. Acrid smoke filled the small roundhouse, making them cough and choke. Rawninn squawked and flapped his wings.

Terrified that Sétna had found them and that they'd just given away their location with coughing, Conall sought Lainn's hand and squeezed it tight. They held all their earthly belongings on their back and waited, frozen in fear, as the unmistakable sound of crunching leaves grew inexorably closer.

Chapter Seven

Crunch. Crunch. Pause. Crunch. Crunch. Crunch. Conall held his breath as they approached. His chest burned and he let it out again. He drew another with a shudder and flicked a quick glance at Lainn. She looked pale, but that could be weak light, peat smoke, or her two-day slumber. Whatever the cause, her lips were pressed into a grim line.

Conall drew upon the brooch's magic, pulling up power through the brooch, up from the earth and through his feet. It made his hands and fingers tingle. He noticed a slight glow, a dim spark underneath his fingernails. He stood ready to do whatever he must to protect Lainn.

A shadow darkened the doorway, cutting off most of the light. With a mix of relief and disappointment, Conall realized this couldn't be Sétna. The tall, thin frame was a far cry from Sétna's hefty belly.

A stranger didn't mean safety, though. He peeked at Lainn and saw the same mixture of emotions cross her face. She remained as stock still as he did.

As Conall's eyes grew used to the darkness, he could pick out details. The man held a tall walking staff, a stout oak branch carved into the head of a wolf. He wore warrior braids and a thick fur brat. His bushy, black beard almost hid his scowling face. The man's low, guttural voice jabbed into the darkness. "Y' don't belong here."

Conall swallowed. "M- my apologies, we'll leave now. We meant n-n-no harm." He hefted the second sack and pulled on Lainn's hand, hoping the man step away from the doorway so they could escape.

The man glanced up to where Conall had repaired the thatch, and his eyes narrowed. Conall inched closer to the door, Lainn silent behind him. "P-please, we'll just go now."

The intruder grunted and shifted to one side, leaving them enough room to slide past. Conall ducked and writhed his way out, Lainn slithering afterward.

Once clear of the doorway, they ran as fast as they could away from the roundhouse, into the woods, westward. Neither even looked back, worried they'd see the hunter following them.

As Conall's hip screamed in pain, he pushed farther until he couldn't ignore it any longer. He slowed, but Lainn kept running. Conall panted, "Lainn! Lainn, wait for me. I have to rest just a b-bit."

She slowed, glancing over her shoulder in nervous worry. "We're not far enough away. He'll come. He'll find us."

As he caught his breath, bent over with his hands on his knees, he furrowed his brow. "You said those words when you woke up. What did you mean? Was it a dream of Sétna coming for us? Or something else? That wasn't Sétna who c-came."

She shook her head, but fear still danced in her eyes. They seemed feral, startled at every natural noise in the surrounding woods. "We can't stay. We can never stay. He's coming."

Her voice no longer had the carefree tinkling of bells when she laughed. Now she spoke low and flat, inflectionless. That change chilled Conall more than the winter wind.

With a glance over his shoulder to ensure they were, in fact, alone, he straightened his back and took three steps. When he stood directly in front of his sister, he placed his hands on her shoulders. "I c-can't pretend to know what's going through your mind and your heart, Lainn. I don't know what happened to you these last few days. All I know is that I'm here to keep you from harm. That's my d-duty and calling. Do you understand me? I won't abandon you, and I won't let anyone t-take you."

A glimmer of his sister's soul shone through her eyes, but then it faded away. Her furtive glances returned, and he drew her in for a long hug, not letting her go even when she didn't hug back. Finally, she melted from a stiff log into human form and hugged him back.

When he let her go, the glimmer was back. Not strong, but recognizable. He even coaxed a half-smile from her lips, and he returned it with a full grin. "Now, let's go forward. We may have lost the roundhouse, but thanks to your t-timely warning, we have our food."

She took a deep breath as they walked down the path. "I didn't know why we needed to pack, I just knew we did. The darkness came closer, and I could feel it, but it took Barnabus to rouse me to action."

"Barnabus? Was he someone in your dreams?"

"No, silly. The bee. Remember? Adhna introduced us."

He gave his sister a sidelong look. Had her dreams stolen her wits? He remembered Adhna's story, but that was just a fancy tale. The old man was full of ridiculous stories.

They walked in silence. He didn't wish to disturb any fragile belief she might have about the random bee, and it didn't really matter. Let her believe it had been one of Adhna's bees. Such belief did no lasting harm.

Crunching ice and leaves beneath their feet became a marching rhythm as they walked. Bare trees reached skeletal arms above them, sheltering them from the frigid sky. Dark clouds chased white clouds, changing the temperature as they danced above. The path wended through the forest, slowly creeping to the west.

Once, they passed a large clearing with a cluster of farmhouses to their left. But smoke seeped through the thatch, and the pungent odor of farm animals and burning peat assured them the houses were well-occupied. They traveled on.

The river no longer marched beside them, but Conall spied a hill in the distance. This might be Uisneach, the druid hill, but he couldn't tell. Mists covering the top of the hill hid all details.

While Lainn didn't want to take chances with the druids, that might be their only option now. His earlier reluctance had given way to concern over their ability to survive. The druids might at least give them supplies for the winter. But he doubted they even had the right hill.

The path rose, and his thigh muscles complained. He wished they could rest, but now Lainn had purpose and energy. Few things got in her way when she was determined. They'd only stop when they found a place to stay the night.

His sister had changed over the last few days. No longer the adorable little sister, she was tall as a young woman in her own right, though she counted but sixteen winters. Her confidence was mercurial, flitting between unstoppable and nonexistent. But then again, his own confidence was only a sham.

He dug the heel of his hand into his thigh, wishing the ache would ease, even for a little while. He stumbled as the path grew rocky and the trees fell away. Soon, they climbed into the fog, dark gray enveloping them. Up, up they traveled, into the misty mystery.

Gray swirling fog obscured everything, even his sister's form fading to a blob. Darkness swayed back and forth with each step in her boy's swagger. The faint click of the beads in both their braids was the only other sound to penetrate the mist, as the world went silent.

Dank, musty fog filled his nostrils. Conall wondered what had happened to the raven when they fled the roundhouse. The bird had fled when the hunter arrived.

Several bare hawthorn trees grew from the gray as they passed, reaching for them with emaciated fingers. A bare touch from one made him flinch and shiver. He stumbled over a small ridge in the land, an oddly precise line of demarcation. Someone might have built a wall there centuries in the past. Now it was a lump along the ground.

A dark shape loomed beyond Lainn's fading figure. As it coalesced in the mist, it resolved into a huge pile of stones. Conall caught his breath, certain they'd found Uisneach. Stones piled atop each other, reaching twice his own height, shaped like a cat crouched, watching a mouse.

Every part of his body urged him to run far away, faster than he'd ever run before. His skin crawled, and the back of his eyeballs itched. Conall's bones screamed at the stone. It screamed back. A woman's voice dripping with rage and longing settled into his blood.

He yanked Lainn back just as she walked near the stone.

"Conall! What are you doing?"

"Don't pass that stone!"

She furrowed her brow. "What are you talking about? It's just a stone."

He stared at the figure, mist still clinging stubbornly to the crevices. "No, it's not just a stone. It's anything but *just a stone.* Can't you feel it? You're the one with druid training. The thing is alive. Dangerous. It's screaming at me."

His sister stared at the stone for several moments. She grew pale and clutched Conall's arm, her fingers digging into his skin. "The stone is moving. Breathing. How could it be breathing?"

Fully expecting the cat to raise its head and blink at them, Conall pulled Lainn back, step by step, until they'd reached the remnants of the stone wall. Once the fog swallowed the stone once again, his heart stopped skipping.

"Conall, what was that?"

"I don't know. I don't want to know. Did your training give you any hint of such a thing?"

Lainn shook her head, her eyes still glued to where the stone hid in the mist. "Nothing. But I'm only one season into my training. Most of my education has been memorizing tales and listening to nature. Stonework is at least sixth season."

"Stonework. Simple words." He shivered, a reaction that had nothing to do with the cold fog caressing his skin. The stone's screeching had faded from his mind, but it lingered in the shadows. The wet kiss of the morning suffocated him. He needed to be elsewhere.

Conall took Lainn's hand and drew her away. Not south the way they came, nor north toward the haunting stone, but to the east, along the low ridge.

As he breathed the thickening mist, his heart raced, and he needed away from this smothering damp. His breath got more labored as he hurried along the ridge, praying for escape from the enduring shriek haunting his mind. The stone pulled upon him, dragging his will back to its seductive danger.

With a wrench of determination, he shut that part of his mind away into a hollow pocket. He kept his aching grief for his father in such a pocket and the guilt for leaving his mother.

The ridgeline cut off, turning into a stone-lined path, dense with packed earth from the feet of many travelers. The path led north once again, but well past the menacing stone.

With a glance at Lainn, he placed one foot upon the path. His hip spasmed, but that single step eased his pain. The lines on Lainn's worried face smoothed out as she followed his footsteps.

Peace and joy suffused through his legs and into his heart as he walked along the bare dirt. No ice formed upon the path, though it sparkled on hawthorn bushes to either side. As the ground rose and they climbed to the summit, his pain and fear slipped away.

Just as a shaft of sunlight burned through the mist, they reached the top of the hill. A stone wall built upon a rampart encircled two large roundhouses, their roofs peeking over the rampart, but no smoke filtered through the thatch.

Conall smelled no livestock, no fire, no midden. The enclosure remained still and silent as the sun bathed it in the preternatural glow of mid-winter morning.

Massive wooden gates stood open, one barely attached to its pole. A breeze rocked the gate, making it creak loud in the strange silence.

Gripping Lainn's hand, Conall walked into the enclosure, senses alert for any sign of life.

Both roundhouses had seen better days. Like the one in the forest, they both needed serious care and maintenance. A firepit in the center hadn't been lit in many seasons. A pile of brush and trash lined the edge of the rampart, shoved by the wind to the corners.

Lainn took a deep sigh, spinning to see everything. "Do you think anyone else will come? Can we rest here?"

"I hope so. Which roundhouse should we t-try?"

She glanced at both and pointed to the one on the left. "The smaller one. It'll be easier to heat."

His mouth in a grim line, Conall took out his belt knife and approached the roundhouse with caution. Lainn walked around the exterior of the building as he entered, nostrils flared for any odors and ears perked for any sound.

Lainn's cry made him dart back outside in an instant, only to find her chuckling with her hand over her heart. "Just a rabbit. Nearly frightened me out of my wits."

He gave her a wry smile. "That's p-p-presuming you had your wits, to begin with. I'm fairly certain I left mine b-back at home, days ago."

She let out a short bark of laughter and shook her head. "Did you see anything inside?"

"You didn't give me a chance, did you? You and your rabbit."

Despite the interruption, Conall's heart slowed, at peace with himself and their situation. Laughter definitely helped, and the roundhouse felt welcoming, warm, and comforting.

But why would a strange, cold, deserted roundhouse feel like home? Why would he wish to go inside, despite the dangers? That sentiment made no sense and thus remained suspect.

Conall gripped his bronze knife until the swirled designs on the hilt bit into his fingers, motioned Lainn to remain behind him, and tiptoed into the roundhouse.

Like the one in the forest, only broken bits of shelf and pottery littered the floor. Dirt and leaves had blown in, swirling and rustling in lonely eddies. A musty odor of neglect permeated the room.

"This place seems safe, Conall. I'm so tired. Can't we sleep? Just for one night?"

Conall shook his head. "Too safe, Lainn. It feels too safe. Why should we be safe here? We're on a hill in the mist, in a place given to the gods long ago. This is no fit place for humans."

She threw up her hands. "Now you're just difficult! Given to the gods. You think this is a sacred space? If anyone held this place in the least regard, they wouldn't have left it to rot. Someone would have swept, repaired, and maintained the houses."

While her logic made sense, it still seemed too odd for this sense of peace to come across so strong. Still, he grew weary after their ordeal.

He let out a yawn so wide, his jaw cracked. "Let me check the other roundhouse, just to be sure. Wait here."

"Oh, no. You aren't going in alone. I'll be right behind you."

He wrinkled his nose but how would he stop her, anyhow? He adjusted the bag still over his shoulder, unwilling to leave it in case they needed to run from whatever hid in the second roundhouse.

Though larger, the other house hadn't fared as well with time. Something had shattered the center pole, allowing the thatch roof to buckle inward. More broken furniture scattered within as if someone had left in a hurry, forgetting essential pieces of their lives in a rush to leave.

Ghosts of prior residents flitted through Conall's mind. Panic and fear seized his heart, urging him to flee before the danger arrived. He steeled his will to keep from running far away.

"I don't like it here, Conall. We chose the right roundhouse."

He didn't want to stay on the hill at all, but they did need rest. They returned to the smaller roundhouse without a word.

Conall set down Adhna's linen bag, his shoulder aching with relief. As he set it upon the packed-earth floor, dust sprang up. The motes sparkled in a beam of strong sunlight, giving an almost magical hue to the air surrounding them.

Lainn had already curled up with her sack as a pillow, dead to the world. To protect her, he curled up behind her, sharing her warmth. He placed his smaller sack under his head and the larger one at his back. With one last glimpse at the door, the noon-day sun now beating through the last shreds of fog, he closed his eyes and found the bliss of slumber.

Chapter Eight

Ice crashed on his head like hammers, pounding his skull until he covered his scalp with his arms. When Conall glanced up, he saw the thatch had fallen away even further from their meager roof, letting in winter hail.

"Blood and bones!" He scrambled to his feet and retreated to the edge. The roof above Lainn was still solid, but his head ached where apple-sized stones had hit him. He rubbed his scalp, trying to ease the pain. The sheer volume of noise from the hail drowned out all other concerns until his bladder informed him that he'd slept all day, thank you very much, and would like immediate attention.

Conall stepped outside and took care of his need, ducking hail. When he went back inside, he checked their supplies. All three sacks were safe, so he rifled in his for an apple. He found the dried venison and a small cheese first, so he ate those. The venison tasted sour; the dried meat would be unsafe to eat soon.

He put the rest out for Lainn and washed down his meal with his flask. Hailstones bounced around on the open floor of the roundhouse. He picked one up, hefting the icy stone a few times with a smile, despite the chill. Then he grabbed two more and used them to practice his juggling. He dropped them and they cracked into many pieces, but he had a huge selection of replacements.

Conall didn't understand how Lainn was sleeping through the racket, and for a moment, worried that she'd once again fallen into an unnatural slumber. But she moaned a few times and turned over.

She woke with a cry, her eyes darting around the room. "Conall! What in the name of *Goibnui's* forge are you doing?"

He blinked several times and held up his ice balls with a blank expression. "Juggling?"

Lainn stared at him and burst out laughing. Conall giggled, unable to keep a straight face. Soon, they both rolled on the ground with belly-laughs, reveling in the hilarity of nothing at all.

Adhna once told him laughter was a salve for the soul. For once, Conall believed the old man's ramblings. After their hilarity subsided, his shoulders felt less achey.

Lainn spied the food he'd left out and fell upon the morsels with ravenous intent. When she wiped her mouth, she glanced at the sky, still spitting smaller hailstones. "I suppose we need to repair that. The hole's a lot bigger than the last place."

Conall studied the gap. "Maybe we can take some thatch and timbers from the other roundhouse?"

The amusement fled from her expression, her mouth in a grim line. "I don't want to walk in there again."

"We don't have to go inside. I can pull thatch from the outside. The job'll go more quickly if you help, though."

She stared at the hail. "What if we build a wicker wall for this half of the roundhouse? The half with the roof?"

"The whole roof needs more support. A section just fell in this storm. Also, a wicker wall wouldn't keep the wind out, and we don't have enough daub for sealing. We have plenty of mud but are short of horse manure."

Reluctantly, she agreed. "Fine. But I won't go inside."

As the storm raged, they swept out the livable space, arranged food on the remnants of shelves, and organized a sleeping area better than bare dirt.

Conall found several stones to create a better hearth and gathered rain-soaked wood. He didn't relish the billows of smoke, but he couldn't find any dry kindling.

His muscles and bones protested the cold, and they'd need a fire as the night came. He couldn't tell the time of day through the storm, but dusk must be soon. They'd slept most of the day.

Lainn kicked in the back of his knee. "Wake up, daydreamer! We've got too much to do in too short a time for you to gather wool."

He scowled at her. "Shut up, Lainn. You sound like Sétna."

Her eyes grew round, and he instantly regretted his words. "Crow dung. I'm sorry, Lainn. I didn't mean that."

Lainn set her jaw and picked up a bundle of wet sticks she'd dropped. She shoved past him without a word. Once she tucked them into a dry spot, she walked out into the storm.

"Lainn? Lainn!"

Her form disappeared into the sleet. With a growl, Conall grabbed both their brats and ran after her.

His skin chilled as icy rain pelted him, stinging his face and ears. He drew his brat over his head, but the cold settled into his bones. His feet crunched as he stalked after his sister, having no clue in which direction she'd run.

Damn my thoughtless words and damn her for running off in this. They still didn't know if this place would be safe, and she'd gone haring off into the unknown in the middle of a winter storm. They'd both freeze to death before he found her.

Conall's foot sank into an icy puddle, dunking him into cold water mid-calf. He cursed again and jerked his foot out, shaking off the excess. In an even fouler mood, he continued.

Something bounded across the path, a streak of gray and brown. He considered trying to catch the rabbit but finding Lainn was more urgent. They'd need fresh food, but he first needed to make certain his sister returned safely.

He spied a lump under a lone hawthorn tree, and he caught his breath. Lainn huddled beneath, her arms cradling her head on her knees. He knelt beside her, tossing her brat around her shoulders and hugging her tight. She flinched away but didn't make him move.

"Come back to the roundhouse, Lainn. We'll freeze out here." He drew her up to a standing position, and she didn't resist. She also didn't look into his eyes. Still, she allowed him to lead her back down the path and to relative safety and dry shelter.

The slush and sleet grew thicker, and he had to push physically through the falling ice, one step at a time. The path blurred before his eyes. When that feeling of peace washed over him, he knew he must have arrived at the smaller roundhouse. The shock of no longer being pelted by ice pellets made them both gasp as they entered.

Conall was bone-weary from just a few minutes in the storm. Lainn drooped as she sat on a log, hands once again cradling her head. He heaved a deep sigh and gathered logs and kindling.

Conall shaved bark with his belt knife and piled the kindling in the center. He pulled out the tinderbox and clacked the flint several times, trying to get the spark to jump on the shaved bark. After about ten tries, he gritted his teeth and pulled on his magic. This would take a feather touch, but he should be able to guide the spark to the right place.

One click, and his magic shoved the spark across the room. A second click and he barely moved it. A third click brought the spark closer, but the bright spot died with a sizzle on a wet log. The fourth one flew true, and he only needed to nudge the spark into place. A tiny wisp of steam curled up from the bark. He fanned the spark, praying for the flame to catch. Soon, with judicious additions of bark and splinters, he had a small, merry blaze going, though the smoke burned his eyes.

As he sat back to survey his efforts, Conall considered the differences between a wood fire and the more familiar peat fire. Peat fires burned low and smoldered for a long time, while a wood fire burned hot, fast, and fierce. Flames licked higher with a wood fire, as sometimes peat had no flames at all, only embers. Peat might even smolder underground.

His father once told him a story of a bog which caught on fire, but no one knew until someone dug down to where the fire burned. A huge billow of smoke enveloped the man and cooked him in a matter of minutes.

A glance at his sister made him smile. She was curled up and asleep again. He supposed he shouldn't blame her. Sleep seemed an excellent idea. He let out another massive yawn.

First, Conall set out the last apple for her and roasted an onion for his own meal. The sweet flesh burned his lips, and he sucked in air to cool his mouth. When he'd licked the last of the charred juices from his fingers, he curled up next to the fire and pulled his brat over his shoulders.

As he shivered under the cloth, his arms felt bonier than he ever remembered. They'd both lost weight.

Despite being exhausted, sleep danced out of his grasp. Conall drifted in and out of dreams, punctuated by hail drumming on the thatch with occasional drips of icy water working through the roof. The fire's toasty warmth made him uneven if he lay on one side for too long. He'd shift and toss, once kicking Lainn in the shin in his gyrations. She grunted and moved to the other side of the fire.

As the rain faded, snowflakes replaced them, drifting in silence upon the now ice-covered surfaces. Conall watched each one fall in lazy circles from the midnight sky, wandering down random paths from the heavens to gather into snow clouds on the ground. Wet kisses from the few drifting onto his face made his skin damp. He rubbed his face with the edge of his brat, but the scratchy wool cloth was still damp from yesterday.

Conall gave up on trying to sleep. He sat up and studied the ceiling in the dim firelight, figuring what he'd need to repair it. Their wood fire gave off better light than peat fire would, though it flickered more, and shadows gamboled across the ceiling, making a true assessment difficult. He'd have to survey the damage in the morning.

He filled their pot with fresh snow and nestled it into the embers. By the time Lainn woke, they'd have soup with the last of the onions and some turnips. They had no meat left, but perhaps he might snare a rabbit soon.

He stared at the pot, waiting for the water to boil. Dark reflections in the liquid shimmered and shone, a black pond under a starless sky. He stared at images swirling on the surface, losing himself in gyrating features. He almost made out the form of a man beckoning to him. The figure looked lean and long, with dark hair and pale skin, his movements seductive and tantalizing. Conall lay back down, images tumbling in his mind.

Lainn's high-pitched screech startled him awake, and he sat bolt upright. He scrambled to his sister and enfolded her in his arms, rocking her for comfort. He whispered soothing sounds, but still she screamed, her voice slicing into his nerves and his heart.

"Sh, Lainn. I'm here. You're safe. No one c-can harm you."

"He's coming. He's coming for us now. He'll find us!"

Conall thought he might find them more easily if she didn't stop screaming. Horrified at his own uncharitable thought, he hugged her tightly, proof against anything in the outside world that might harm her. "I'll protect you. I'm here. I won't leave you."

He rocked her back and forth, praying for her calm and her silence. Eventually, her screams subsided to whimpers. Lainn cried in time to his rocking, back and forth, sob and breathe. Back and forth, sob and breathe. Her wet tears mingled with the melted snow on his face. Somewhere, a raven cawed in the night. He glanced up to see if Rawninn had found them, but nothing stirred in the crumbling roundhouse.

Ages later, Lainn slept again. As difficult as this had been for him, this ordeal must be a thousand times worse for her. His sister had morphed into a new person. She looked like a boy, now that he'd gotten used to her clothing and hair. She'd subsumed her entire identity in this mad escape. Conall wondered if he'd ever get his old sister back, the carefree, delightful young girl who skipped through summer storms and laughed while picking wildflowers.

When reluctant sunlight filtered through the lingering snowstorm, flickering shafts of light found Conall's face. He'd fallen asleep holding Lainn in his arms. His sister still slept, drooling from the corner of her mouth. He wiped it and laid her gently on the floor, using both his brat and hers to cover her.

He'd completely forgotten about the snow in the pot. It had almost boiled away, so he added more snow. When this melted, he chopped the remaining onions and turnips in, adding the rosemary. Conall wished he had salt or garlic. He eyed the wood-ash, knowing it had a salty flavor. With a sigh, he swept some up and sprinkled the ash in. He didn't care for the charred taste, but it added a tang.

Several hours later, the savory aroma of the stew must have woken Lainn, for she moaned and turned toward the fire, opening her eyes. Her nostrils flared, and she sat up, rubbing her eyes. "How long did I sleep?"

"Forever and a day, good sister."

"Brother. Call me brother."

He cocked his head. "We're alone, though."

"It doesn't matter. If we're traveling and someone hears by accident, things might go wrong. Promise me, Conall."

He let out a sigh. "I p-promise, Lainn."

"Thank you. Now, what delectable delights have you cooked for our morning meal?"

He smiled at the glimmer of his sister's irrepressible optimism and gestured with the spoon in a dramatic flourish. "Your meal will be a delicious stew with onions, ash, and turnips, should it please you. At least you had the forethought to sleep long enough to allow the stew to simmer."

She tossed him a half-smile before she stood to retrieve the bowls. "And if it shouldn't please me? Then what would you do?"

He gave a casual shrug. "Throw the slops to the pigs and find you a rabbit."

She handed him one bowl. "I wouldn't turn down meat. Do you know how to set snares?"

He nodded as he served them both. "Father taught me before he left. Sétna never bothered with such things, but I should remember. I need to find a sapling flexible enough to bend."

She glanced up as a drop plopped on her forehead. "I should be able to help, but I think the roof repair has greater priority. What'll you need for that?"

While he listed off supplies, including stout branches for the frame, dried grasses for the thatch, and twine to hold it all down, he blew on his stew to cool it down.

Lainn watched him and let out a giggle. She grabbed a handful of snow and dropped a bit in each of their bowls. In moments, the snow melted and cooled both bowls to eating temperature. He stirred his and took a sip, grinning at his clever sist… brother.

He tried to wrap his mind around thinking of her as a boy. If someone heard them in casual conversation as they walked, or even came upon them here in the roundhouse, any innocent remark might be dangerous, as she said. Even as a boy, she'd be in danger. But she'd be in less danger than a girl.

"Why don't I teach you the snares? That way you can set several while I gather the things for the roof. The snow has stopped, so we can work after our meal."

Lainn nodded, taking another sip of her soup. "Sounds fair enough. You use willow switches, right?"

"Sometimes. You can use braided sinew or twine, but I'd rather save the twine for the roof repair. I have sinew in my sack. If you use a switch, cut the branch and strip it thin." He held his fingers up to show how thin. "Bend the branch into a full circle. It should be flexible enough to tie a slipknot at the end. The branch also needs to be stiff enough to stand up along the rabbit trace, so the loop catches around their neck as they run through."

She nodded, closing her eyes. "I think I can visualize it. How do you find the nests?"

"They'll be sleeping for the winter, but some are up and about. I saw one yesterday when I chased you down." He frowned but she still had her eyes closed. "Search for hollows and depressions, lots of brown leaves and shrubs. If you can find a trail leading from it, with broken branches or trampled leaves, that will be your best spot. I'll make one and show you how, then you can do more."

"Will you need help gathering the supplies for the roof?"

He shook his head. "I think I can get most of what I need from the other roundhouse. I'll need help with the actual repair, unless I want to risk breaking my neck."

"Right. I'm done with my stew. Give me your bowl, and I'll clean them. Then we can set a snare!"

Luck was with them, and they found several young willow trees. He sawed one down with his belt knife, stripping the sapling thin and showing her how to set the knot. Then he let her loose to find the rabbit nest.

With a few false starts, she found one. He showed her how to tie the trap to an overhanging branch and moved several thorn bushes to each side of the path, so the rabbit had to pass through.

"Not a beautiful trap, but it should work well enough. Think you can do three more?"

She nodded, already stripping more of the willow switch. He watched her for a few more moments before heading back to the roundhouses.

On the way back, Conall gathered several stout branches, testing each one for dampness and sturdiness. Two, he discarded as unsuitable after one shattered in his hand and the other crawled with spiders. The latter he flung away as far as he could and brushed at his arms and hands, desperate to remove every crawling thing. He shuddered and hurried back, not daring to pick up any more branches.

The second roundhouse had three solid supports that might suit for repairs. After a lot of wrestling and grunting, he removed them from their moorings. Conall dragged each to the smaller roundhouse and stacked them against the center pole. Then he found lighter branches for a thatch framework.

Most of the other things in the larger roundhouse had rotted away. He took a deep breath and headed back to the trees to find more. This time, he examined each prospect before picking it up in case more spiders swarmed.

Eventually, armed with seven good branches, he concentrated on the thatch itself. Most of the larger roundhouse had decent thatch, but when he tried to remove the straw, it crumbled. Disgusted, he harvested some from the underside, where weather had not yet taken its toll. He'd need to supplement the old stuff with fresh straw.

No river ran nearby for sedge grasses, but he thought he glimpsed a pond in his wanderings. Perhaps he'd find water grass to harvest for thatch. In the meantime, he needed to wrestle the beams into place before he could fix anything else.

Conall surveyed his bounty, hands on his hips, as footsteps sounded behind him, crunching in the dry leaves. The cadence didn't sound like his sister, so he pulled out his belt knife and turned to face the intruder.

The breath he'd been holding burst free. Lainn approached, with her boy's swagger. He couldn't even recognize his own sister's step any longer. The world had tuned upside down.

As he sheathed his knife, she grinned. "I set three more traps. Are you ready for my help?"

"Do you want me to check them?"

She shook her head. "They aren't elegant, but they should work. So, those beams go up there? In a wheel pattern from the center?"

He nodded. "Each one should rest on the center pole once I tie them in place. The other end rests on the outer wall. First, we should shore up the wattle on this part of the wall. Otherwise, the beam might be too much weight and pull it down. What do you think?"

"Agreed. I'll fetch mud and more flexible branches. The vertical poles seem sound enough. It needs more filling, right?"

"Good idea. I'll see if I can find stones or a stump to stand on to lift the beams in the center."

He'd just managed to roll a stone into place, with a little help from his magic, when he heard a rabbit squeak in alarm. He scanned the clearing, looking for Lainn. Her head popped up from some bushes to one side. "It worked already?"

"Sounds like it." He gripped his knife and strode toward the gate. Lainn shuffled up behind him, her own bronze knife ready.

He gestured for Lainn to lead the way. The first snare was still in place, as was the second. The third, however, held a struggling young rabbit, still mottled brown and gray from his autumn coat.

The rabbit squealed in panic when he saw Lainn. She lifted her knife and placed the blade against the rabbit's neck, but hesitated. Her eyes grew wide, and she visibly swallowed. Her jaw twitched, and she moved the knife away from the struggling creature. Then she took a deep breath and tried again, but had to stop when a massive sob wracked her frame.

Tears fell down her cheeks. "I can't do it, Conall. I can't. Gemmán taught me to sing to the rabbit, not to kill it."

He gripped her shoulder. "You need to, Lainn. If I can't hunt, you have to learn. Try again."

She shook her head so vigorously, she almost fell over from her crouch. "I can't! Don't you understand? I can't! Gemmán said a druid should always seek another path from violence."

Conall wanted to shout at her, but instead nudged his sister aside and slit the rabbit's throat himself, ending its pain and panic. He loosened the snare and reset the loop, carrying the corpse by the feet. He helped Lainn to her feet and led her back to the roundhouse.

"I'm sorry, Conall. I should have done it, but I couldn't."

He didn't look up as he sliced the rabbit's belly, preparing to skin the corpse. He kept his tone even as he worked. "We have to eat, Lainn. You know that. It's a matter of survival."

"I know. I know we have to eat. But I couldn't kill!"

As much as he wanted to comfort her, he needed to skin the rabbit. He steeled himself from the urge to take her into his arms and tell her everything would be all right. What would happen if he got hurt? She'd have to hunt.

If she didn't kill, they'd die from starvation well before the winter faded. He couldn't tell if he was angrier with her or with himself. Either way, he mustn't let frustration get hold of him, like their stepfather did.

Conall concentrated on pulling the skin off each leg, then the back, then the neck. He sliced the membranes, pulling it away from muscle, nicking each tendon so the skin slid off.

When he finished skinning the rabbit, he chopped up the carcass into four sections. He dumped more snow into the pot and settled it back into the embers, fetching more wood for the fire. He waited while the water boiled, still unwilling to glance at Lainn.

His sister sobbed while sitting with her back against the roundhouse wall. Her cries were a gentle counterpoint to the crackling fire.

Chapter Nine

Over a moon later, Conall wished he'd thought to dry some rabbit meat, rather than stew it all for that meal. They found no other rabbits, no other game, not even any late apples or nuts. They subsisted on a few foraged mushrooms and one lone fish he'd coaxed from the pond. Their stomachs grumbled constantly. The pain made him double up and hold his stomach sometimes.

He might ask if she was hungry, but she wouldn't answer. Lainn's inability to kill the rabbit had been her last comprehensible words to him. Try as he might, Conall hadn't been able to coax his sister out of gloom. He spoke to her, sang her stories, and rocked her in his arms, but nothing helped.

Lainn would take food if he handed it to her, but she wouldn't move from her huddled space along the edge of the roundhouse. She hummed to herself, ululating without the semblance of a tune. It made the hair on his arm stand up as if someone breathed on his neck. He wished Barnabus would fly in and answer her, but bees slept in the dead of winter. Somewhere, he swore he heard the echo of male laughter.

Conall did complete the roof repairs, though he had to draw heavily upon his magic to lift the thatch and supports into place.

Snow fell each day, trapping them in place. While he had plenty of water and some hazelnuts, he didn't know when he'd find more food. He doled those precious few nuts out one a day for each of them. Only three remained.

During the day, when light still filtered through cloudy skies, he kept his hands busy. He found flat reeds and wove sleeping mats. Conall foraged wood and carved them into bowls, mugs, and utensils until his hands ached. He drew mathematical diagrams and problems to solve, using calculations Sétna had taught him in his masonry training.

As he glanced at his sister, singing tunelessly to the otherworld, tears formed in his eyes. His heart ached with the need to help her, to heal her, to lead her back to humanity, but he had no idea how.

While he roasted the last three hazelnuts, then crushed them into a paste, he fed all three to Lainn. He fed her as he had when she'd been a babe, unable to hold her own spoon. A bit dribbled down her chin, and he caught it, making sure every bite made it into her mouth. Then he held the mug of water to her lips, making her drink.

She batted at him and whimpered in fear, but he persisted until she'd drunk at least half. Conall relented when she knocked the mug from his hand and growled at him, retreating into a ball. The smell of her soiling her clothing reached him, and he grimaced. He'd have to change her *léine* again and wash the stains.

Conall almost wished Sétna would find them. At least then, Lainn might return to her human self. Had the Fae stolen her soul? As far as he knew, she'd touched no Faerie stones or accepted a gift. She hadn't spied them dancing in the moonlight or drunk of their nectar. She simply refused to kill a rabbit.

In the past weeks, he'd prayed for guidance. He had prayed both to the Christian God and the ancient gods, whoever might be listening. As he fed his sister the final bite of hazelnut paste, he sent his appeal to any being that might help them.

With little hope for an answer, Conall knelt as the late afternoon light faded into wintry darkness. "Please, we need help. We need food, or a way to escape to someplace with people. A place that will shelter us from harm. My sister needs to find her soul again. If you can hear us, anyone, please help."

A sudden freezing cold wind tickled the back of his neck. He shivered and drew his brat more closely around his shoulders. The fabric had worn thin. Maybe he could sew rabbit fur along the neck edge.

A raucous caw made him jump back, his eyes wide in startled terror. An enormous raven watched him from the eaves. The bird hadn't been there when he closed his eyes. At first, Conall felt a wave of relief that Adhna's raven had found them, but then he realized this bird looked larger than Rawninn, its black-sheen feathers glinting in the fading light.

Crawling backward, away from the raven, Conall retreated to Lainn and hovered in front of her. If the raven meant harm, he'd protect her against all interference, be it natural or Fae.

"You called for help."

Conall was staring at the raven, and the bird's beak hadn't moved. With growing fear, his eyes darted around the roundhouse and saw the man-shaped shadow near the doorway. The shadow moved subtly, but not as a human would move. His arms and legs moved with a liquid flow, more graceful than any dancer.

The shadow let out a low, musical laugh and morphed into human form, with skin as white as summer clouds. His hair flowed into midnight-dark locks. Pointed teeth gleamed as he smiled. With languorous steps, he approached with his arms spread wide. His voice was honey and ashes. "I am here to help you and your lovely little sister, Conall, as you requested. Will you disdain my generous offer?"

Conall fumbled for his belt knife, but it was out of his reach, next to the food shelves. He grabbed Lainn's hand, though she moaned at his tight grip. She yanked on his hand, and he glanced back. Her eyes had flown open, staring at the creature.

He swallowed and turned back to the intruder, with his too-white skin and his ink-black hair. The sharp teeth were more like a feral cat than any human. The aromas of lilac and burnt bone tickled his nose.

"You shouldn't be afraid, mortal child. Truly, I'm here to help. Have you never seen a member of the Fae court before?"

The creature's smile chilled Conall to the bones. "Now, Conall, I must ask you a question 'ere I offer more than my simple help. Are you indeed the spawn of the human called Fíngin?"

Startled at his father's name, Conall nodded before he could stop himself. Lainn had stopped whimpering, but her hand had grown ice cold.

"Excellent, excellent. He gave you a trinket, I believe. A gift from his own mother, is that not true?"

Conall couldn't remember if the brooch came from his grandmother. He clenched his jaw and held himself still, despite his quaking bones.

The Fae waved his hand. "No matter. I can sense the magic within you. Now, please believe me when I vow, as a member of my Queen's Court, that I have no interest in harming you. Rather, I've been sent to watch over you and to come when called. You have called for help, and therefore I must come to offer the same. With that in mind, will you accept my help?"

Conall found his voice, though it cracked with fear. "Wh-wh-who sent you?"

The Fae's smile deepened. "The only being who can command my actions is my own dear Queen, mortal child."

Conall realized the stranger hadn't quite answered his question. "Why would she send you to us?"

"That is not my tale to tell, youngling. Will you accept my help? I can bring you to warmth, safety, and sustenance for however long you require such things."

"However long? You mean until you kill us?"

The melodious laugh caressed Conall's ears like a long-lost lover. "Such a fierce protector you are! No, I will not harm you, remember?"

What he'd said was that he had no interest in harming them. But the Fae's last statement seemed a stronger promise, and Conall allowed himself to breathe.

With a glance back at his sister, still alert and unmoving, he asked, "Fae food? Or human food?"

The Fae's laugh echoed against the walls, fondling Conall's skin like the softest rabbit fur. A shiver ran down his spine. "Human food, of course. As I said, I have no wish to trap you into a contract or a promise. This is simply the repayment of a debt incurred long ago. Now, will you consent to come with me?"

If the Fae's presence could drag Lainn from her madness, he only had one choice.

With trembling legs, Conall stood, pulling his sister to her feet, but he kept between them as a shield. He grabbed his sack, Adhna's, and Lainn's. He made certain his father's brooch was hidden within his own, and packed what little they had left before he took his sister's hand again and turned to the Fae. "Very well. I accept your help."

"You both must accept, child. My dear Lainn, do you accept my assistance?"

Conall held his breath, both eager to hear sensible words from his sister and dreading her answer. With silent urging, he begged her to deny the creature and remain sane.

Lainn's eyes darted to Conall, and a spark of defiance flashed deep within her soul. She shut her eyes upon that flicker and turned to the Fae. "I accept your help, Ammatán."

Before they left the chilly roundhouse, the Fae required them to leave anything iron.

As they rifled through their belongings, Conall whispered to Lainn. "How did you know his name? Have you met him before? He knew our names!"

She shook her head and said nothing, her motions abrupt and jerky as if someone moved her limbs for her.

Out of the corner of his eye, Conall watched the Fae. He stood perfectly still. Not even his chest moved with breathing, nor did the breeze flutter his hair. Perhaps he stood in a moment of frozen time.

With furtive movements, Conall palmed the ancient bronze knife Adhna had gifted them. The Fae's gaze burned into him, his regard like a heavy load upon his shoulders.

They removed their iron pot, several utensils, and three nails from their sacks before he would lead them away.

As he dropped the last piece of iron from their belongings, he turned to face the creature. "I need you to promise me two things before we go with you."

Now the Fae moved, his delicate eyebrows raised in surprise. "You think to dictate terms, mortal?"

Conall tried to show much more confidence than he felt, an illusion which shattered as he stuttered. "I d-d-do. You must promise to help heal my sister and to never allow harm to come to her."

The creature narrowed his black eyes and considered Lainn. She had picked up her own sack, lighter by several iron items, and took Conall's hand with a quick, fierce squeeze.

The Fae smiled, his lips curling away from his pointed teeth. "I do promise I will do what I can to help Lainn find and retain her missing sanity. I also promise I shall not allow Lainn to come to harm if it's within my power. Further, I shall promise to show you how to return to your world, if you should wish to return."

Conall realized he'd get no better promise. However, the bargain still hadn't been sealed. "What will you ask in return for this promise?"

The Fae walked around Conall, one hand lingering on his shoulder, trailing down his arm, and he couldn't suppress a shiver. Then he touched Lainn's shoulder in a similar caress until he stood where he started. "I ask nothing in return for this promise, human child."

Conall glanced at Lainn, who shrugged. "I don't understand. Fae always want something in return for their help."

"I've already received my payment."

The creature's eyes turned blacker than the blackest night, and Conall felt himself fall into their endless depths for an eternal moment. He wrenched himself back into his body with tearing pain of will and grasped Lainn's hand. Turning to her, he whispered, "Are you sure? Are you ready for this?"

She blinked and rubbed her eyes, as if waking from a long sleep. "I'm hungry, Conall. He's here to help us."

Hoping vehemently that her words weren't the result of a fever dream, he turned to Ammatán. "We're ready. What must we do?"

With an even deeper grin, the Fae held out his hand, elegantly long fingers curled in supplication. "Come away, O human child, to the waters and the wild."

Despite his rising terror, Conall placed his own hand in the Fae's, while holding fast to Lainn's with his other. Ammatán's hand felt cold and firm.

Conall prayed he wasn't making a horrible mistake with their lives and their souls.

Chapter Ten

The darkness enveloped Conall, and he felt neither the Fae hand nor his sister's, though he still clasped hard upon flesh. Stars twinkled past his eyes and into his mind as he flew through the dark void, spinning until he grew dizzy.

With a suddenness that made him nauseous, the spinning halted, and he fell on his knees. He tried to suppress a cry, but a whimper escaped.

Lainn cried out, and a wave of relief swept through him. He tightened his grip, finding her hand once again in place.

Conall blinked, but he saw nothing but blackness. He groped around, but his fingers found nothing solid. Hollow sounds removed from reality surrounded them.

A light flashed, so bright his eyes screamed in pain. He squeezed them shut and held his head in both hands, trying to ease the agony. Belatedly, he realized he'd let Lainn's hand go, and he tried to find her again. When he touched her shoulder, he drew her in for a tight hug, refusing to let her go again.

"We've arrived, human children. Be not afraid. You are safe in my home."

He cracked one eye open a sliver. The light was still much too bright, but he squinted and eventually, opened his eyes. The colors alone made him gape in wonder, for such vibrant colors he'd rarely seen. Only in the full bloom of spring had he witnessed such vivid blues, oranges, and yellows as assailed his senses.

At first glance, it seemed a simple place. A large round structure, albeit with impossibly delicate arches across the top, stood beside a sparkling pond. Flowers surrounded the pond with small insects that seemed like butterflies, but not like any Conall had ever seen.

A menacing black shape darted toward Conall's face, and he flung his arms up in defense, only to hear Ammatán chuckle as the enormous raven alighted upon his shoulder. "Have no fear of Sawchaill. He likes bringing drama where none exists. To intrude upon an already dramatic moment was more than he could resist."

The tender smile the Fae gave his raven eased Conall's fear more than anything the Fae had said. Such obvious affection for another creature gave Ammatán a more trustworthy standing than any words might have done.

"Now, we must get you settled and allow you to rest. It's been many moons since you've slept well. Sawchaill, do go and find our guests some food, will you? Nothing insectoid. They need meat. Nothing human, mind you!" The Fae had to raise his voice as the raven flew away, intent upon his assigned mission.

A chill returned at the Fae's last words. No human meat? Did this creature actually want to care for them? Or was he fattening them up for his own feast?

Conall found it difficult to believe in such carefree hospitality of anyone, much less a Fae. But then he remembered Adhna, and his theory about the old man not being quite human. Perhaps some Fae were kind, after all.

Lainn was curled up against his side, not fallen back into the madness which had gripped her before, but no longer as coherent as she'd been before their journey to Fae.

Ammatán held out his elegant hand to help them to their feet. Once again, Conall took a deep breath and allowed his assistance. The hand seemed cool and dry within his own, cooler than any human, yet solid and much stronger than he'd imagined.

Together, they got Lainn to her feet, though she stumbled with half-opened eyes and mumbling complaints.

The Fae led them into the roundhouse, under a soaring stone arch which sparkled. Conall searched for the sun, but light seemed to come from all directions rather than a single source. This odd light held the warmth of a late spring day, full of buzzing insects, floral perfumes, and even a pleasant breeze. As they entered the shade of the shelter, motes of magic danced in the beams of light criss-crossing the space, entrancing him.

Conall placed a hand on the arch, trying to determine the type of stone, but the surface seemed vibrant, not like stone at all. The substance felt warmer, smoother, almost like the small bone flute Lainn played.

"The bones of ancient animals, captured from human history."

Ammatán's voice intruded upon his thoughts, but this time it didn't seem jarring. Rather, the information made an odd sense. Conall saved that bit of knowledge in his growing list of oddities in the Faerie realm.

In the center of the room stood a delicate table, entwined with living vines rising from the floor and then again to the roof beams. This table held massive bowls of fruit, bread, and, as Sawchaill winged in and dropped a mass upon one end, a chunk of salted bacon.

"There! Well, I suppose he might have chosen better, but at least it is meat. This is a type humans eat, correct? The flesh of swine?"

The savory odor made Conall wipe away a thin drip of saliva from the corner of his mouth. He nodded, unwilling to speak. He saw Lainn's eyes light up at the feast.

After handing each of them a sweet, yellow fruit, Ammatán warned them, "I think one each for now, then sleep. I understand it has been some time since you've eaten, yes? Humans cannot eat so much at once after deprivation. I learned this once."

Conall nodded, biting into the fruit, unable to identify it. The sweet, tangy flesh stung his chapped lips, but he licked each drop anyhow, eager to capture every drop of the delicious juice. Next to him, Lainn did the same, licking each of her fingers and gnawing on the flesh of the fruit down to the core.

"Now, to sleep. While you slumber, I shall create a true welcome feast."

Conall wanted another piece of fruit so badly, he almost cried out in protest, but he understood the wisdom of waiting. His stomach rumbled in argument, and Lainn's echoed his.

The Fae led them next to a small chamber with a fluffy pillow filled with feathers. "This is for sister Lainn. Does this not look luxurious, my child? Come, lay your head and curl in comfort. No human harm can find you here in my demesne."

Lainn's eyes glazed over at the warmth and solace of the small room. She let go of Conall's hand and nestled into the huge pillow, asleep as soon as her head settled upon her folded hands, curled up like a babe in her mother's arms.

Conall wiped a tear from his cheek, horrified lest the Fae witness his affection. "Come, Conall. I shall find an equally relaxing place for yourself."

Once again, the Fae took his hand, drawing him into the next chamber. Despite his mind screaming to stay alert, to distrust, to run away with Lainn and the brooch, that voice faded into the somnolent ease of tender sincerity the Fae offered.

The next chamber looked much like Lainn's. The feather bed looked enormous, large enough for three adults to sleep upon it. When Conall sat on the shifting mass, he decided he'd never touched anything so soft in his life.

"You'll watch over Lainn while I sleep? You promise?"

Ammatán ran one pointed finger along Conall's cheek, which sent shivers down the young man's spine. "I promise, human child. Even if I had not previously vowed my service, I would do so for you."

Conall wanted to protest he was no child, but he closed his eyes, despite his efforts to remain vigilant. As he drifted off to sleep, he wondered once again how Lainn had known Ammatán's name, and how he knew theirs.

Something tickled his nose.

When he dragged his soul from a deeper sleep than he ever remembered, Conall rubbed his face. Crusty bits of sleep scratched his eyelids, and the faint touch of a fluttering cloud brushed his hand. He blinked several times, trying to shove through the haze of slumber.

The golden non-sunlight shone through tall, airy windows, not warm on his face, but not chilly either. After an eternity spent in winter, the lack of cold was a salve to Conall's aching bones. His hip didn't hurt for the first time since he'd fallen on it and he took a long moment to savor that lack of pain.

A flicker of color caught his eye, and he steadied his gaze upon a fluttering insect with iridescent blue wings. Golden light shone upon the wings, making prismatic flashes of color across the walls, a dance of ethereal radiance to rival dancing god-lights on winter evenings.

He'd only seen god-lights a few times, in the middle of the night. White glowing illumination had swept low on the northern horizon. His father told him the lights were a festival of the gods, where they celebrated their own power and life, just as humans did at the harvests and fire festivals.

What did this delicate creature have to celebrate? Living in this magical land seemed blessing enough. No cold, no wind, no night, no pain. What more would any being crave?

As Conall remembered the delicate touch of the Fae lord, his heart raced. His breath caught, and something that had been swimming in the back of his mind came forward.

Conall imagined himself touching Ammatán's face in return, and that made his heart race even faster, had his skin tingled with warm desire. In a strange way, he now knew the answer to what he craved.

Should this be how he reacted when Aoife had touched him? Is this what other men experienced when they lay with their wives? The reaction frightened him.

He knew men who lay with men and women who lay with women. Lainn's own mentor, Gemmán, had mentioned his lover. But Christians disapproved of such pairings and often shunned or attacked those folks.

Here, in the middle of nowhere in the land of Faerie, perhaps they might be safe.

Conall's bladder told him he'd been asleep far too long for mortal bodily functions. He threw off the feather-light blanket and searched for a night basket. He found none inside the soaring structure.

Then Conall peeked in on his sister, still sleeping in her room. With a tender hand, he brushed her hair behind her ear, evoking a slow sleepy smile from her. He echoed her smile and went outside.

Ammatán wasn't around, but the raven was. The bird cawed in greeting and Conall waved, not at all certain this was a proper response. He found a bush with no thorns and sighed in relief.

Then he surveyed the small, peaceful glade. Other than the bones of Ammatán's home, everything appeared alive and thriving. Bushes with colorful flowers crowded around the structure, while a small grass-covered glade surrounded the still pond. Large water lilies and pads floated on the surface, and at least one fish poked his head up, sending lazy ripples to the edge.

A small path wound through the trees to one side, where it disappeared among the oddly colored leaves. Silvery trunks sported blue, green, orange, and red leaves, though some of these shifted in color even as he watched. Not the slow shift of the autumn season, but a rainbow shimmer of change.

The sound of footsteps made him turn around to see Ammatán approach. The Fae had changed from the short, white *léine* he'd worn when he found them. Now he wore something more like a long robe, with yellow and red vertical stripes. The riot of color against his pale skin almost hurt. "My sleeping beauty has awoken. I regret I wasn't here immediately, but even Sawchaill couldn't find me so rapidly. You must be hungry, Conall. I've set a meal for you both. Has Lainn arisen?"

He shook his head, unable to resist smiling at the Fae. "She's still snoring away. Neither of us got good rest in recent months."

He shivered. "Such a cruel place, your world. How do you stand the cold? I know it gets warmer, but I've not been willing to stay in such a place to find out how long it takes."

"Several moons, at least. Half the seasons are cold, and half warm, though all have plenty of rain."

With a half-smile, Ammatán placed a hand on Conall's shoulder. "We have no rain or cold here in Faerie. There are storms, but only windstorms, and often caused by one of us in a fit of anger."

His expression turned bleak, but his smile returned in a flash. "Not to worry about that. As long as you don't insult the Queen, your weather should be fair."

Conall giggled, somewhat nervous. "I've no plans to insult anyone." His stomach betrayed him with an audible rumble. "You mentioned food?"

The Fae laughed, a rippling tumble of water over a spring brook. "Perhaps you will help me prepare the food in a human manner?"

Together, they set up a cooking fire, using a bronze pot to heat water. Conall showed Ammatán how to chop the vegetables and simmer them in the pot. Ammatán appeared fascinated with the process but made no move to help. "Such labors aren't for the Fae. If we cannot do it by magic, we are, I'm afraid, much more likely to ask human help. This is why such things as milk, honey, and bread are so valuable. They require human labor to create."

Remembering Adhna's particular favorite, Conall asked, "Like cheese?"

Ammatán laughed again. "Precisely like cheese. While it's not my favorite, I know some Fae who would move mountains to gain a steady supply of cheese."

Conall grinned along with Ammatán, his laugh infectious. It seemed like so long since Conall had been so at ease, and yet he felt a strange tension, a waiting as if something should happen. He wished he knew what.

After the stone next to the fire grew hot enough for Conall to fry bacon upon it. Lainn finally roused. The smell of frying bacon would be enough to rouse the dead.

Her red hair stuck out at odd angles where it had escaped the days-old braids. She looked like a wilted dandelion, but at least she was awake and smiling. A glimmer of the old Lainn showed through the dirty boy's clothing and grim visage.

Without a word, she narrowed her eyes at both Ammatán and Conall, selected a fatty piece of bacon and scooped it up, transferring it from one hand to another as the sizzling meat burned her fingers. With delicate bites, she nibbled it like a squirrel, looking much more human when she'd finished.

Her eyes wide, she glanced around.

Conall let out a chuckle. "Outside, as far as I can tell. Unless you have a night basket hidden somewhere, Ammatán?"

His brow furrowed. "I'm unfamiliar with the term."

"A place to relieve herself. We keep a basket with sand in it, so we don't have to go outside in the snow."

The Fae's eyes grew round, and he laughed. "Oh, I understand. Fae don't require such things unless they live in your world for extended times. I've no special basket for it."

With a desperate nod, Lainn ran out of the room into the bushes. A cloud of non-butterflies fluttered away, and Sawchaill cawed in response to the swarm.

Conall cocked his head to one side, studying the Fae as Ammatán watched Lainn leave. "Ammatán, why did you help us? Whose promise were you keeping?"

The Fae shook his head, his straight black hair falling over one eye. "That I cannot say. I have a *géis* upon the information and betraying that trust would be dire."

"Does it have to do with my father?"

Ammatán's eyes flickered with anxiety, darting back and forth. "I truly can't tell you, Conall."

"Is that how you knew his name and ours?"

The Fae moved to within an inch of Conall's face, and his eyes grew harder and darker than he'd yet seen. "I cannot answer your questions, human child. You will not ask them again."

Conall's heart skipped a beat at the danger and desire flowing through his blood. This Fae had the strength to crush him, kill him with a touch, if angered. Yet when he stood so close, the Fae's soft skin pulsed with anticipation. Conall raised his right hand and cupped Ammatán's cheek.

The black eyes turned soft, and Ammatán's fierce expression eased. He placed his hand over Conall's and closed his eyes.

When Lainn entered the roundhouse, she giggled. "I tried to catch one of the insects, but they're much too fast for me. They wouldn't even let me sing them back."

With guilty speed, Conall dropped his hand and stepped back from Ammatán. He let out a shuddering breath and busied himself with slicing one of the odd yellow fruits. Lainn glanced between them with a narrowed gaze, grabbing another slice of bacon.

Ammatán took a slice of fruit and nibbled at it. Not one drop of juice dared to fall on his clothing. "The beings here are not the same as in your world. They sing a different song. However, if you know the songs of their paler cousins, you might learn theirs in time."

This news made her eyes light with anticipation and glee. Conall handed her three slices of the fruit, which she shoved into her mouth, barely chewing the sweet flesh.

"If you teach her magic, can you teach me something as well? Or can we do anything to earn our keep?"

"Earn your keep? Please forgive me, Conall. I spend little time in your world, and you speak many phrases with which I'm unfamiliar. Your modern slang evolves too quickly for me."

Lainn wiped her mouth and reached for another yellow fruit. "What are these called? And when did you last live in our world?"

"We call them Brid's apples. She created them many generations ago, but they cannot be grown in the Outside."

Conall bit into another piece, delighting in the tangy juices. "Brid? Like in St. Brigit?"

Ammatán hissed and the air chilled. His eyes turned hard and dark, boring into Conall's own like stakes. "Brid is no demi-god in the dead god's pantheon, human child. She is a true goddess of the Tuatha Dé Danann, the people of Danú. She is to be honored and worshipped as is her due."

The fruit caught in his throat as he coughed, and Lainn patted him on the back. When he'd recovered, Ammatán had backed down and returned to his pleasant host mask. Still, the dangerous Fae hovered beneath a shallow veneer. Conall must remember to choose his words carefully.

The Fae lord smiled at Conall, cheerful once again. "Now, young human man, what does the phrase 'earn your keep' mean? What are you keeping?"

"It means earning a living. Doing work in order to afford food, shelter, all the things a person needs to live their life."

Ammatán furrowed his brow and blinked. He glanced at his roundhouse, then at Sawchaill. The raven cawed and fluttered his wings in a gesture so much like a shrug, both Lainn and Conall burst out laughing.

The Fae's frowned deepened. "I don't see the question as a jest. Am I missing something else, human?"

After wrestling his mirth into submission, Conall shook his head. "No, there's no joke. Sawchaill just… well, he's funny."

Conall suddenly realized he hadn't stuttered once since he'd entered the world of the Fae. What if this wasn't real? Maybe this whole adventure was nothing but a fever dream. What if they'd been trapped in eternal sleep in the deadly winter on the hill of Uisneach? They'd never survive. In the spring, their frozen bodies would thaw from the melting ice.

Ammatán put a slender hand on his shoulder, his feather touch a tender caress. True affection and concern reflected in his black eyes. "Child? Is aught amiss? You've turned pale for your kind."

He swallowed, his mind buzzing with worry. "I just realized I'd lost something I never thought I'd miss. It's nothing that matters. Lainn, have you noticed?"

She stared at him, her eyes growing wide. She nodded once and took another bite of her Brid's apple. The juice dripped down her arm, and she licked it before it reached her elbow.

Conall rubbed his temples to dispel these ideas all tumbling together. He'd never puzzle things out all at once. He needed some time before he could untangle the possibilities.

Taking another fruit himself, he turned back to the Fae. "Did you have any ideas of what I might do here? Something to make myself useful. Your roundhouse doesn't seem to need any repairs. Maybe other Fae houses need work? Or something to be built? You said Fae don't like to do things that magic won't create. I can make cheese, milk, or bread. I love working with stone but will need new tools. The few I had were mostly iron, so I had to leave them behind."

Ammatán shivered and drew his hand back, his pale-white skin tinged green. "Iron. We can have no cold iron here. However, there are places which would welcome a mason's artistry if you can do delicate work. We must find you some tools to work with. Will silver do? Or bronze?"

Conall considered his options. "Bronze is too brittle for all but the softest stone. I can use an abrasive to sand stone down, but that takes a lot of effort and time. Antler or flint might work with slate to chip off flakes, but fine control of carving will be impossible for the harder stone. To do the best work, the finest details, I would need the chisels and hammers made of iron, like Sétna used."

Ammatán jumped up, startling Lainn, Conall, and Sawchaill, his face lit with enthusiasm. "Aha! I know of just the thing. Wait here."

The Fae dashed into the roundhouse, leaving the children to their fruit. Conall took another bite of the tangy flesh, finishing his bite just as Ammatán returned with a small black oblong object in his hand, his face full of glee and anticipation. "Will this work? I can get more! We can shape it however you like."

Conall took the soot-colored item, about as long as his arm. It flared at both ends like a bone, but the color looked as black as wood-gall ink. "What is it?"

"Burnt bone. But Fae bone is harder than human bone. It should be stronger than your evil cold iron."

Conall dropped the bone to the dusty ground, and Lainn backed up several steps. She stared at Ammatán. "Fae bone? Did you… did you kill him? Who was he?"

A flash of anger, followed by a moment of sheer pain, flickered across the Fae's face. However, the impression disappeared in a moment as the Fae laughed. A tinge of hysteria made Conall nervous, and the siblings exchanged a glance.

He detected no cruelty in the laugh, but Fae might mask such things more easily than humans. They stared at the blackened bone, lying inert on the ground.

126

"I did not kill him. Believe it or not, Fae can die of natural causes or accident. We are not sentimental of our empty bodies as you humans are. Our spirit, as you call it, goes to Tír na nÓg. Fae bones are quite useful, as are other parts of our flesh."

Still loath to touch the thing, Conall knelt to examine the bone. He gazed at it from several angles, finally picking it up by one end and gingerly turning it in his hand. He picked at the surface with his nails, tried to scratch it with a stone, and knocked it over his knee to break it. The piece remained intact.

With a reluctant nod, he handed it to Ammatán. "If you can make me three sizes of chisel and a blunt hammer, I think I can use this, as long as the stone is relatively soft." He held up his fingers about as wide as his thumb. "This is the middle chisel size. The others should be half as small and twice as large. The other end of each chisel should be blunt and flat so I can strike it with the hammer. Like this." He drew a picture in the dirt from several angles.

The Fae tapped a finger to his lips and nodded. "We can craft that. Will you come with me to approve the details? I know several young Fae eager to learn something new. Perhaps you can even teach them some of your stonemason skills."

Conall's stomach dropped. "I'm no master. I've only begun learning myself last year! I can't teach others!"

The stricken look on Ammatán's face, hurt and confused, made Conall sorry for his words, but he couldn't retract them. Dead silence fell upon the glade until Sawchaill squawked and took flight, circling the clearing several times before flying away.

"I'm sorry, Ammatán. I didn't mean to snap at you. It's just that I am not good enough to teach someone else my trade, even if I had permission. I'm only a student."

Ammatán still stared at the ground. Conall walked to the Fae and took his hands, cold as they were. "Will you forgive me?"

The Fae looked up, wearing an unreadable expression. "I have difficulty judging human ages. How many of your seasons do you count?"

"I've seen seventeen winters now."

"Is seventeen a short time?"

"For a human, yes. I'm barely an adult. I might live to be fifty winters, or seventy. Or I might die tomorrow. But I've probably stopped growing taller now."

Ammatán gave a half-smile and glanced at the top of Conall's head. "You have a good height. You are even taller than I am, which is pleasing to me."

This made Conall grin. "How many seasons do you have?"

"We do not count time in Faerie. The exercise is futile, as so many of us can manipulate the passage of seasons in the human world. Most of us can only go forward, as I can, but some can travel back, or stop time. Here we have no seasons, no drought, no famine. Our rulers do not die so easily as human rulers, so counting by the seasons of power does no good, either. If I used your world's seasons. . ." Ammatán considered, his eyes shifting back and forth as if doing complex computations in his mind. "I first lived perhaps one hundred and fifty of your seasons ago. I am not certain, as many of us are not born and grow like humans. Some of us started as humans, but my parents were both Fae."

One hundred and fifty years. Far longer than any human Conall had ever known, except perhaps Adhna since he wasn't human. What wonders had Ammatán seen over the years? Perhaps he'd met Saint Patrick himself or the great chiefs of history.

Lainn's thoughts must have run parallel to his own. "Will you tell us tales of your long life, Ammatán? I'd love to hear of the people you've met and the events you've witnessed."

The corner of his mouth curled into a half-smile as he turned his gaze upon her. "I can do as you ask."

Lainn clapped her hands together in child-like delight. Her action caused Sawchaill to fluff his wings in annoyance, and he cawed at her.

"I can tell you a tale now if you crave one. Would you like to hear of the Faerie Court?"

Lainn nodded with child-like vigor, which made Conall grin. When he turned that smile to Ammatán, the Fae flushed his white skin shading into gray.

The Fae cleared his throat and sat cross-legged, gesturing for both humans to do the same. Sawchaill winged back to the glade and settled on Ammatán's shoulder. When they'd settled into their circle, he cleared his throat again and spoke. "Many years ago, when I was but a youngling, I witnessed a great meeting of the Faerie Courts. Now, most of the time the courts jealously guard their territories. One Queen daren't set foot in another's land, and they respect their boundaries with extreme caution. A Faerie war is not to be taken lightly."

He cleared his throat and pursed his lips. "This meeting was of the southern Courts of Ériu. Representing the parts of Faerie attached to the human lands of *an Mhumhain*, *an Chláir*, and *Tiobraid Árann* came the most royal Queens, Áine, Aoibheall, and Oonagh. Our own Queen in *an Mhí* is Gréine de Leicne Bán, though rumors say she once lived further west and held Oonagh's domain."

Conall's head already swam with all the unfamiliar names. He would never be able to keep track of all of them.

"I, a minor courtier in a sea of Fae, awaited the Queens' arrival." Ammatán drew himself up, as if the queen watched him now.

"Our Queen sat in serene patience upon her throne, placed in front of the royal palace to greet her guests, her Consort by her side. He had but recently been chosen and stood uneasily upon his lesser throne. He'd been a courtier, Master of the Queen's Hunt, before his elevation in status. Another Fae, Bodach, took his place as Hunt Master when he became Consort."

Now Ammatán frowned, and Conall guessed he didn't care for Bodach. He glanced at Lainn, but she was listening with rapt attention.

"As the first sound of hooves echoed across the golden plain before the palace, the entire host stood silently as a human grave, craning our necks high to catch the first glimpse of the visitors. When the first chariot crested the hill, a collective sigh swept across the courtiers, a sigh of wonder and awe."

The Fae stood and swept his arms wide, his head thrown back. "Nine white horses drew the elaborate chariot, each perfectly matched in size and conformation. The Queen herself stood proudly in the front of the chariot, a handmaiden by her side."

He sat back down, a delighted smile on his face. "As the second chariot came into sight, also drawn by nine white horses and containing a Queen and her handmaiden, our Queen frowned and glanced at her Consort.

"The third chariot came into view, again with only a handmaiden to accompany the Queen. Queen Gréine flicked her hand at her Consort. Both Consort and his throne disappeared with a pop and the odor of oily smoke. I briefly wondered if she had destroyed him or merely banished him out of duty as a polite hostess. If her guests hadn't brought their Consorts, she couldn't have her own in attendance."

Ammatán paused as if trying to remember what happened next. "Each Queen's chariot ground to a halt in front of Queen Gréine's throne. Each Queen disembarked with grace and beauty. Each Queen flicked her hand, and the chariots vanished, without even a pop.

"Queen Gréine stood and opened her arms to welcome her guests. 'Be well come to my domain, sister Queens. Eat of my fruit and drink of my mead. Be merry and happy.'"

Sawchaill squawked, and Ammatán glanced at the bird. "I'm getting to that! Have patience, my friend."

"Let me describe each of the Queens to you. Áine came from the south, a land of rolling hills and lush forests. Her own curves were strong and lush as well. Her silver-white hair shone, twinkling with sparks of fire and starlight."

He stroked Sawchaill's feathers as he spoke. "Aoibheall came from the west, a land which embraces the ocean. She stood thin and tall, willow and ash. Her hair shimmered like the sea on a stormy day, blues and greens shifting with the breeze."

Sawchaill cawed again, and Lainn beckoned to him. The raven cocked his head, fluttered his wings, but remained where he was.

"Oonagh came from the mountains, her skin gray and black and pebbled like granite. She stood strong and stout, a massive woman of obvious physical power.

"Our own Queen had evergreen hair and dusky red skin. She represents the heartbeat of the center of our island, both full of passion and life.

"Together the four Queens stood. Tension grew like a physical pressure upon all, as each waited for one of the Queens to break the silence."

Sawchaill hopped down from Ammatán's shoulder and took one step toward Lainn, but stopped.

"Queen Áine broke out into a grin, holding her arms out to Queen Gréine. 'Sister! It has been long since I've looked upon your fair face. Let us sup together in peace and love.'

"Once the dam had broken, each Queen offered her greetings in kind. Soon, each Queen exchanged court gossip and giggled like girls."

Sawchaill took another hop. Ammatán frowned down at the raven. "I didn't know how we should react to such a strange sight. I glanced at the other courtiers, but they seemed as confused as well.

"A few had crept away, unwilling to risk being witness to the Queen's odd behavior. I didn't consider such an action as wise, as she'd never dismissed us. To turn your back on a Queen invites dire punishment. To turn your back upon four? I daren't contemplate such a course. And yet, it seemed we, the courtiers, had become unneeded and unwanted in this regal audience. I had almost taken a step backward myself.

"But then our Queen spun in place, her eyes literally blazing with fury, and blasted each of those Fae who had dared to leave into piles of crumbling cinders. No warning, no mercy, simple instant destruction."

Ammatán swallowed now, his face turning ashen, perhaps recalling how close he'd come to destruction. "With no thought to the Fae lives she had destroyed, our Queen turned back to her chat with a pleasant laugh, an answer to Queen Áine's last question, and a flip of her luxurious green hair. I gazed upon the blackened piles of ash with a rising dread within my heart, knowing I'd been moments away from making the same fatal decision."

Conall shivered and grabbed Lainn's hand. Her skin had turned icy as she gripped his own. Sawchaill took another hop toward her.

"I needed no reminder since that day to fear my Queen's wrath and imperious nature. She is not to be trifled with by even the most privileged of courtiers."

Sawchaill let out a caw and hopped back to Ammatán's shoulder, and the Fae stroked him. "One of those who she destroyed had been her own beloved son, a Fae of great power and regard. He now languishes in Tír na nÓg with the dead."

He glanced at both Conall and Lainn, growing apprehension on his pale face. "I've disturbed you too much, I see. I shall halt our tale and continue another day."

Silence grew heavy after Ammatán stopped speaking. Conall's sense of ease and safety had fled in an instant, and Lainn's eyes shifted to the trees and the pond with nervous flickers.

"Fear not, Conall and Lainn. You are under my protection. No lesser Fae may harm you, and I will do my best to keep you from the wrath of those above me." Ammatán clapped his hands together and chuckled. "And now, I have part of my vow to keep. Now that your sister has regained her health, I shall show you the way to your world, should you choose to leave."

Conall truly hadn't expected that and now felt shame that he had doubted the Fae's word.

Like anxious ducklings after a mother duck, Lainn and Conall followed Ammatán as he led them around the pond. As they passed the first path, he pointed. "This leads to the Faerie Queen's palace. Do not take that path unless she has summoned you."

Lainn shuddered and grabbed Conall's hand. He squeezed it for reassurance. When they came to the path across from the roundhouse, Ammatán paused, almost causing Conall to crash into him. "Do not touch the stones when we arrive, do you understand? It can cause great confusion and transport you to an unknown place in your realm. Only touch if I tell you to."

Conall nodded, as Lainn did beside him. They glanced at each other as Ammatán walked down this path, sudden apprehension growing in Conall's heart. Did the Fae mean to take them to a dangerous place, after all? Had this been some elaborate trap or a way to bind them to this place? To make them afraid to return home?

With cautious steps, they followed the white-skinned one. Tall reeds soared on either side of the path, cutting off any view of the countryside. Lainn put her hand out to touch the reeds, but Conall slapped it down. "He said not to touch anything!"

"He said the stones. These are reeds."

"It doesn't matter. Don't touch."

She scowled at him but kept her hands at her side.

The reeds fell away to an empty glade, clear except for five soaring black stones, jutting in a circle in the center. Each one glittered with silver bits, despite the lack of sun. Entranced by the beauty, Conall let out a sigh of wonder.

Lainn smiled and reached out her hand. Before Conall could stop her, she remembered Ammatán's instructions and froze. She glanced at the Fae, and he shook his head. She dropped her hand.

"These stones are attuned to your plane, the human world."

"There are other worlds?"

He nodded. "There are many. Faerie is just one, standing between your human world and Tír na nÓg, the land of the ever-living. Other worlds are elsewhere, such as Tír fo Thuinn, Emain Ablach, or Mag Mell. Other sacred people live in other lands, but these are the lands bound to your island."

The ideas of so many realms jumbled in Conall's mind. Lainn asked, "How do we travel to those other planes?"

Ammatán shook his head. "You do not. Not unless one of the Fae or the Tuatha Dé Danann bring you there. The planes of other deities are forbidden. The only place you may travel without assistance is your human plane and Faerie. Even then, you must honor the gateways and know their secrets."

Conall ached to touch the stones as Lainn had almost done and wondered if a magical compulsion lay on them. He gripped his hands together to ensure his obedience. "Will you teach us these secrets?"

"Some of them, yes. Those you need to know."

What other secrets might Ammatán know? He had known his father's name. Did the Fae know what happened to him? The idea itched at Conall's mind, but Ammatán had already made it quite clear he wouldn't speak of this subject.

"When you approach the stones in your world, it should be during a sun feast or fire feast. You know of these days?"

Lainn nodded. "Sun feasts are the solstices and the equinoxes. Fire feasts are the midpoint days between those."

Conall didn't know these words and looked at his sister sideways. This must be part of her druid lore.

The Fae nodded his smile wide. "Just so. You've studied such things?"

"With the druids."

Ammatán's smile fled, and he took a troubled swallow but continued. "If you approach the stones from Faerie, however, such times mean little. You may depart on any day. Even in your world, the passage is possible on other days, but the way is more difficult."

Conall nodded, praying Lainn would remain silent about the druids. Ammatán clearly cared little of them.

"Approach from the north and walk around them in a circle. Go the opposite direction the sun travels, three times. This will attune your human bodies to the stones. They will warm and hum, signaling their readiness."

He continued instructions and Conall tried to memorize them, but he knew if he missed any details, Lainn would recall them. Part of her training as a druid must be to train her memory.

As they returned to the roundhouse, they settled for a meal. Conall ate his food with a half a mind, thinking about what his father might have done with this information. Perhaps he didn't die, but escaped to Faerie? Might he be wandering around one of the planes, alive and well? How could Conall find out without breaking Ammatán's *géis*?

A raucous call brought their attention to the sky. Sawchaill dove down among them, and they all covered their heads from his talons. Instead of attacking, though, he dropped a small package.

When he'd fluttered to the thatched roof to groom his wings and cast a gimlet eye upon them, Ammatán threw him a dirty look and picked up the package.

The exquisite box looked like chased silver and gold in filigree patterns, not unlike the designs on Conall's brooch. The overpowering smell of lilacs, rain, and musk made his head reel.

Ammatán opened the box with care. When he lifted the delicately carved lid, rose light engulfed the clearing and Conall caught his breath. Pressure upon his lungs and mouth shoved him to the ground. Lainn fell next to him leaving only Ammatán still standing, the box in his hand.

Several layers of a booming, feminine voice echoed through Conall's bones, from the earth below him and within his mind. "I have a task for you, courtier. You will attend upon me at once."

As abruptly as the pressure came, it disappeared. Conall could breathe again and took in several ragged, deep breaths, coughing as dust tickled his savagely dry throat. Lainn coughed beside him, the whites of her eyes tinged with panic.

Ammatán's darted between them. "You must both stay. Into the roundhouse. I must leave. Now!"

With no further explanation, Ammatán transformed into a large bird and flew away. Black and white feathers mimicked his Fae coloring, and the bird looked much larger than Sawchaill. He vanished into the dim Faerie light.

Lainn tugged on his arm. "He said to go inside, Conall. Come on! You can't think that voice is one to disobey, can you?"

He shook his head to clear the cobwebs and let his sister take him to safety.

Chapter Eleven

Conall hadn't gotten used to the lack of any time in this place. No sunrise, no sunset, no darkness, no storm, no stars. Nothing to mark the hours, the days, or the weeks. He only grasped that Ammatán left a while ago. In the meantime, they ate, rested, and explored the roundhouse.

The Fae's home stood larger even than Sétna's luxurious roundhouse. Six alcoves radiated off from the central hearth and main room.

No dust from the thatch floated in the air. Instead, the sweet aroma of wildflowers and honey permeated the room. Flowers bloomed in the ceiling and vines wrapped around each wooden support. Each of those was a living tree, entwined with a central trunk. The entire roundhouse shifted and rustled in spite of a lack of breeze as if breathing.

One alcove held food and tools for cooking, though most of the food didn't require actual heating. Like Adhna, Ammatán preferred fruits, vegetables, nuts, and mushrooms. Foods to gather or forage, rather than bake, cook, or boil. No bread, no meat, no milk, nor cheese sat in his larder. While Conall did spy a small pot of honey, he suspected this was the product of trade with the mortal realm rather than something the Fae gathered.

Ammatán's sleeping alcove contained rich, brightly dyed fabrics, but Conall didn't pry further into the Fae's personal space. He didn't know if Fae had a sense of privacy as humans did, but it seemed common courtesy.

Lainn helped him make a meal of nuts and fruit, offering several choice items to Sawchaill, who accepted each morsel with dainty dignity. The raven preferred to take items from Lainn's hand.

For a moment, Conall resented his sister's talent with animals but squashed it. He could work stone and had his father's brooch, both considerable talents. Why should he envy her abilities as well? That was just greedy.

With a smile, he grabbed three Brid's apples and juggled them, making Lainn giggle. Sawchaill didn't seem to grasp the demonstration. He cocked his head back and forth several times as if trying to get a better look at the spinning fruit. The bird squawked, settled on his perch, and turned up his beak at the performance.

With a chuckle, Conall bit into one apple, offering Lainn another. "Why don't you sing us a song, Lainn? Something to soothe both us and our raven companion until Ammatán returns?"

At the mention of their host, the memory of the terrible voice returned, stealing the warmth from the day. The light dimmed, and his terror returned. He closed his eyes and concentrated on his breath, forcing himself to take each one with measured concentration.

When he opened his eyes again, the world had contracted, as if pushing on him with a gray force, pressuring his vision into a narrow focus. Then, as rapidly as the panic arrived, it fled once again. Conall sat at the large wooden table and raised his eyebrows at his sister. "Well?"

With a glance at the raven, she sighed and rolled her eyes. "Fine. How about the story of the birth of *Cú Chulainn*?"

Lainn must have remembered the hero had always been Conall's favorite. He sat back, crossing his arms and closing his eyes. Conall had heard the tale many times but had never heard his sister sing it, not since she'd gotten training at the oak grove.

She sat with her back against the roundhouse wall, a mug of water at her side. Conall settled, his hand on Sawchaill's silk-feathered back as they both listened to the tale of the hero *Cú Chulainn*, who had been born Setanta.

"Many moons ago, in the dawn of the age of man, a chief named Conchobhair mac Nessa lived and ruled in Ulster. While he inherited his chiefdom through unusual means, he became a mighty chief out of legend, with many great deeds to his name, but this is not his story.

"Conchobhair mac Nessa had a daughter named Deichtire who also served as his charioteer. On the wintry eve of her wedding, a mayfly few into her cup of wine. She drank the mayfly and fell into a deep sleep, a sleep full of dreams and portents.

"Within this dream, Lugh of the Long Hand told her she must come with him, along with her fifty handmaidens. They transformed into a flock of shining white, exotic birds and burst forth from their chambers. The wedding guests exclaimed with alarm and wonder at this, but when they discovered Deichtire and her ladies had disappeared, searched for them for a full year.

"All the chiefdom had given up hope of finding their lost daughter. However, the following year, to the very day, the same flock of white birds reappeared in the skies. These birds descended upon the land and ate every blade of grass and every winter berry."

Sawchaill cawed at the mention of berries, and Conall stroked his feathers, just as he'd seen Ammatán doing.

"In fury and determination, the men of the chiefdom, with Conchobhair in the lead, went on the hunt, chasing the bare hint of the exotic flock of birds. In and out of the clouds this flock flew, flirting with their hunters through the short day and long night. Nine flocks of silver birds winked white against the black winter sky, each led by two, and the whole mass led by three. Across the land, they followed, from *Sliabh Fuaid* to *Fir Rois*.

"This mass of birds drew the Ulstermen to a lonely cottage on the edge of the land, in a glade of spring flowers, seemingly apart from the snow-clad hills surrounding it."

Lainn stopped and took a long drink of water before clearing her throat to continue. "The cottage appeared poor and crumbling, with barely enough room for three people, and yet the hunters found no other shelter. The host came out and invited them inside with grace and a smile. One hunter, Bricriu of the Bitter Tongue, declared the place too poor and small, yet he entered anyhow.

"When he approached the cottage, a well-lit house stood in its place. Within this large home, their host welcomed him. He asked if Bricriu searched for anyone.

"'Indeed, I do! We search for Deichtire, the daughter of our chief. Is she here?'"

Conall grinned as this was his favorite part of the story.

"The man grinned and opened his hands. Fifty maidens appeared before him, each more beautiful than the last. He spied his chief's daughter among them but held his tongue. He decided he should receive a reward from his chief if he could take credit for finding Deichtire, so he'd bide his time until that became possible. 'I must have a token of this wonder to bring to my chief.'

"With narrowed eyes, the host offered a fine cloak of purple and gold fringe, a truly regal gift. Bricriu took this cloak and brought it to Conchobhair. 'Our host offers this gift to his guests. We can go inside to rest this night.'

"The hunters piled into the building, all fitting comfortably inside no matter the exterior appearance. Despite their comfort, they got little rest. Their host greeted them but excused himself. He attended upon his wife, who was in labor. The screams of the woman vied with the screams of a mare, also giving birth in the stable. Throughout the darkness, female screams ripped at the hunters' ears, almost driving them mad with the sound."

Lainn stopped again and drank more water. This time, Sawchaill hopped next to her, and she petted the bird. He trilled with pleasure.

"When the morning dawned, each hunter woke and stretched, unable to understand why they could see the winter clouds above them. The cottage, modest or large, had disappeared. Icy hills had replaced the spring glade.

"Conchobhair rose and found Deichtire and her fifty maidens, a newborn babe, and the mare with her two newborn colts.

"Each of his hunters wanted the honor of raising this child of mystical birth, but Conchobhair bade them all wait until their return home. Once there, the druid passed judgment on the fate of the child.

"'Let he learn the craft of ruling from Conchobhair, the craft of speaking from Sencha, the craft of war from Fergus, and the craft of learning from Amergin. Until then, Dechtire and her husband shall raise him as their own.'

"And so they named the child Setanta, child of all men and of none."

Just as Conall stood to get more food, Ammatán flung the door wide. The Fae's eyes were white-rimmed and darted around the roundhouse with nervous energy. His hair appeared ashen and mussed. "You are both safe. Good."

With quick movements, he entered and shut the door securely behind him. Ammatán stood with his hand on the door for several moments before he turned to them, taking a deep breath. "I'm not certain when or by whom, but your presence has been reported to the Queen. I've delayed her demand to see you, but I must prepare you."

Conall's stomach knotted into a cold lump and his hunger disappeared. He sat with his back against the wall, finding solace in the unyielding, reassuring object. Conall glanced at his sister, but she didn't seem worried. He envied her serenity.

Ammatán sat down, crossing his legs and placing his fingertips to his temples. He screwed his eyes shut for a minute before opening them and blinking. He turned to Conall with a sad smile. "Your arrival has already come to the Queen's attention. This discovery had been inevitable, but I'd hoped to have more time. Still, we have a few hours before you are due."

Lainn snorted. "Hours? How can you count hours here?"

Conall waved her into silence. "What do we need to do?"

"Good lad. First, we must clean you. To be presented to the Queen in any less than your best would be a prime insult. Luckily for us, she does not currently have formal Court, so you needn't be in full regalia. Sawchaill? Will you fetch something appropriate for each of our guests?"

The bird cawed and fluttered his wings but didn't fly away.

"Don't ask me! You're far more familiar with Court fashions than I am. Shoo!"

With another squawk, the raven batted Ammatán with his wings and darted off into the distance. Only once the sound of his wings had faded did Ammatán speak again. "Now, into the pond, both of you. You'd best strip off those clothes. We should have done this when you arrived, but I sensed you required food and rest first, and then I was too eager to tell tales. Now we need clean! Come now, up!"

Conall rose and hesitated, not wanting to be naked in front of a stranger, and stranger than most. Lainn had no such compunctions and peeled off her boy's clothing, revealing her nude curves. Grime hid within each crease in her skin, making her freckles dim in the low light. Her hair hung in bedraggled warrior braids.

She removed each of the twine knots from the braids and pulled them out until her auburn hair looked like a mass of dead winter vines, crackling out to a bramble patch.

His sister put her hands on her hips and glared at him. "Well, Conall? What are you waiting for, doom? I'm not the only one going in the pond, I'll have you know."

Abashed at his own shyness in the face of her boldness, he pulled his *léine* over his head, hearing the rotten fabric rip despite his care. He eyed the discarded pile of clothing with both distaste and wistfulness.

Each piece of the mortal world he pulled away from himself severed another link to that world. Would he ever return to everything he held dear? Or had they become trapped forever in this bizarre, darkly singing countryside?

Lainn had such a free spirit, she'd make a home wherever she wandered. Conall didn't think he would adapt so easily.

Still, needs must win over wants. He pulled out the twine and simple beads in his own braids, one by one, until his own hair resembled that of his sister's, though his dead winter vines were black while hers were copper. He scratched his scalp vigorously once all beads and braids had been removed, closing his eyes in sheer pleasure at the sensation. Lainn smiled and did the same before they both stepped into the still pond.

The water felt warmer than he'd imagined, enveloping them in comfort. The river at home stayed cool throughout the summer. This had a low fire simmering underneath. Not hot, but sinfully sybaritic. He sighed as he submerged, raking his fingers through his tangled hair. They caught, and he yelped trying to get them clear.

Despite his earlier agitation, Ammatán laughed and went into the roundhouse. He came back with a large comb made of bone. "Come, sit in front of me. I'll tame that tangled mess. Then you can do the same for your sister."

Conall's skin stung from the warm water and more nervous energy, he sat in front of the Fae. With gentle fingers, Ammatán began at the ends of his hair, brushing each section until smooth, working his way up to the scalp. Then he worked on another section.

Conall closed his eyes, surprised at how luxurious such care felt. Ammatán's hands brushed his shoulders now and then, making his skin pebble. For a moment, he wished Lainn elsewhere. Ashamed at such an uncharitable thought, he glanced at his sister.

He'd gotten so used to seeing her in boy's garb and hair, to see her diving under the surface like a selkie gave him a shift in perspective, almost as if he had lost his sister at one point, only to regain her now as a grown woman. Her curves had increased over the winter, and he averted his eyes as she burst through the surface, sluicing the water from her still-tangled hair.

He wondered why she had so easily shifted back to a girl, but he supposed she was in less danger here than in the real world. Except for the Faerie Queen, of course.

Ammatán stopped grooming him, and Conall wished he hadn't. The Fae placed a hand on his shoulder. "May I rebraid your hair, Conall?"

With a gulp and a nod, Conall let out a long breath, waiting for every stray brush of the Fae's hand. Did he imagine it, or did Ammatán sit closer now? He could feel the Fae's cool skin against his back, stirring sensations within him he'd only felt in dreams before. The center of his being tingled, as if he'd leapt into a river, the sheer joy of anticipation an incredible build up and release.

When Ammatán finished the last braid, Conall had to wait before he could stand. Embarrassed, he waited until the Fae had walked back into the roundhouse before he motioned Lainn over. "Sit where I did, and I'll do your hair and braids."

She sat in front of him, and he worked as Ammatán had, smoothing the bottoms out first. Her hair curled like his, but with larger curls. He took much longer to smooth out her locks, matted and tangled. When he'd finished, they both stepped out of the pond to find Ammatán.

He stood inside the roundhouse, regarding four sets of clothing, a finger on his lips. Sawchaill sat on his perch, preening one wing with viscous energy, while Ammatán cocked his head at the first set. This had varying shades of brilliant blue, from aqua to near purple. Each diagonal stripe leapt from the cloth.

The second set consisted of abstract splotches of red, mostly deep and sanguine. This robe could have been the dropcloth beneath a grisly murder.

The third was pure white, with feathers and sparkling bits that shone even in the shade of the roundhouse, while the fourth showed no color at all. It blended in with the table beneath it so well, Conall almost hadn't noticed the fabric, except where the translucent substance draped past the edge.

With a grunt, Ammatán picked up the red one, holding it up to Lainn's neck. He eyed it from several angles and glanced back at Sawchaill. The bird fluttered and shook his head. "You're right. The color clashes horribly with her bright hair. I think the fourth one for her."

"I prefer to dress as a boy."

Ammatán shook his head. "Impossible before the Queen, Lainn. One cannot hide their true nature from her, and any attempt to do so may trigger her uncertain temper. Now, the blue… the blue works wonders. Come, try it on and go out into the light."

When Conall saw the brilliant blue stripes against his sister's red hair, she looked far lovelier than even Aoife, a true goddess in human form.

She picked at the sleeve's edge with her mouth curled up. "Close your mouth, Conall. You understand I hate this."

"You look lovely, Lainn. Truly, you do."

She blushed and cast her gaze down, the perfect image of a modest maiden.

Ammatán turned to him. "Now for you, my lovely human. The red would look striking against your dark hair."

He put his hands up, shaking them. "No, no, I'd look like a murder victim."

With a low chuckle, Ammatán held up the scarlet garment. "At least try it on? For me?"

With a roll of his eyes, Conall drew the robe up and secured it in front. It seemed wrong not wearing a traditional léine, and the open front exposed him far too easily.

"No, like this. This side ties all the way around." Ammatán untied the belt and reached around him. His skin prickled again as the Fae's arm rubbed his chest. His breath came shallow, and he stood frozen, not trusting himself to move.

When he'd tied the robe, Ammatán surveyed him, hands on each upper arm. Their faces were barely a handspan apart, so close he could smell the Fae's sweet breath. His flat black eyes glistened in the light, and Conall's heart raced faster.

The Fae stepped away, his white skin shaded gray. Is that how he blushed? Conall's mind grew fuzzy as Ammatán examined him in the new clothing. "That should do fine. What do you think, Lainn?"

His sister's eyes twinkled with mischief. "You hate this as much as I hate mine, don't you, Conall?"

He nodded, mute.

"Good. Then they're perfect. Ammatán, you said we needed to prepare. We're clean and clothed. What else will we need to do?"

With Ammatán's final instructions in mind, Conall and Lainn followed their host down the first path to the Faerie Queen's Court.

In his childhood, he'd imagined such a journey with four matched white horses drawing a fancy chariot. In reality, they marched across the bizarre and ever-changing Faerie countryside.

The light never changed, even as they moved past something which ought to cast shadows, like those gyrating trees with oddly colored leaves. Non-butterflies and bees flitted around them like children playing ball.

A small, furry creature with stripes and a bushy tail crept into the bushes beside the road at one point, but Ammatán warned them both against trying to coax the animal out.

They passed rivers, ponds, and boglands, just like in their world, but despite the similarities, each had an odd quality, like someone had drawn the land rather than created it. The flat light made each object less real.

146

In the distance, a faint bright object grew into a single white beacon, a spire rising above the landscape. As they approached, it resolved into a shining tower.

Conall realized his hip should have long since been aching by now, but it didn't hurt at all. Like his stutter, the ache had disappeared when he arrived in Faerie and hadn't returned. That both frightened and pleased him.

The tower grew into a silver needle, soaring high into the dim sky. Staring at the structure made Conall's eyes ache, but still, he couldn't tear his gaze from the graceful lines of the building. His mason's training tried to analyze what stone the palace had been crafted from as they got close enough to see the walls.

Ammatán stopped them before they came to the arched entrance. "Remember what I said, Conall? Lainn? Keep your eyes down and bow or kneel when you greet her. Say nothing unless asked a direct question. Answer with a simple yes or no if you can. Do not eat or take anything offered, even if someone insists."

Lainn scowled. "I thought you said eating the food here wouldn't trap us?"

"Eating *my* food won't, but I cannot give assurances about anyone else. Unless the Queen offers food. She is above such petty trickery, and all understand a gift from her is a signal honor and proof of her regard. Touch no one. Do not turn your back on the Queen. Do not insult the Queen in any way imaginable. Do not leave until I tell you."

"What shall we call her?"

"She is Queen *Gréine*, but if you must address her at all, it would be wiser to call her My Queen."

Conall's stomach churned with each step and now grew into a full revolt within him.

The elegant arches they walked beneath attracted his eyes, and studied the details as they passed, almost stumbling into Lainn. Ammatán grabbed his arm and gave him a warning squeeze. Abashed, Conall kept his gaze to the path.

No one lingered in the hallway, and a heavy silence reigned in the courtyards. Through a maze of arches and doorways, they made their way to the center, the grand throne room.

The space was large enough to hold hundreds of dancers, yet it seemed utterly desolate. Soaring, delicate arches met at the center of the ceiling, grander than any cathedral Conall had ever imagined, all crafted from white and silver stones.

At the head of the echoingly empty graceful hall sat two massive thrones. One made of black thorns, curling cruelly up and around the seat, and a second, larger throne made of wild green vines. This larger throne writhed and twisted even as they watched, growing with each step closer.

The thrones both stood empty.

Ammatán whispered, "Keep moving. Just because you can see no one there doesn't mean She cannot see."

Stone floor tiles glistened with a high polish, making Conall slip in his steps. They reflected everything like a still morning pond, making him dizzy and disoriented. The ceiling looked shiny as well, though the roof curved with arched supports. He imagined a thousand reflections of them all walking through countless abandoned halls, with the Queen watching each set of humans in a different world.

As they came near the thrones, his steps felt heavier, until it was difficult to even raise his legs. Lainn frowned, glancing at her own feet, and soon they could move no farther.

Ammatán glanced back to see what kept them and stepped back to stand beside them. He addressed the empty thrones, bowing low with a dramatic flourish and a forced smile. "We have arrived as you requested, my Queen."

The silence grew denser, pushing upon Conall's ears and eyes. His head pounded with pain, and when the voice came, it brought blessed relief. A terrifying, multi-toned voice echoed through the massive hall. "Step forward, human girl child."

Afraid for his sister, Conall fought the urge to step in front of her, to shield her from the invisible Faerie Queen's wrath. He was rooted to his spot, however, unable to so much as move a muscle. Lainn stepped forward with halting movements, like a puppet on strings. She knelt with difficulty.

"You're almost a pretty child, despite the stink of mortality. Turn for me."

Like a toy, Lainn turned with her arms out stiff. Her still expression betrayed no emotion, but she kept her eyes to the floor.

"Now the boy."

Conall's legs moved of their own volition. He had no more power to stop them than he did to fly away into the Faerie sky. His body took three steps until he stood next to his sister.

He bowed in a jerky attempt at grace. He also turned in a circle, his hand knocking Lainn's ear as he turned. She couldn't move out of the way, and he couldn't pull his hand back.

"You have chosen lovely playthings, Ammatán. They are siblings? Even more precious. Will you keep them both? Perhaps you should breed them."

"If it please you, my Queen."

"Have they any magic?"

Conall held his breath. Had Ammatán discovered the brooch? What about Lainn's druid training? It might be unwise for this formidable Faerie Queen to have control over such powers. But even less wise to lie to her.

"The boy can carve stone, my Queen. The girl can sing."

"Bah. Singing is nothing. Who cannot sing? The least courtier in my Court can sing more sweetly than any mortal could hope. But stone carving, that might be useful. Yes, useful indeed. You were wise to find me such a resource just as I needed it, Ammatán. This will increase your favor in my eyes. Send him after the next meal. I have a project for someone with such a talent."

"As you command, my Queen."

The pressure that held them vanished and both humans fell into heaps on the ground. Conall heaved a sigh of relief, almost a sob. His muscles still wouldn't obey him, but at least nothing else commanded them.

Ammatán knelt beside them, a gentle hand on Conall's shoulder. "She's gone. You can stand now."

Every muscle protested as he tried to scramble to his feet. He slipped several times, and he ached as if he'd run all afternoon. Each bit of him throbbed in pain, but the Fae helped him gain his balance, and then they helped Lainn.

As they left the throne room, Conall studied the arch more closely, trailing a finger across the fine grain of a base. "What sort of stone is this constructed from? I've never touched anything like it. Smooth, light, yet sturdy enough to hold so much weight."

Ammatán gave a casual shrug. "The stone is quarried from the land of Tír na nÓg."

"Tír na nÓg? The land of the ever-living? Is that not where we are?"

Ammatán shook his head and pulled Conall by the arm, away from the stone. "Tír na nÓg is where we go after our time in Faerie. It's the afterworld, where the gods and goddesses have retired. A human can travel there, but never back again. Only a few have tried and all have died. I'll not allow that to happen to you."

The entreating look in the Fae's eyes made Conall's throat constrict. "What stone would I work with for the Queen's project, then?"

"I cannot say. Her plans are not given to the likes of me, and her palace is complete. I would have rather kept you to myself, but as the Queen commands, so must we obey. At least she has only called you and not Lainn."

Conall didn't think this to be a blessing, necessarily. He wanted to spend time with Ammatán, not work for the Queen. However, if his labors would be the wage he must pay for time with the Fae, so be it.

He hoped he'd be up to whatever task she asked of him. His own inadequacy haunted him on the journey back. What if he should fail? What if he insulted the Queen? Would he punish Lainn? Ammatán?

Did their lives and sanity rely upon Conall's imperfect knowledge of masonry? He was only an apprentice. Every criticism Sétna had ever given of his work crowded into his mind, jumbling together for attention.

The weight of his unknown task grew heavy across his young shoulders as they returned to the roundhouse. Sawchaill cawed twice at them as they ate a silent meal. When they finished, Conall glanced at Ammatán. "She said after the next meal. Must I return alone? Do I go to the same place?"

The Fae drew him outside, away from Sawchaill and Lainn. Now, in some modicum of privacy, Ammatán drew him close, murmuring in his ear. "I will walk you there but must leave you when she arrives. You must be strong, you must be obedient, and you must be smart. Can you do those for me?"

Being this close once again made Conall dizzy, and the Fae's breath in his ear gave him shivers. "I will do as she commands to the best of my abilities. What if she asks something I can't do? How do I tell her?"

Ammatán touched one long finger to Conall's jaw, tracing the line down to his chin. Conall shuddered and shut his eyes. "Explain it's beyond your powers. She understands power and believes mortals have none. She will have tools far superior to any I can provide. High quality bronze and bone, antler and stone. She might even have diamond dust for grinding surfaces."

The Fae's fingers touched Conall's lips in a velvet caress. "Ask for whatever you need, as long as you don't mention iron. Never mention cold iron, not even once, understand? She might destroy you on the spot for such an insult."

"Why would she even need my help? Can't she create what she wants with magic?"

He shook his head, his finger moving to Conall's chin. "She can create a glamor, that's true. But she'd need to work to maintain the illusion, and if this is to be a place of relaxation, such a construct would defeat that purpose. Only a mundane, physical construction would last beyond her conscious magical effort, and we no longer have such masons. We must draw upon human talents from time to time, and this time, she has chosen you."

Conall nodded, wishing the Fae would caress him again. He put his hand on the Fae's shoulder, drawing him closer. Slowly, their lips pressed together in a chaste kiss, and tingling spread from his lips to the bottom of his stomach.

Ammatán pulled him into his arms, and they embraced with heated ferocity before a squawk from Sawchaill made them pull apart.

The Fae took his hand, and they headed back toward the palace. "We must go. Promise me to be careful. I don't wish to lose you."

Chapter Twelve

Conall touched the odd stone. While not the same substance as the palace archways, it still felt smoother and finer than any of the limestone or granite he'd worked in the past. The Queen had called it marble, and he saw veins of gold, blue, and silver throughout the black. The sheen entranced him, but he needed to experiment to see how it worked with his techniques.

He chose a small piece to crack with his new tools, sitting down next to the worktable. At least she permitted him to wear a simple, utilitarian *léine* for this work. That court garb would be utterly impractical for stonework.

Bronze and quartz chisels, diamond dust, and flint tools had also appeared. However, the Queen herself didn't attend, only her voice. As he had never worked with such materials, he turned to where the Queen's voice came from, his head bowed low. "May I request time to master these unfamiliar tools?"

"You may. However, my patience had finite limits. Learn quickly."

He bowed lower. "I shall do so, my Queen."

The marble seemed softer than the granite and limestone he'd worked with in the past, and the slate he'd worked on once. The grain felt fine, and he'd be able to carve much greater detail into this new stone.

With the bronze chisel, he tapped a small chunk, both softly and harder, learning the limits of the medium. Then he chose the flint tool and tested that, along with the quartz chisel.

Once he formed the chunk into a perfect cube, he used the diamond dust to wear the edges to a fine edge. Each flat surface shone in the light, and each edge was almost sharp enough to cut his skin.

With a grin, he then sanded near one edge of the cube to see how thin he might cut the marble without breaking it. Thinner and thinner he wore down near the edge, making an almost translucent piece. He held it up and discerned a faint light through the stone. Was this a magical trick of Faerie? Would it work in his world?

With his hands, he tried to break the thin piece. It took effort, and it flexed before it snapped. He ran a finger along the sharp edge, noting the uniform break.

He used the flint tool to flake the marble into thinner and thinner pieces, like the slate he'd used for a project last year. The slate flaked in long, flat pieces, but the marble had a less uniform tendency. It usually broke how he intended, but sometimes cracked in places he didn't intend.

It took a great deal of experimentation to discover the right angles, pressures, and percussions until he decided he had a decent understanding of the marble's properties, and what his new tools could do.

Now that he had an understanding of his materials, he deemed himself ready to speak to the Queen about what she wanted and how he'd make that happen.

Conall stood, shaking the stone dust from his *léine*. He arranged his new tools and the practice pieces in a neat row, and addressed the surrounding air, as she'd instructed him.

"I am ready, my Queen."

So far, he'd only heard her powerful voice from all around him. She hadn't yet appeared to him. He counted himself blessed for this, as the voice was plenty to inspire terror within every bone of his body.

While her appearance would be beyond beautiful, he doubted his own body's ability to respond to such a creature with any semblance of courage or sense. The voice vibrated through the ground and into his bones. "You have assessed your abilities with this substance?"

He swallowed, wishing for some water for his parched throat. "I have. What would you like me to build?"

Conall must have imagined the hesitation. The Faerie Queen must know what she wanted. Still, he noticed a measurable space of time between his question and her response. "They built the palace long ago, before my time. While it is supremely beautiful, I would prefer a private retreat to reflect my own tastes. I enjoy open spaces, delicate ornamentation, but a sense of seclusion and peace. A retreat, a hideaway from Court where I might relax and be silent. Can you create such a thing with the stone I have provided?"

He gave another bow. "I understand, my Queen."

"The stone will be the framework, as I'll want gardens and animals to keep me company, but no Fae. An oasis of peace for my own."

The idea a Queen of Faerie might crave solitude almost made her seem human in Conall's mind, though to say such a thing out loud would be a grave insult. Perhaps *approachable* or *relatable* would be better words.

Conall considered his options and his tools. He might create a space with this delightful stone, with floral shapes and curving lines. Such a light, strong stone would make a skeletal arch above a bower.

His mind wandered back to the beautifully planned chaos of the interlocking stones in the druid's garden, the peaceful fountain in the oak grove. To create his vision, he'd also need living things, flowers, and vines, to complete the atmosphere of a secluded retreat.

He glanced up toward the voice. "May I recruit the help of someone with a talent for growing things?"

"Granted. I shall send someone when you need them. Begin now. I will allow you to return to Ammatán's home periodically to rest. You will be provided with human food."

The voice vanished, leaving him breathless with weak knees. Conall sat abruptly on the ground, his spine tingling from the impact. What had he gotten himself into? What if his creations displeased the Queen?

Could he complete this task? Would he even survive this task?

With a sense of fatalistic urgency, he searched the tools for a piece of the chalk he'd requested. He sketched out five designs on the black stone, each one reminiscent of curling vines and flowering trees. The first would be the simplest, clean lines and gentle curves. The last had fancy curling vines and braided details, something he thought he'd have in both the marble and in the living trees. It incorporated the planned chaotic beauty he had observed in the druid's garden, back in the human realm, the organic shapes melding into each other with seamless crafting.

The nostalgia of his lost home almost made him crumble into tears, but he swallowed them down and continued to draw.

After what must have been several hours, Conall stood and lifted his arms. His back cracked as he surveyed each of his samples. Would Ammatán help him choose the best one for the Queen? Or should he call for her again, and offer them for her approval?

"Your final design pleases me the most."

The surprise and the power of the voice made him flinch and retreat to the edge of the clearing, but the voice disappeared as soon as it had come.

That meant the Queen could watch him. If she didn't watch him directly, she might have a creature keeping him under a watchful eye, ready to inform her of anything she needed to know. Valuable information.

After wiping the first four designs from the slab, he planned out the carvings he must complete. He determined how many blocks of the new stone he'd need, with a few extra in case of breakage or mistakes. A larger chisel would be useful and more abrasive dust. In addition to his new tools, he'd need non-stone materials. Soft wood, a strong adhesive, and a fine cloth to finish the polishing to a brilliant sheen.

The sheer amount of work before him seemed daunting. Hundreds of hours just in carving the stones, much less sanding and polishing, building the armature, and adding the living elements. Years of work lay before him, in just one being's personal retreat.

For the retreat of a Faerie Queen, he had little choice in the matter. She had not asked his consent.

His memory of the visit to her palace shrouded in his mind. Conall remembered that he'd met the Queen but couldn't bring her image to his mind.

He tried to picture what she looked like. Was she tall, bigger than life, like a goddess? Or compact like Lainn? Did she have a curvy, voluptuous body like Aoife? What color was her hair?

He couldn't remember seeing any other Fae except for Ammatán, though he must have done so at the palace. Did they all have snow-white skin and black hair? Ammatán stood tall with long, lean muscles. His fingernails and teeth were pointed, giving him an almost feral appearance. His smile, however, warmed Conall's heart, and he hoped he'd be allowed to see him soon.

Always keeping in mind that the Queen could watch him, Conall sketched out the number of marble blocks he would need and a reasonable draft of the other required supplies. When he finished, he leaned back on his heels and wiped the excess chalk on his *léine*, satisfied with his work.

"I suppose that's the best I can do for now. I've planned every step. Once I get the other tools, I can start the actual work."

A raven's caw in his ear made him jump to one side and fall on his hip. "Blood and bones, Sawchaill, did you have to sneak up on me like that? May the devil use your backbone as a ladder to pick apples in the garden of hell!"

The bird flapped his wings and hopped three times. He glanced back at Conall and cocked his head.

"What, am I to follow you? I'm working on the Queen's project."

He squawked again and hopped three more times. Another glance over his shoulder made Conall narrow his eyes. "Are you sent to take me back to Ammatán's for my rest? Is that it?"

The bird nodded thrice and hopped again. With a prayer he was interpreting the raven's actions correctly, Conall took a deep breath and followed.

The trip to Ammatán's roundhouse seemed much shorter than the first trek had been. Maybe anticipation and fear had colored his sense of time, or maybe distance was a mutable variable in Faerie. Possibly both. Either way, by the time he reached the now-familiar roundhouse, his limbs felt leaden.

Ammatán exited the house as Conall approached, called by Sawchaill's caws. Lainn ran to him, hugging him tightly. "You're back safe! I worried she might chew you up into little quivering bits for the birds to feast upon."

He laughed with a slight edge of hysteria at the gory vision her words evoked but hugged her back. "I've got a commission and one that will take me a long time. At least I'll be useful, earning my keep."

He smiled at the phrase and glanced at Ammatán. The Fae looked drawn around the edge of his eyes, and the lines in his face looked deeper. He'd been worrying.

After extracting himself from Lainn's embrace, he stepped to the Fae and took both his hands. "I am safe back, Ammatán."

The Fae's hands felt warmer than he'd remembered. Ammatán's skin normally felt unnaturally cool, like the wood of an autumn tree. Now warmth flowed through his hands, almost warmer than a rock in the summer sun. Conall drew in that warmth, thankful for its healing effect. He squeezed the Fae's hands and drew him in for an embrace.

Conall no longer cared if Lainn watched, or if Sawchaill disapproved. He put his arms around Ammatán and hugged him tightly, thankful the Fae returned his ardor with fierce affection.

Ammatán gripped him with his own need, his elegant fingers digging into his back. Pain and pleasure from those nails kindled an intense fire within Conall's belly.

With an apologetic glance to his sister, he drew Ammatán into the roundhouse. Lainn shrugged and headed toward the trees. Sawchaill flew to accompany her.

Now that he'd made his choice clear, Conall grew nervous. He perched on the edge of his cot, pulling Ammatán down next to him, still holding one hand. He didn't know how to proceed. Luckily, Ammatán had no hesitation.

The Fae placed a finger on Conall's jaw, turning his head so they faced each other. His soft kiss tickled his lips and made the hairs on his arms stand up, especially when Ammatán leaned in and their teeth scraped.

Conall leaned back as Ammatán leaned forward. Soon he lay on the cot, the Fae above him. Ammatán kissed his neck, sending shivers all along his body. He didn't want Ammatán to stop. Every muscle, every bit of skin tingled with anticipation and longing, and he wanted this amazing sensation to last. He'd never felt so alive, so vibrant, as in this moment, in Ammatán's arms.

The Fae's long fingers traced his chest, down to his belly button, along the tops of his thighs, and back up again. In return, Conall ran his hands along the muscles in Ammatán's back, down to his buttocks and up along his waist.

With breathless frenzy, both removed their clothing, so they could touch all over. Every place his skin touched Ammatán's burned with desire and quivering nervous energy. Conall wanted to caress everywhere at once, but he also wanted this to last forever.

He stroked the thin skin along Ammatán's neck and watched as the Fae closed his eyes. Then the Fae shivered and gave a wicked smile, making Conall smile back. He kissed Ammatán's neck, shoulder, and down his arm. Ammatán caressed the nape of his neck with his other hand.

When he reached the fingers, he kissed each one with gentle care. With a pointed fingernail, Ammatán drew a line down Conall's chest, putting just enough pressure to leave a red line in his skin. Not enough to draw blood, but the mark didn't fade immediately.

Then he licked along the line, down from the hollow of Conall's neck to his belly button. A few black hairs circled this area, and Ammatán played with them a few times before shifting lower.

Conall held his breath, afraid someone, anyone, would burst in upon them, denounce them as unnatural, and kill them both.

The anxiety grew so strong, he gasped, making Ammatán glance up. "Did I hurt you, my dear?"

"No, no, you did nothing wrong. I just," Conall swallowed, trying to find the words to explain, "this is nothing I've done before. I'm not sure what to do."

With a puzzled frown, Ammatán placed his hand flat on Conall's chest. "You need do nothing if you don't wish to. You are under no obligation for anything. Would you like me to stop?"

"No! No, I don't want you to stop." Conall had to grin, despite his fears. Ammatán echoed his smile, made more feral by his pointed teeth, and he bent to kiss Conall's hip. He nipped with those sharp teeth, making Conall squirm, but he kept smiling to show Ammatán that he wanted more.

A loud caw broke into his thoughts, and the raven swooped into the roundhouse, flying at both their heads.

"Damn that bird to the bottom of the Morrigan's fen!" Ammatán glared at the bird. "This had better be important, Sawchaill."

After settling on his perch, Sawchaill cawed several times, bobbing his head. Ammatán glowered and shifted to the side of the cot, much to Conall's consternation. His excitement drained as Ammatán stood and dressed.

The Fae stopped to caress Conall's jawline. "I am so sorry, my dear. I am being summoned. We must continue another time. Forgive me?"

With a startled nod, Conall blinked back disappointed tears, unwilling to show how upset the news made him. Ammatán exited, with Sawchaill following, leaving Conall to pull his *léine* over his head and calm his arousal.

Conall had never imagined such need for another being before. His dreams, as exciting as they'd been, never came close to this fire, this burning frenzy. His heart, mind, and body craved Ammatán's gaze and touch. How had he become so smitten? He'd only met the Fae a few days ago.

Had it only been a few days? He tried to count the number of times he'd slept. Two? Three? More? Time had no measurement in Fae, no convenient way of counting the hours. Conall considered the possibility they'd been in Fae for over a moon, and daren't discount the notion.

However long they'd been here, Ammatán had filled his days, except his time in the Queen's garden. Even with Ammatán out of his sight, dealing with whatever Sawchaill fetched him for, Conall couldn't stop thinking about the curve of Ammatán's smile, the sting of his nails down the skin of his chest, and the tingling of desire both created.

Once again, his ardor rose, and he glanced down in frustration. He'd been about to go outside to discover what kept Ammatán, or if Lainn was close by, but now he'd have to wait.

Sawchaill's call cut through his thoughts, and the bird didn't sound pleased. Concerned, Conall sent a firm reminder to his manhood it needed to calm down and waddled outside.

As he reached the doorway of the roundhouse, he spied Lainn skulking behind a tree along the edge of the glade. Her gaze flicked to him, and she gestured urgently for him to join her. Quietly, he made his way to his sister.

Ammatán stood toe to toe with another creature, even taller than him, with pale green skin and a tangle of hair so wild it looked like winter bracken. If he squinted, he just made out tiny, bright pink flowers in among the snarled strands.

His stance radiated threat and anger. Ammatán's reflected hostility, though the difference in height made Conall nervous. He didn't know Ammatán's status in Faerie, nor his power, physical or magical. This adversary might kill his would-be lover on the spot, and Conall had no way of stopping it.

Except that he did. Ashamed that he hadn't thought of the brooch's power first, Conall quested for the familiar thread of magic, just in case it might help Ammatán.

Conall sent his will down through his feet and into the earth, searching for the anchor the brooch provided, to pull that power in through his body. But as he pushed his will into the Faerie dirt below him, he grew so dizzy he had to grasp a tree trunk to keep from collapsing. The land itself swirled with a maelstrom of power, twisting and eddying through his mind in confusion and pain.

He dug his fingers into the smooth bark of the tree, trying to focus his concentration. Down, through this bewildering storm of enchantment, he finally found an echo of familiar magic. Twice, he reached for the brooch with his mind and twice he failed. The third time, he pushed with the center of his soul and latched onto the metal artifact. He cried out in triumph, making Lainn glare at him. "Quiet, fool! They'll hear you!"

Too late, both Ammatán and his adversary swiveled their heads to look at the humans. Conall wanted to shrink into a tiny non-butterfly, away from the censure of both Fae. They'd obviously seen him, so he stepped out from behind the tree. If he had the chance to direct their attention away and keep Lainn safe, he must.

With unsteady steps and false bravado, he stumbled forward. He maintained a death grip on the tenuous thread of magic to his brooch, ready to shove the other Fae into the sky at the first attempt of physical threat to Ammatán, Lainn, or himself.

The tangle-haired creature furrowed his brow and asked Ammatán a question, but the other Fae shook his head. Despite his concentration, Conall couldn't hear the words, only a raspy voice.

Conall finally reached them and stood next to Ammatán. The Fae said nothing but raised his eyebrows. Conall gave him the barest hint of a smile.

"What is this creature, Ammatán? Does the Queen know you've found a pet?"

"She knows, Bodach. He is doing work for her."

The other creature narrowed his eyes. "Hmm. Indeed. So, you found a pet with talent, eh?" He sniffed a few times, leaning toward Conall. "He stinks of human magic. How can you stand that stench?"

Startled, Ammatán smelled Conall, his eyes growing slightly wider. "I smell nothing unusual, Bodach. You must have grown ill with some strange human fever. That's what you get for haunting them so often. Speaking of such, don't you have some child to terrorize?"

The impossibly wide, savage grin that spread across Bodach's face chilled Conall's spine. His teeth looked more wicked than Ammatán's, like an enormous, ugly pike. Conall fought every muscle in his body not to turn and bolt in the other direction.

He gritted his teeth to clamp down on a scream and wished he was anywhere but here. His bronze knife would be incredibly comforting to hold just now.

"Why yes, I have several current favorites. One might even go completely mad tonight if my craft is strong." His grin morphed into a frightening frown. "You used to enjoy our jaunts, Ammatán. What's changed?"

Ammatán's gaze flicked to Conall and then dropped.

Bodach stared at Conall and back to Ammatán, his smile once again growing to alarming proportions. "Oho! I see how it is. You never could keep your heart straight, silly creature. One of these days, your penchant for a romp will land you in a world of trouble. If not with your lovers, then with your Queen."

The white-skinned Fae waved his hand in dismissal. "Neither of those matters are your concern, Bodach. Are you done here?"

With another amused glance at Conall, Bodach nodded. "I suppose I'll get no more answers from you on that matter. If you hear anything more, though, I expect a complete report, understand?"

"You'll get information when I'm ready to send it."

Bodach's pale green skin turned dark, and he bared his teeth. Rather than a smile, this was a palpable threat. Conall inched closer to Ammatán, tugging on the brooch's magic, but Ammatán hissed, "Get back, you fool!"

Reluctantly, Conall took a half-step back, allowing the two Fae to face each other with only a hand-span between their noses.

"I tolerate no insubordination, Ammatán. Not in my ranks."

"And bullying will not encourage my loyalty, Bodach."

Bodach lowered his woody eyebrows. "You have bullied many people in your time."

"Even the Fae can change, Bodach."

After one painful, silent moment when even the leaves didn't sway in the breeze, Bodach burst out laughing. His voice boomed across the countryside, shaking the branches, the thatch of the roundhouse, and forming tiny waves on the pond.

Conall's legs turned weak, and he almost fell down before he locked his knees.

"You are so lucky you're funny, Ammatán. Any other Fae I would have squashed like a beetle. Go, then, have your little fun. I have other places to search for my prey."

With a final, calculating glance at Conall, the green Fae faded away. When the last hint of tangled green had disappeared, Conall let out a long breath and gave in to his weakness.

He sat on the ground, crossed his legs, and cradled his head in his arms. Ammatán knelt and squeezed an arm around his shoulders. "You fool! Why did you come closer? Bodach could have snapped his fingers, and you'd be nothing but a pile of gray dust!"

Conall took several deep breaths, trying to regain his wits and calm his thoughts. "I wanted to distract him from Lainn. And I couldn't let you stand against him alone!"

Ammatán closed his eyes, shaking his head. "Conall, my dear, stupid human. Do you have any idea how little power you have compared to Bodach? Or even to me, for that matter? Here in Faerie, you are about as helpless as a mouse is in your own world. That's the word for the small, furry creatures living in the thatch, right?"

With a nervous giggle, Conall nodded. "Yes. They like cheese."

This earned him a sad smile from Ammatán. "Well, some Fae enjoy cheese, too. I know one who would kill for it. At any rate, under no circumstances are you ever to confront another Fae, do you hear me? I won't have you obliterated for misplaced bluster."

He pulled Conall to his feet, and Lainn emerged from her hiding place. "This encounter has rattled us both, and I'm sure all three of us would appreciate some food and rest. What say you?"

With shaky legs, Conall allowed the Fae to lead him back into the roundhouse. Lainn followed, with Sawchaill on her shoulder. Ammatán then made them both eat, though Conall didn't taste the food. He didn't remember what he'd eaten.

Soon, Ammatán tucked him into the cot and commanded him to sleep. "Tomorrow will be a new day, as you humans say."

Conall mumbled, "There are no days here. No nights. It's… strange."

Ammatán brushed a stray hair from his eyes. "All things are strange in this world and the next."

He kissed Conall's forehead. Calm spread across his body, and soon he slept.

A raven's caw dragged Conall from an intense dream of Ammatán's hands all over his body. He glared at the blasted bird for interrupting the sweet intensity of his fantasy, but then glanced around, in case Ammatán himself might be nearby to finish the dream.

Alas, no one else seemed inside but the raven. "Did you wake me for a reason, Sawchaill? Or just to be mean?"

The cursed creature chirped with all innocence, fluffed his wings, and preened underneath, ignoring Conall.

He took this to indicate no immediate urgency and stretched his aching muscles. Yesterday's tensions still held tight to his body, both the terrifying and pleasurable situations. Would he have time with Ammatán before he must return to the Queen's work?

The Fae in question popped his head in. "Oh! Good, you're awake. I've food before you must leave. We've worked out a more convenient mode of transportation."

Once Conall had dressed and eaten, Lainn and Ammatán led him behind the roundhouse. Lainn's grin threatened to crack her face in two. "My suggestion! Ammatán helped with the magic, of course, but this should make your journey much easier."

She opened her arms wide in a dramatic flourish, revealing a raft. Five tree trunks lashed together with twine.

Conall, still yawning, crossed his arms. "This? How is this going to help?"

Lainn lifted her eyebrows. "Ammatán? Would you be so kind?"

Ammatán winked at her and lifted one hand, palm up. As he did, the raft rose into the air.

Conall looked sideways at the Fae. "Is that allowed?"

"The Queen won't mind, and she's the only opinion that matters. If she mentions something, it's to make certain you arrive at your task rested and ready to work."

Conall might have moved the raft himself, with the magic from the brooch, but he'd arrive each day tired and nauseous from the effort. Also, using such magic in front of the Queen made it dangerous.

He didn't know what she'd do if she discovered the brooch, but he didn't want to find out. Conall hadn't even told his sister or Ammatán of the magic. Perhaps he'd never need to.

"Besides," Lainn poked the dirt with her toe, looking bashful, "I needed to do something, too. I can't spend *all* day watching butterflies."

"They are… I don't know the human name for them. Festival wings?"

"Festiwings! I can call them festiwings." Lainn skipped around as several of them landed on her head and hands.

Conall chuckled, hefted his pack of tools, and climbed onto the raft. "Maybe you should try to learn their song."

She stopped and cocked her head. "I think that is a delightful idea."

Thrilled that he had his sweet sister back, Conall turned to the Fae. "Will I need to bring my tools here each day, or can I leave them in the Queen's glade?"

"Do you think any creature would disturb anything in the Queen's own retreat?"

"Fair enough. Will this take me home when it's time?"

Ammatán blinked over glistening black eyes. "Do you consider this your home, Conall?"

His throat caught. Had he upset Ammatán with his temerity? "Only if you want me to. You're the host, and I'm merely your guest."

Ammatán pulled him in for a warm, fierce hug. "It's your home for as long as you wish."

After he climbed on, the raft rose to half his height and drifted away from the roundhouse. Conall wished he might have stayed and wiped the glistening tears from Ammatán's face, but he mustn't keep the Queen waiting.

With increasing speed, the raft swept along the path, zipping around the occasional bend around trees, bushes, and through the last glade. It drifted gently next to the workspace he'd been in the day before.

Had it only been a day? It had felt like a week since he'd been here last, but still, his sense of time had become useless.

Tales of Faerie always had issues with time. Some travelers came back twenty seasons when they'd only been gone a few nights. In some cases, the opposite held true. Other tales told of hundreds of seasons missing. No reliable correspondence between the mortal world and Faerie existed, or none Conall understood.

All the supplies he'd requested the day before were arrayed before him, stacked in precise ranks. He let out a deep sigh and studied his sketched plans.

His first task would be to create the base blocks, those with the least amount of filigreed decoration. That way, he could practice his carving skills on the larger curves and twists, gaining skill as he worked. Maybe Ammatán had suggestions for the more delicate artwork as he got further along.

Conall wanted to move some of the blocks but grew wary of using his magic. Yesterday had proved the Queen kept surveillance upon him. Would such a show of power be foolish? Or unnecessarily delaying his work?

He tested a small use of power. He tensed himself for contact with the Faerie earth, keeping in mind the madness that almost sucked his soul yesterday.

This time, the pull didn't feel as disturbing, but he had farther to travel to find the brooch's magic. It may be the brooch lay too far away to… no, there! He grasped it with a feather's touch, drawing it to his body.

Once he held that whisper of power, he shifted a chisel to one side while looking the other way. Then he waited.

The small use of magic resulted in no reaction. That might not mean much, though. The Queen's minion may not watch every minute but might notice later if someone had used magic. Conall worked on one block while he waited for any backlash from his magic use.

Conall finished rough-carving the first block and started on the second before he tried another sliver of magic. He moved three tools on the bench, the scrape drowned by his chisel on the marble.

By incremental tests, he worked his way to larger and larger uses of magic, finally shifting his fourth block into place with half power, half muscle. Once he'd carved that block, he leaned back on his heels and wiped the stone dust from his face. Even in Faerie, he sweated and stank after so much work. He longed to take a cool dip in the pond at Ammatán's home.

At the thought of Ammatán, Conall's hand stopped just before he hammered the chisel. He recalled how the Fae's snow-white skin looked against his own freckled chest and let out a sigh of longing. His mouth stretched into a sensual smile, yearning to run his fingers through the Fae's hair rather than work on the Queen's creation.

Perhaps, if he completed this project to her satisfaction, he'd be permitted to spend eternity with the Fae.

With renewed motivation, Conall bent to his task. Soon, he was moving blocks around as needed with no heed to the consequences of his magic use.

With the eighth block, he'd finished the base. As per his design, these eight blocks would rise into delicate arches, merging into four and then one in the center. Each arch started simply at the base and then increased in delicate detail until the top formed a translucent, woven mat of marble, accentuated with vines and summer flowers.

Eight blocks had been a great day's work, and he felt every inch of it in his muscles. He lifted his arms high, stretching his back until it cracked. Conall stretched his neck and then twisted his torso to relieve the bunched muscles. Out of the corner of his eye, he noticed the raft had drifted back up into the air.

He spoke to the air, presuming his guardian listened. "Does this mean it's time to go to Ammatán's roundhouse?"

The rafted bobbed a few times and then moved right next to him. It nudged him several times until he laughed. "Right! Right. Time to go."

Conall arranged his tools neatly on the workbench and cast a glance over the space, satisfied that all was in order. Then he climbed onto the raft.

He'd barely settled before it sped off, almost dislodging him. He gripped the edge as it wended through the path, dodging trees and bushes once again, faster than the first time.

Soon, the raft came to an abrupt stop at Ammatán's roundhouse, almost making Conall flip forward when it halted. With difficulty, he pried his fingers from the wood on the edge and staggered off. When Ammatán emerged from his home, he watched for a moment and then laughed.

"It's not funny! That thing tried to kill me!"

His mouth twitching from a suppressed grin, Ammatán put a hand on Conall's shoulder to steady him and lead him inside. "I shall gentle the magic to ensure a reasonable speed, my dear. Will that make up for my laughter?"

"Barely." Conall sat gratefully on the bench once inside, taking a long drink from the waterskin. "Also, can I bring this tomorrow? My throat's parched with stone dust. Some fruit or bread would be helpful since I'll be there so long each day."

Ammatán raised his eyebrows and handed him a yellow fruit. "Anything else you should require, my lord?"

Conall grinned. "If I think of anything, I'll let you know." He glanced around. "Where's Lainn?"

"She went off after what she calls festiwings. I think she's trying to learn their song."

Conall smiled, remembering the bees in the oak grove. At least Lainn had found something to learn. "Are you hungry? I'm starved. Shall I make soup?"

"That would be lovely." The Fae turned to his raven, resting on his perch. "Sawchaill, do fetch Lainn."

The raven cawed and shook his head.

Ammatán rolled his eyes. "Very well. If you would please invite the young human to return, I would be most grateful."

The bird cocked his head and then flew away as Ammatán smiled. "That bird gets more unruly every day, but I'd be lost without him."

"How long has he been your friend?"

The grin deepened, showing his teeth. "Since I was young. They give every noble child a chance to impress a raven. Long ago, each raven had been fully sentient, able to talk and teach the child about magic and etiquette within the Fae court. However, their abilities have declined as Fae faded from the human world."

"Their abilities? What about their intellect?"

Ammatán shrugged. "Who can tell? Without the ability to speak with mouth or mind, we can only guess how much they understand. They speak their own language, but neither Fae nor humans understand it well."

Conall considered Ammatán's pantry and decided fish would be a welcome respite. He'd noticed several dried pike and selected one. He grabbed several turnips, an onion, and some herbs for soup. "Why would the Fae fading from my world make the ravens forget how to speak?"

With a shrug, Ammatán took a drink from the meadskin. "No one ever discovered why. Our greatest scholars studied it, crafting complex spells to discern the cause, as we love our ravens. We even stooped to asking human druids for their opinions, as much good as that did." Ammatán shuddered.

Conall filled the bronze pot with water and set it on the hearth. "Did it happen all at once? Like a magic curse?"

Ammatán shook his head with a wistful glance at Sawchaill's empty perch. "No, the ability to speak just faded away. Each generation grew less vocal, less able to form words."

The raven swooped through the door and landed on his perch just as Lainn said, from the doorway, "What if they could write?"

Both Ammatán and Conall stared at her. The Fae asked, "What is *write?*"

"Writing is marks made to represent words. The monks do it."

Conall chopped parsley and thyme and threw her a scowl. "How can that help? He has no fingers to hold a quill. Besides, I don't know how to write. Do you?"

She shrugged, grabbing half of his remaining nuts. "No, but many humans do. Ammatán might find someone who knows, have him teach both the Fae and the ravens, and then they could communicate more fully. A raven could scratch the words on a slate with their talons."

Ammatán paced around the central hearth, his hands fluttering in agitation. "I don't understand how marks can represent words. You cannot draw sound."

Conall wiped away bits of herb and took one of Ammatán's hands in his own to calm him. "No, she's right. My father knew how to write. He'd known a monk who'd taught him some words."

Ammatán's face flashed a series of emotions, from incredulity to anger to stubbornness. "It can't be that simple. The greatest powers of Fae couldn't discover a solution. How could one human child have such power?"

Lainn shook her head, taking Ammatán's other hand. "I didn't invent writing. I simply suggested it. This isn't power, its knowledge."

He ripped both his hands from their grips and stalked outside, muttering to himself. They glanced at Sawchaill, but the raven slept, his beak tucked under one wing. Lainn walked to the bird and laid a gentle hand on his back, a pensive look in her eyes. "What if someone taught him to write, Conall?"

"He's smart enough to argue with us. But neither of us can write."

"I asked Gemmán once about writing, and he almost bit my head off. He said no self-respecting druid would commit the sacred mysteries to such a medium, exposing the risk of the uninitiated discovering them."

Conall shrugged as he chopped turnips. "The point is moot, then. We can't teach the raven what we don't know ourselves."

Lainn didn't answer at first, caressing the soft black feathers. She glanced up after a few moments. "We might train him to communicate better. Teach him set responses that meant set words. Just because we don't know what drawings mean what sounds to the monks, doesn't mean we can't make up our own."

He paced as Ammatán had just a few minutes before. "How would that work, Lainn? You mentioned you didn't invent writing. Isn't that exactly what you're proposing now?"

"I don't know, Conall! I don't know. I just think we should try."

Chapter Thirteen

When Ammatán returned, he refused to speak. No amount of coaxing from Lainn would get him to talk. When Conall sat beside him and tried to hold his hand, he pulled away. Conall handed him a bowl of soup, but the Fae ate with the minimum of movement.

After a long time of awkward silence, Lainn took Sawchaill outside, leaving Ammatán and Conall alone. This time, when he fumbled for the Fae's hand, Ammatán did not pull away. Instead, he squeezed Conall's hand without looking up.

Using his free hand, Conall tried to move Ammatán's face up to gaze into his eyes. When the Fae relented, his eyes glistened with suppressed emotion, and his jaw twitched as he clenched his teeth.

"Ammatán, what did I say to upset you? Whatever I said, I apologize."

The Fae took a deep breath and swallowed several times. "You didn't upset me, Conall."

"Then I apologize on my sister's behalf. She meant no harm."

"Lainn didn't upset me, either. But her ideas did."

"But she only suggested teaching the ravens to write. I don't understand what's so upsetting about her idea."

With another sigh, Ammatán turned on the bench. Conall also turned so they faced each other, and the Fae took both of his hands in his.

"I must explain to you about the Fae, Conall. We are slow to change. What Lainn proposed is an enormous shift in a long-standing belief, a paradigm the Fae accept as a final truth. Such things do not change so easily."

Conall cocked his head. "Do you think her idea is dangerous?"

The Fae shook his head and cast down his gaze. "I'm not certain. I must think about the implications. Her mind is as quick as lightning. This makes sense for humans, as their lives are so ephemeral, but Fae are slower, more deliberate in their considerations and actions. As much as I hate to admit Fae have a failing, it is their entrenchment in their ancient ways."

"Haven't those ancient ways served you well in the past?"

He gave a shrug. "In some ways, yes. In some ways, no."

Ammatán stared at the fire crackling in the hearth. When he turned back to look into Conall's eyes, his flat black eyes glittered. "This is not something we can settle now. You're finished with your work for the day, and the only rest I've offered you is conflict and philosophy. Can we not spend the rest of your free time in a more pleasant activity?"

Conall gave him a shy smile and blushed glancing down to their clasped hands. Ammatán let go and cupped both his hands under Conall's jaw, drawing him in for an unutterably sweet, slow kiss.

His lips tingled with the magic of the moment, and Conall wanted that kiss to last for days. The Fae's tongue explored his mouth with mounting frenzy, and he responded in kind. Soon they clutched each other in frenetic need.

Ammatán stood, drawing Conall to his feet. Conall's entire body vibrated with desire and anticipation. The Fae led the human to his sleeping alcove. While they stood next to the cot, the Fae ran his hands up under Conall's *léine*, drawing it over his head with a fluid, graceful movement.

By the time Conall had worked free of the garment, Ammatán also stood naked, his white skin glowing in the dim light.

Goosebumps formed all over Conall's skin, despite the warm comfort of the roundhouse, as Ammatán drew a fingertip down the center of his chest, circled first one nipple, and then the other. He bent to kiss the left nipple and Conall caught his breath.

Ammatán nuzzled Conall's neck, pushing until he lay on the cot, lying next to him and propped up on one elbow. The Fae gazed into Conall's eyes with a half-smile on his lips. "What would you like me to do, my dear? What is your desire?"

Conall hadn't stuttered since he'd arrive in Fae, but now his tongue tied with embarrassment and trepidation. "I... I don't know. I've never done this."

Ammatán raised his brows. "Not even with a human woman? Don't men couple any longer in your world?"

Conall blushed harder, certain his own inexperience would be repulsive to the Fae. "They do, but I haven't. There *was* a girl, but I didn't want her. She wanted me, but I wouldn't—"

"Shh, it matters not. I shall teach you what I've learned, and we can find out new things together."

When Conall woke, Ammatán still lie beside him, his arm curled around Conall's waist. Tenderly, he caressed the Fae's arm, the skin hairless and velvet soft. Even in his sleep, the Fae's mouth curled in an endearing half-smile.

Every muscle in his body ached, and Conall felt certain he'd regret the sometimes acrobatic and body-twisting antics of their lovemaking as he worked today. Still, he wouldn't have changed a thing.

Now, he'd become Ammatán's, and Ammatán had become his. He now glimpsed the love that his mother and father had shared and realized without a doubt she never shared such a bond with Sétna.

Thoughts of his father brought him back to Adhna's words and the notion that perhaps his father still lived somewhere. Would his mother leave Sétna if Conall brought Fíngin back to her? Would they become the family they'd once been? Could he return that incredible bond to his parents?

Ammatán stretched with a sensual groan and a crack of his back. Conall caressed his side, moving his hand around to the Fae's buttocks. Ammatán, his eyes still closed, brought his arms down around Conall's neck, pulling him in for a slow kiss. "Have you rested well, lover?"

Ammatán's arms continued down Conall's back, tickling him until he squirmed. "I'm not sure we should call it rest, but I slept, yes. Stop that! It tickles."

Ammatán opened his eyes. "Are you certain you wish me to stop? You told me not to last night." His hands had now moved to Conall's groin area, waking another part of him.

Now Conall closed his own eyes and moaned, inviting Ammatán to do whatever he wanted.

When they were both panting and covered with sweat, Ammatán sat back. "For a human, you have a great deal of stamina. But you must need to eat and drink before you work, so I shall give you a respite."

As Conall prepared for the day, groaning now and then as he bent to get dressed, he remembered his idea. "Ammatán? Did you say you knew my father?"

Ammatán straightened the cot, as their night had left it in considerable disarray. "I said I know of him, yes."

"Do you think he might be alive still?"

Ammatán froze. Conall wished he'd asked the question when he could see the Fae's face. "I'm not certain."

"But don't you see what this means? If he's still alive, I might find him! I might bring him back to mother."

The Fae turned slowly, an inscrutable expression on his face. His black eyes appeared bottomless. "Your mother?"

"Yes, Ligach. She married this other man, Sétna, but she can't love him. If I found Father and got them back together…"

Conall's voice faded as he realized Ammatán's expression had darkened. The scowl frightened Conall, a fear that sank to his stomach and bowels.

In a flat tone, the Fae said, "Ligach isn't… you shouldn't try to find Fíngin and you shouldn't bring him back to Ligach."

He shouldn't try to find Fíngin. Which means the Fae believed him to be alive somewhere. Otherwise, he'd say Conall *couldn't* find Fíngin. Hope sprung within his heart.

The Fae gripped his shoulders, his nails digging into his skin. "Promise me, Conall. Promise me you'll not leave to search for him." Ammatán's flat voice took on a hint of anger.

Conall nodded slowly. "I have a duty to your Queen, and I must finish that before I can entertain any further adventures."

"That wasn't a promise." More anger flickered at the edges, and his voice took on a multi-tonal quality, similar to that of the Faerie Queen.

The cold spot in Conall's bowels took over his entire body. "I promise! I promise not to search for my father. Not yet." The air shimmered slightly, a wave of distortion across his view.

Ammatán's expression lightened, a cheerful smile blossoming across his face. He brought Conall a bag with nuts and a loaf of bread "Thank you, lover. Now, this should bolster you through the day. Here's a water skin. Before you leave, though, I must speak to you."

After taking both items, Conall squinted at him. "Isn't that what you're doing right now?"

The Fae took a deep breath and stared at his toes. "I must leave."

"Leave? Leave where? For how long?"

"Leave here, but I'm not sure for how long. I have to find someone, but I'll be back when I find them."

He lifted his gaze, a plea for understanding in his eyes. "You and Lainn are free to stay here while I'm gone. I must entrust Sawchaill into your care. Can you watch him for me?"

Conall's skin grew cold, and his heart raced with fear of the unknown. Feelings of betrayal and injustice warred within Conall. "But we just… you can't leave me so soon! You made me promise not to leave, but you're leaving? That's not fair!"

"Nevertheless, I must. I would never leave you so soon if I had a choice. You understand this, Conall, don't you? After last night, when I pledged my heart to yours? We've shared a piece of our soul now. We are forever connected in a way I can never explain, but we can both understand."

Ammatán took Conall's hand in both of his own, kissing him on his palm. "I wanted one night with you, one sweet night we'd both hold in our memories before I left on this mission."

Conall wanted to storm off and sulk until Ammatán changed his mind, but if the Faerie Queen had commanded Ammatán somewhere, he must not disobey her, no matter what emotional pouting his lover did. He nodded, not trusting himself to speak.

"Then you must go, Conall. Go. Work on the Queen's project. Take Sawchaill with you today. Please her with your wonderful vision and skill. And I shall return before you realize it."

Ammatán drew him into a fierce embrace. Conall's tears made him tremble. Why did he feel so deeply, so intensely, after just a few encounters? They'd spent one night of love, just one, and his heart was being ripped from his chest and torn ragged.

When his sobs eased, Ammatán loosened his hug and held him at arm's length. Conall whispered, "Ammatán, Can I… can I keep a lock of your hair?"

The Fae's eyes grew wide, his expression darkening once again. "You don't understand what you ask, Conall."

Too late, Conall remembered tales where locks of hair, bits of fingernail, any piece of a body might be used for heinous spells, to bend another's will to your own.

He shook his hands, hoping Ammatán would forgive his mistake. "Nothing sinister, I swear! Not for an enchantment or a spell. I wouldn't know how to do one anyhow. I just want to keep something of yours. Something to sleep with at night."

His eyes shifting toward the road which led to the Faerie palace, Ammatán jerked the knife from his belt sheath. His rapid action made Conall take a half-step back, certain he'd offended the Fae beyond repair. However, the Fae simply held out a lock of his hair and sliced it with the knife, kneeling as he offered the gift to Conall. "Take my love and my trust with this gift, my mortal beloved."

Tearful again, Conall accepted it, curling trembling fingers around the precious lock, midnight silk against his skin. "I will keep it secret and safe, Ammatán."

Ammatán, still kneeling, bowed his head. "I must go now."

He faded into nothing.

Chapter Fourteen

With a heavy heart, Conall climbed the floating raft with Sawchaill on his shoulder, and zipped through the windy path to his work area for the Queen.

He went through the motions, following his own plans and diagrams with little thought for the artistry or the future. He needed to keep going forward until Ammatán returned.

Sawchaill perched on one of the dressed base stones when he began that day. He fluffed his wings now and then but stayed silent. Conall offered some of his bread to the raven, but Sawchaill disdained his offering and flew off.

When he returned, a small, unidentifiable creature, some type of blue rodent, wriggled in his beak. The bird eviscerated the creature, leaving bloody stains upon the base stone.

Watching the ferocity of the raven's meal gave Conall a measure of satisfaction. Perhaps tearing something apart would make him feel better, too. After casting around for a suitable target, he spied a fallen branch with purple leaves still clinging to it.

He stalked to the branch, picked it up, and shredded each leaf with violence and growing frustration. They didn't tear like normal leaves but stretched and snapped. He needed to yank each piece apart, or they went back to their original shape. Finally, he stood in a pile of purple scraps. The frenzy had marginally calmed his temper.

Conall returned to his block and resumed work. He was now constructing the second tier of stones, more detailed than the base, with the first hints of a vine crawling through the marble veins. He must leave twining stripes in relief, rising from the bottom and ending at the top in two or three branches. This required careful drawing and carving, something his magic wouldn't help with.

Just as he'd hammered the chisel on an essential part of the third branch, Sawchaill cawed, startling him out of a day's growth. He'd almost ruined the branch, and he blurted out, "Blood and bones! Sawchaill, don't *do* that!"

The bird squawked back, fluttered his wings, and bobbed his head. Conall rose, wiping the dust from his hands. "In fact, go on back to Lainn. You're only distracting me here. Go on, shoo!"

He flapped his hands at the bird until he flew away, chattering back at him as he left. Closing his eyes and letting out a deep breath, Conall calmed himself once again and sat to continue his carving.

When he returned to the roundhouse, his feet dragged, and his head drooped. He'd gotten little rest the night before, though for excellent reason, and the day had drained all his energy.

Conall shuffled into the house and found Lainn and Sawchaill staring at the floor. She'd made several scratches into the dirt floor, and they both glanced up as he darkened the doorway.

Lainn jumped up, giving him a hug. "You're back! Excellent. Soup is on the hearth. I'm teaching Sawchaill symbols. Want to learn when you're done eating?"

He shook his head, not even wanting to expend energy answering. Conall scooped some lukewarm venison soup into a bowl, ate ten bites, and collapsed into his cot.

Sawchaill's raucous call in Conall's his ear made him leap out of bed, scramble to his feet, and then glare at the black bird. "What in the name of all the gods did you do that for?"

Lainn's giggle behind him made him whirl around, which caused her to burst out in mischievous laughter. As he glared at her, she laughed harder, holding her side and bending over. "Your face! You should see. . . your face!"

He stomped to the night basket to relieve himself and used the wash basin to clear the sleep from his face. When he'd finished, he rounded on his sister. "Can't you even let me sleep in peace? I swear, I wish I'd left you with the druids."

She waved her hand at him. "Oh, don't be mad, Conall. I was just having a little fun. Besides, I needed to prove Sawchaill understood what I drew."

"What you drew?"

"Yes, silly. Remember? I'm teaching him how to communicate with drawings. He drew symbols to tell me he'd grown bored. I drew symbols asking him to startle you awake."

Conall scowled, rubbing his gritty eyes. "Did you at least let me sleep long enough for a full night's rest? I still have work to do and need sleep."

She nodded, her giggles subsiding. "Stop being so surly. You'll be fine. Sawchaill has a better sense of time than Ammatán does and can tell when a day has passed. He's lived in the world a bit more. Would you like to eat?"

Still sullen at the jest, Conall had to admit admiration for her ingenuity and Sawchaill's willingness to learn. Maybe it would keep her occupied while he worked, and she'd have less idle time for dreaming up ways to drive him to madness.

In the back of his mind, he drew great relief from the realization she was comfortable here, enough to play jokes and laugh. This salved his soul, as it still stung from Ammatán's sudden departure. If he couldn't find joy, at least his sister might.

Back at the work area, he assessed his progress. He'd work on two more stones of the second level today and would still have three more to go until the third level.

With eight levels, and each one being more complex and delicate, he daren't even calculate how much time the full project would take, even if he had a method of measuring time other than when he woke and slept.

Did his body remember the rhythm of the human world? Did he get sleepy and wakeful with the cycle of day and night he'd lived with all his life? Or would this human memory fade into a mix of endless nights and short naps? He never realized how much his body relied on the basic rhythm he now missed.

"How dare you sleep, mortal!"

For the second time that day, Conall clambered awake, terrified of the sound of the Queen's echoing voice, ricocheting off the marble blocks and assaulting his ears from all directions. "My Queen! I am so sorry. I only dozed off for a moment, I swear!"

"Why have you come to this task without sufficient rest? I have left time for your recovery each rest period."

"I'm so sorry! My sister woke me earlier—"

"Your sister is the creature at fault?"

Belatedly realizing his mistake, he shook his head so hard his brain hurt. "No! It wasn't her fault! I swear!"

A loud crack sounded behind him, and he turned to see Lainn, crouched and bewildered, holding a small stick. She must have been carving out a symbol for Sawchaill.

She rose and glanced around. "Conall? What's—"

He hissed at her, "Be quiet and stay still!" Turning back to the work area, he addressed the Queen's voice. "My Queen, this is no one's fault. I apologize for my slip and vow to be more careful in the future."

No answer came, and he held his entire body tense, waiting for the dreaded consequences. Lainn reached for his hand, and he squeezed it.

The light dimmed to almost twilight while a tiny bright light formed in the center of the work area. Larger and larger the light grew, shining so strong Conall had to squint against the pain. Within the center, a figure formed, voluptuous and sensual, while imperious and strong.

As the brightness dimmed, the twilight dissipated, returning things to normal, except for the Faerie Queen before them.

She stood taller than any human Conall had ever known. Long green locks danced in a windless breeze, ranging in color from the freshest spring green to the deepest moss in the shade. They encircled her head and caressed her body as if alive, and perhaps they were.

Her perfect skin faded from dusky red to pale rose, changing even as he watched. The Queen's garment shifted, a cloud of rainbow webbing which accentuated her figure, fondling it with sensual movements.

Despite his own fondness for the male form, Conall grew uncomfortable watching the fabric shift and stroke around her curves.

Her face might have been carved from the marble Conall had worked with, sharp angles and cold eyes regarding them both with distaste. Her deep, sanguine lips parted, and before she spoke, Conall felt her voice deep within the marrow of his bones. "You have displeased me."

These four words almost made Conall's knees fail in the wake of his gibbering fear. His heart raced and he could barely breathe. They shot through his soul like an enchanted arrow, intent upon destroying him.

He prayed harder than he'd ever prayed before that Ammatán would come protect them. Despite his trembling knees, he stepped in front of Lainn to shield her from the Queen's mighty wrath.

The Queen stared at him for what seemed like long hours. Her red eyes bore into his mind and ripped open the careful layers of soul he'd grown during his lifetime. One by one, she shredded his defenses, his humanity, and his compassion.

When she exposed the central kernel of his being, the edges of her lips curved into a wicked parody of a smile. Those tempting, terrifying lips parted, and she laughed.

Her laugh boomed across the work area in harmonic tones, shaking the ground and causing both Conall and Lainn to fall to their knees. Pain from both the fall and the laugh made Conall curl into a protective ball around his sister. "Now I know what you most hold dear, human flea. You displease me, but I shall not punish you. You will finish your work for the day now."

Conall felt certain he misheard the Faerie Queen. She wouldn't punish him after all?

"This will hurt you far more."

Another bright flash of light made them both squeeze their eyes shut, and when Conall opened his, the Queen had disappeared. The glade returned to normal. The birds chirped and the festiwings fluttered by.

Lainn sat next to him, staring at the spot the Queen had stood.

"She's gone, Lainn. It's all going to be fine. She's left us alone."

"You're wrong."

Conall got to his feet and put his hand out to help Lainn rise. "True. She may return or do something to us later. But for now, she's left us whole. For a moment, I thought us both doomed."

Lainn didn't take his hand and continued to stare ahead.

"Lainn? Come on, stand up. You're sitting in the spot I need to be in to finish this block."

She put her hand out near where his was. Puzzled, he grasped it and pulled her up. She staggered and turned to him, though her eyes stared at his forehead.

"Lainn? What's wrong? Are you hurt?"

She let out a short, sharp laugh. "I suppose you might say that. I can't see."

Conall's stomach dropped, and he realized the Queen had punished him with what he held most dear. His sister.

Conall had never seen his sister so dejected. Not when Sétna would take her into the stables in the evening, not when boys teased her for being too smart, not even when their father disappeared. This complete disinterest in everything that life offered rocked him to the core. Her joy in life had vanished with her eyesight.

He hated leaving her alone all day while he worked, but he had no choice. If he failed in his duty again, the Queen might take Lainn's life or gift her eternal pain. He couldn't risk that.

To keep Lainn safe, he learned to communicate better with Sawchaill. Using his own words and the symbols they'd crafted, he made certain the raven would watch over Lainn all day and come tell him if she needed help or tried to do something rash.

Each day, when he finished his work, he rushed home and tried to tempt Lainn into loving life. With Sawchaill's help, he found beautiful, unusual flowers, exotic fruits, brilliant festiwings, new birds to sing for her. None of these made a chip in her armor of despair.

Conall told her stories from the past, both funny and heroic. Sometimes he'd deliberately tell them wrong, to try to goad her into correcting him. He'd make up silly jokes, aching to hear her child-like laughter.

His sister only sat cross-legged in front of the roundhouse, staring across the pond with eyes that could not see.

After at least twenty sleeps like this, he'd made great progress on his work with the Queen's project, but none with Lainn.

His own tears came unbidden at random intervals. It broke his heart to see his sister, so vibrant and joyful, reduced to this husk.

When Ammatán returned, would he help? Could he restore sight removed with the Queen's magic? Should he beg the Queen to change her mind? Or would that simply make things worse?

What would they do if Lainn could never see again?

Before he felt into just as deep a hole as Lainn, he paced around the roundhouse, glancing outside to reassure himself Lainn remained safe. Sawchaill now brought Lainn treats without direction from Conall.

Piles of flowers, fruits, and shiny rocks were strewn around her in a circle, like a shrine to some foreign goddess. The raven must care about her happiness, and yet even working together, they were never able to rouse Lainn from her misery.

Every morning and every evening, Conall scanned the horizon in all directions, searching for Ammatán's return. He made certain Lainn rose, he washed her, dressed her, and made her eat.

His sister allowed him to feed her, to help her to the bathroom, but she initiated no actions of her own. She wouldn't speak. She wouldn't cry.

The last broke his heart more than all the others. He knew what a blessed relief tears could be to pain.

Each evening, he made her eat again, drew her along on a walk around the pond, told her stories, and sang her songs. He considered juggling to make her laugh, but she wouldn't even see his comic antics. Even when he sang silly or off-key, hoping to goad her into some sarcastic remark about his lack of talent, she stayed frozen.

Sometimes, he hugged his sister as tightly as he dared, wishing he might give his eyes to her, so she'd smile again. Lainn stayed stiff and unresponsive as if he hugged a straw figure built to scare the crows.

Maybe if he brought her back to the human world, she'd regain her sight? He didn't understand how that might work, but he'd ask Ammatán he returned.

One day, as Conall climbed upon the floating raft, he nodded to Sawchaill to watch over Lainn. The raven drew a symbol in the dirt, acknowledging that he'd watch over Lainn. Conall swallowed down sudden tears as the raft sped away down the path.

He only had one final stone to complete, the center keystone in the arches. Just a few more passes with the polishing cloth today, a couple final touches, and he'd be ready to shift the last two rows in place. It would take all his magical strength to balance the stones, as he had no scaffolding or forms to hold them until the keystone held them in place.

As he completed each task, he glanced back toward Ammatán's home, wishing he was there.

Several hours later, he sat back on his heels and examined his creation. The black marble shone, even in the diffuse light of Faerie. The polished surface glittered with inclusions of blue, silver, and gold, casting a magical sparkle on the entire glade.

Conall stood, wiped his hands, and closed his eyes. He spaced his feet apart and leaned against a tree trunk to brace himself for the effort. Today, he'd brought the brooch with him so he'd have more strength.

He pulled it from his pouch and unfolded the precious artifact, gripping it in his palm so tight that the sharp edges bit into his flesh. A small line of red formed on one finger, blood to seal the magic.

He quested with his will down from his mind, into his arms, and through his chilled fingers. When it reached the brooch, scarlet light burst forth from the red stones, bathing the glade in a sullen, sanguine glow.

He drew this power back through the bones of his spine and into his legs. Further, it twisted, into the earth, into the stones, into the very heart of the land.

Visualizing pillars of red energy, he lifted the first stone into place, balancing it to where it needed to wait. Keeping that stone in place, he lifted the second one.

With quavering strength, he held both of those in place as he lifted a third and glanced at the fourth. With a deep breath, he then lifted the fourth stone, the final except the keystone.

Each stone grew heavier than the previous ones combined as he pushed his will, draining his own strength. With nail-biting precision, it settled into place amongst its brethren.

One more stone to place. One more effort of will and magic, and he could finally rest.

Conall closed his eyes, prayed for luck and skill, and lifted the keystone.

At first, it wouldn't budge. This was the most elaborate of them all, with filigree decorations climbing up around the top and into a translucent, swirling point. The bottom had to fit exactly into the beautifully chaotic entwined shapes of the block below it. One mistake, and the entire construction would fall and shatter.

Bracing himself by placing a hand against the tree at his back, and the other still gripping the brooch, Conall tried again, careful to keep the four stones in place as the keystone crept up, up, up to the pinnacle of the marble arch.

When he judged the stone to be in the right place, he gently lowered it into its spot, careful and delicate with his magic.

The keystone clicked, and with gentle, feather touches, Conall removed the glowing red energy supports on each of the other stones.

One by one, red light faded, leaving his final creation. He held his breath for several moments before he dared to let it go.

When the arch held, Conall sank to the ground, sweat streaming down his forehead. He laughed and cried at his own success, wiping his face and trying to see through sweat-blinded eyes. "I did it. I did it! I did it!"

He rose on shaky legs and pranced around, flailing his arms like an idiot. All his worry about Lainn, the project, his own impending doom should he make a mistake, came rushing out in a surge of relief.

After far too long running around like a madman, he took a deep breath and surveyed the site. Though he cleaned after each day's work, his space was littered with chips, stone dust, and his tools. Five blocks lay to one side, extras in case he broke one. He'd needed none of the additional blocks. That in itself seemed worthy of celebration.

With giddy energy, Conall cleaned the stone dust away with a flick of magic. This project had helped him practice with the brooch's power, honing his control and strength. Despite his enormous effort with the stones, he had enough left to arrange his tools on the piece of leather to store them. He rolled them into a bundle, tying the leather strap.

Once the area looked clean and presentable, he took a deep breath and stood back from the center of the glade. He still needed to find someone to help with the living vines, but his portion of the creation was complete. "I am finished with the stones, my Queen."

The light dimmed again, but this time, he shut his eyes to guard against her brilliant entrance light. Even through his eyelids, the bright white glow of the Queen's arrival shone.

Today, her hair seemed darker than before, almost brown-black with glints of green. Her skin, rather than dusky red, seemed closer to pale human flesh. Her eyes still flashed red, and Conall braced himself for her critique.

She examined the construction in minute detail, running her long, elegant fingers along the relief carvings of flowers, birds, and vines. Her eyes traveled to the top, where eight branches combined into four arches, meeting at the central block. Her lips curved into another smile. Conall tried to shut away the instant terror her smile inspired.

"You have pleased me with your art, human. I did not think you would."

A wave of sweet relief swept through his body, almost as powerful as the sensation Ammatán had coaxed from him that one sweet night they shared. After the incredible physical and magical effort of the day, he was ready to collapse. Still, he had a duty to complete.

"If it please you, my Queen, might I ask a boon for completing this project?"

She spun around, the locks of her hair hissing at him like so many serpents from Greek tales. Startled, he stumbled back, the sheer panic returning five-fold. When she didn't smite him for his temerity, he stammered out his request. "M-might you grant my sister her vision again?"

The Queen's eyes bore into him. He had no defense against such an assault, so he stood as still as possible, hoping he'd survive a second attack. Layer by layer, she peeled away his soul again. His mind screamed in agony against the intrusion, urging him to flee with all speed away from the terror.

"You have performed admirably. I may consider the request."

She clapped her hands, a sound which thundered across the glade and shook the stones of the new archway. He shut his eyes, certain she'd destroy him on the spot instead. When doom didn't come, he cracked one eye open.

The glade had disappeared. She'd sent him back to Ammatán's roundhouse. Lainn sat in her normal spot, staring at the pond with sightless eyes.

Conall abandoned his glimmer of hope that the Queen had restored Lainn's sight and sat beside his sister in resigned silence.

More sleeps passed with no regard to light or dark and no purpose but misery and survival.

Each time he woke, Conall dressed and washed his sister, helped her relieve herself, made her eat, walked her around the pond, and tried to rouse her from eternal apathy. Sawchaill tried to wake her with his cries, to similar effect. Eventually, both stopped trying.

After a dozen sleeps, he lost his patience. Once he fed her the morning meal, he took her by the shoulders and shook her. "Wake up,

Lainn! Enough is enough. You've got to live again. Losing your sight is tragic, yes, but it isn't death. You're alive! You can sing, you can tell stories, you can dance, you can run. You are more full of life than anyone I've ever met! Come back, Lainn!"

Sawchaill squawked agreement, and landed on her shoulder, nuzzling her neck.

Neither attempt elicited a response from the silent girl.

Conall dropped to his knees, hugging Lainn around her middle and clutching her tight. "Please, Lainn! I can't do this without you. I can't survive without you by my side! You're all I have left. Please, please, come back to me!"

Still, no sound came from her lips, and her dead eyes stared at nothing.

"This is my fault, Lainn, and I don't know how to fix it. I need your mind, your talent in puzzling out the way to make things right. We're a team, and I need you! I need your bright smile and sweet voice. I need your joy and your optimism. I love you! Come back!"

Tears fell down Conall's cheeks as he held her, rocking back and forth, having no idea what to try next.

When he'd exhausted himself with sorrow and grief, he stumbled to his feet and washed salty tears from his face. He led his sister around the pond as he'd done so many times before, and knew he'd do so many times hence.

When Ammatán finally returned, many sleeps later, he found them both sitting cross-legged, gazing out at the pond. He scanned the still water to figure out what they stared at, but nothing moved. Not even a festiwing flew across their path.

The Fae crouched next to Conall, his hand upon his lover's shoulder. "Conall? What's happened? Lainn?"

Sawchaill cawed from the roundhouse and winged out. Ammatán held his hand up for the raven to land upon. Instead of landing on the proffered perch, however, Sawchaill winged to a halt and settled on Lainn's shoulder.

A dark cloud crossed Ammatán's worried face. A cruel laugh behind him made Conall turn with dull eyes to his friend.

Bodach stood behind Ammatán, holding his side from laughter. Ammatán turned to the other Fae, thunder in his eyes. He hissed, "Be quiet, fool! Can't you see something tragic has happened?"

With a gasp for breath, Bodach pointed a gnarled finger at Ammatán. "Ho! The only tragedy I see is your raven has changed masters!"

Steel crept into Ammatán's voice. "Begone, Bodach. We've completed our mission, and I require privacy."

Ammatán turned his back on the other Fae, whose chuckles faded away as he vanished. Once again, the white-skinned Fae placed his hand on Conall's shoulder. Conall's eyes felt raw and gritty. He must have been staring too long.

In the time since he'd completed the job for the Faerie Queen, he'd had no tasks, no project, and no purpose. Each day, he sat next to his sister as she watched nothing on the pond. Each day, he slipped farther and farther into a depressive slump, with no interest in anything but watching, eating and sleeping.

He dressed, fed, and washed his sister upon waking and before sleeping. Sawchaill sometimes communicated needs or desires, and they both tried to coax Lainn from her stupor, but neither had any success.

Eventually, they'd both stopped trying.

Now Conall's world shifted. No longer did he live in an endless cycle of ennui and tedium. His lover had returned, but it took some time for Conall's mind to realize that.

Ammatán's anger faded, and his expression turned to pity and concern. "You need care, my love. Come, let me help you up."

With gentle hands, the Fae lifted Conall to his feet. Together, they made Lainn stand. They led her to the roundhouse, to sit on the low bench near the table.

Waving his hand in front of Lainn's eyes with no reaction, Ammatán glanced at Conall for an explanation. "How long has she been like this? How did it happen?"

Conall hung his head, mortified. "It's all my fault."

Ammatán placed his hand on Conall's chin, forcing him to look up. "What's your fault? Conall, what happened? I can smell the Queen's magic upon her."

Conall batted away Ammatán's hand. "I fell asleep while working. The Queen came and dug into my memory, or my mind, or something. She found what could hurt me the most. Lainn."

Ammatán's jaw tightened, and he glanced at Conall's sister, with Sawchaill perched on her shoulder. He took a deep breath and let it out again. "This is something I might be able to heal. May I try?"

A glimmer of hope blossomed within Conall's heart, forcing him to smile, and the answering light in Ammatán's eyes made the very air around them brighten. "I may need help, but I have worked similar magic before. We must prepare. Will you assist me?"

Conall glanced at his sister. "Did you hear him, Lainn? We might be able restore your sight! Ammatán wants to try!"

She betrayed no reaction, but Sawchaill cawed and fluttered his wings, gazing mournfully at her eyes.

With a thoughtful expression, Ammatán tapped his chin. "I'll need supplies. There's a special plant that grows in the Westlands which just might help. It isn't certain, but it's a chance. Unfortunately, the only Fae who knows where it grows is Bodach."

"The Fae you returned with? Why is that unfortunate?"

"Because I'd need to ask him a favor, and he's cruel and demanding with his favors. Many evil stories of our kind in the human world stem from the games he plays for prurient pleasure."

Conall swallowed, knowing some of those stories, and the fate of those who dealt with the Fae. Most humans did not fare well in such encounters. Other than a simple death, a human might get a club foot, a hump on their back, utter madness, or even cursed luck onto seven generations. It all depended on the whim of the Fae.

After remembering Bodach's harsh mocking earlier, he didn't relish the idea of Ammatán dealing with the malicious creature. Still, if it would help Lainn's sight restoration, and Ammatán wanted to pay such a price, Conall would do whatever needed.

"I've missed you so much, Ammatán. I had no idea what I should do about Lainn."

With a sad smile, Ammatán held his lover's hand, caressing the top with feather-light touches. "We'll find a way. You don't mind if I help?"

"Of course not. She's my sister."

A flash of inscrutable emotion swept across Ammatán's face as he glanced to Sawchaill on Lainn's shoulder. "And you love her. As you should. She's a sweet child, and if she were my sister, I would do the same. What else can I do for my love, than help those you hold dear?"

Conall's voice choked with emotion, and he squeezed Ammatán's hand, brushing his own eyes with the other.

Ammatán bent to kiss the tears away, and Conall's spine shivered with desire and anticipation. "As much as I hunger to spend time together after my travels, I think our reunion should wait until we can heal Lainn. Will you forgive me for the delay?"

Conall's cheeks burned. "Of course."

The Fae rose, glancing around the roundhouse. Empty bowls and cups lay near the wash basin, and the sleeping alcoves were in similar disarray. Conall experienced a surge of shame for his own laziness and indolence. "I'll clean up while you're gone, I promise. I'm sorry to have taken such poor care of your home."

With a half-smile, Ammatán shook his head. "All I care is that you are alive and well. For you to be well, we must ensure your sister is well. I should return after a few sleeps, my dear."

When Conall glanced up again, his Fae love had vanished.

With a sigh and a groan at unused muscles, Conall pushed himself up from the table and, with the cautious creak of renewed hope, cleaned the roundhouse.

He washed the dishes, stacked them on the shelves, and shook out the blankets. He offered Sawchaill some chopped turnip as he prepared the evening meal, but the raven turned his nose up.

With a low chuckle, he instead gave the raven dried fish, which the bird accepted. Lainn still sat on the bench, her hands clasped in her lap, staring forward at nothing.

He slept poorly. When he woke, he was full of hope, but when he grew tired again with no sign of Ammatán, he fell into another fitful sleep. And again the next one. And again.

Conall didn't know how many human days the Fae had been gone, and he'd had dreams of his lover's return many times. Had he dreamt Ammatán's return that first time? How could he tell if this one was true?

"Sawchaill, did Ammatán return? Or did I dream it?"

The raven nodded, marking in the ground the symbol which meant *truth*. Conall's relief broke into a wide smile, and he gave Sawchaill more fish. "For a moment, I thought I'd gone mad, Sawchaill."

A deep, sardonic voice from the doorway said, "Don't eliminate that possibility just yet, human child."

Whirling to face the intruder, Conall was both relieved and nervous when he recognized Bodach. He inched toward his cot and surreptitiously palmed the ancient bronze knife. "Ammatán went to find you."

The dark Fae nodded, his mottled brown skin shifting in the light like the bark of a tree. "He found me. I gave him directions for the plants he seeks. However, I thought about his problem, and I don't believe I'd need such an ingredient to affect the change he needs."

Cold gripped Conall's heart, and he stepped closer to the door, positioning himself between Bodach and Lainn. Sawchaill cawed and perched on her shoulder, a menacing glint in his black eyes.

"I'd rather wait until Ammatán returns. He'll know best."

With languorous steps, the dark Fae sauntered around the edge of the roundhouse, but Conall matched his pace, still keeping himself between the Fae and Lainn. The hilt of the bronze blade grew warm in his palm.

"Oh, but he has little experience in transforming humans. Besides, he owes me a favor after this last mission. I have performed many such magics in my life, child. I can puzzle out what the Queen has done. Then, I can reverse the curse if you will just allow me."

Still, he circled, spiraling in, coming closer to the central table. Conall's blood chilled, his fingers tingling with the need to act. He drew upon his brooch's power, ready to wield it in defense of his sister if needed.

He had no idea if the power would be sufficient against this Fae, but he'd damn well do his best. Would the knife or the magic be more damaging? Would either do anything?

"Such a tame little bird you have there, human girl. May I pet him?"

Conall had never heard the raven hiss before, but the harsh sound warned Bodach he wouldn't tolerate the Fae's touch. A quick peck with his beak made Bodach withdraw his hand. "Foul creature! As if I desired such a moulty pest."

Conall tried to get between them again, but Bodach would not back away. Pulling on his power, Conall pushed against the Fae, but he didn't budge.

"Come now, all it takes is one touch of my fingers. I will not harm your dear sibling in the slightest. Would you not like her to see all the wonders of the world again? Would you make the decision that doomed her to the darkness for her entire life? If Ammatán cannot make this magic work, you will sentence her to darkness forever, you know."

With a nervous gulp, Conall glanced at Lainn. She stayed frozen. If only she'd give him a clue, an idea of what she wanted. He didn't want to make such a momentous decision for her. If Bodach had the power to heal her sight, how could he deny her the chance?

"Yes, consider your sister, human. Consider her well. I shall not make this offer again. This is your one and only chance to restore her vision. Choose wisely."

Conall gripped the bronze knife handle tightly and spoke through gritted teeth. "What is the price? There's always a price."

"Of course, there is. I ask for little from you. Others will pay my price."

Paid by others. How could he condemn another to pay the price for his sister's sight?

"Come now. I will not hurt you, nor your sister."

Never make a bargain with the Fae. Wise words he'd heard all his life. Every tale, every story, emphasized this basic truth.

And yet he'd come to Faerie with Ammatán, in a bargain that had saved their lives. He'd made a deal with the Faerie Queen and escaped alive. Maybe it just required being smart enough to avoid being tricked. Maybe he had the trick of it now.

A surge of confidence burgeoned in his heart, telling him he could come out of this unscathed. The tales never spoke of bargains done well. He must trust they existed, as he'd already seen the truth with Ammatán.

Bodach's whisper drilled through his mind. "Ammatán has left you, human child. Why would he ever come back to you, a mere human boy? He's found another lover, a better lover."

Conall screwed his eyes shut and covered his ears, trying to block the Fae's insidious words.

"I'm your sister's only chance, human child. Say yes to me."

Bodach's voice whispered into his ears, the tendrils reaching into his mind. Urging him, begging him, commanding him to say yes. Conall shook his head, wishing he might run away and escape the hissing words. If he ran, his sister would be helpless to Bodach's cruelties. Conall could never leave her.

"You are the reason she is blind, human. Shouldn't you be the reason she can see once again?"

The Fae's logic made horrible sense. With a desperate glance at the door and a prayer for Ammatán to arrive and save them both, Conall closed his eyes, gripped the knife so tight his fingers went numb, and gave a single, solemn nod.

"What's that, human child? Was that an agreement? I must have it in your own voice for the bargain to be binding, you know. Come, delicious human. Speak to me. Give me your assent."

With his eyes still closed, Conall said, "Yes, Bodach, I agree to your terms. Please restore my sister's sight."

The chuckle began slowly, increasing with volume as Bodach circled the table once again, to face Lainn. Conall opened his eyes as a green glow formed around Bodach's knobby brown fingers, like leaves sprouting from twisted branches. This glow entwined around Lainn's head, and Conall knew instantly he should have waited for Ammatán.

Power thrummed through the earth, a deep hum that rattled his bones. Flashes of pale green sparked within the deeper green glow, and Lainn gasped, clapping her hands over her eyes. She cried out, an anguished scream of raw terror.

Conall rushed to his sister, putting his arms around her shoulders to shield her from further harm. Her skin felt icy and stiff, but she was alive.

Laughter boomed through the room, assaulting his ears and mind. What had he done? Why hadn't he trusted Ammatán to return? Thumps and bumps sounded through the roundhouse, but Conall couldn't watch.

All he could do was hold on to his sister with all his might and try to save her once again from his own poor decisions.

Wind swirled through the roundhouse with furious force, whipping their braids around their heads. Noise and power pummeled them until he thought he'd go mad.

With the suddenness of a thunderclap, all sound and fury ceased. Cracking one eye open, Conall found no one else in the roundhouse amidst the destruction. He and Lainn were alone.

Except for Sawchaill, who was sprawled on the ground.

Lainn blinked several times, glancing around her with trepidation and blossoming wonder. Her eyes grew wide until she noticed Sawchaill. With a cry, she jumped to his side, cradling the still raven in her arms.

Her wails echoed through the roundhouse with more agonizing pain than the furious wind had.

Chapter Fifteen

What a difference a few days can make.

Conall had lost all hope in life, sitting next to his sister as she wasted into death by her blindness. His relief at Ammatán's unexpected return and the subsequent disaster with Bodach made him question every tale about fate, curses, and destiny.

He'd fallen asleep while he worked for the Queen, and his poor decision resulted in Lainn's blindness. Then, he'd agreed to allow Bodach to cure her, and that resulted in Sawchaill's death. Sawchaill, who'd helped Lainn through her blindness, had become her dear friend and support. Sawchaill, who'd helped them countless times through their stay in Faerie. Sawchaill, who'd been his own love's dearest companion since he was young.

The lifeless body of the ink-black bird turned stiff, but Lainn still cradled the large raven in her embrace. She sobbed so hard it turned to hiccups, trails of snot and tears all down her cheeks.

He knelt beside Lainn and placed a hand on Sawchaill's cooling body, tears running down his face and arm, mingling with hers.

Conall didn't know how long they knelt. Both ran dry of tears, but still, they couldn't rise. He imagined it must be time for supper and sleep, but he felt no hunger. His exhaustion wasn't the sort he could sleep with. This exhaustion meant every disastrous moment replayed in his mind, stealing sleep from the horizon. He'd find no rest.

Ammatán said he'd be gone several sleeps, but Conall had no way of tracking of time now. He couldn't sleep, he didn't want to eat, and he could do nothing but care for Lainn.

The dead raven in Lainn's arms was his only focus.

A gasp from the doorway made him glance up with dread in his heart. Ammatán's stricken face stabbed him to the quick. Conall wanted to explain, to try and shield his love from the grief, but he only sat next to Lainn while she held Sawchaill's cold body.

In an instant, Ammatán was next to them, pulling the raven's body from Lainn's arms. The stiffness of death had faded with time, and his limp wings flopped as Ammatán cradled the raven in his arms.

Lainn cried out and tried to take the raven back, but Ammatán turned, rocking the dead bird and humming a tearful tune.

When she placed her hand on Sawchaill's head, Ammatán hissed, clawing at her with his sharp nails. He drew blood in three parallel scratches and she screeched, stumbling back.

Conall dragged her away from Ammatán and the raven. "Lainn, we must rest. Leave Ammatán to his grief. We've taken our time to mourn. We must allow him the same."

She gulped and managed a tiny, sad smile as he brushed his hand across her braids. "We both need to bathe properly. I'll fix some supper."

Finally broken from the spell of mourning, Conall made Lainn wash instead, and he prepared a meal, though he knew the Fae would have no appetite.

The hearth had long since burned down and Conall added wood, stirring the fire back to life. Lainn helped him sweep and straighten the roundhouse, all the time working around the Fae, who sat cross-legged near the hearth, still holding Sawchaill's body.

Once, Conall stepped too close to the grieving Fae, and Ammatán growled at him. He didn't scratch as he had with Lainn, but whether this was due to a mellowing of pain or the desire to hold Sawchaill more closely, Conall didn't know.

It didn't matter.

His heart ached to comfort his love. He wanted to take Ammatán in his arms and make him forget his anguish, to wipe away the suffering and distress.

Ammatán said he'd been linked with Sawchaill since he was young. Conall didn't know how long that meant in human years, but they'd been friends for Ammatán's entire life. Sawchaill had been a best friend, a confidante, and a companion. If someone had murdered Lainn, Conall might feel the same level of agony.

A glance at his sister allowed him finally to grasp the fact her vision had returned, and as a result, she'd returned to the land of the living. She swept the sleeping alcoves as he drank in the sight of her moving on her own accord. Despite his horrible decisions, he'd finally done right by her.

But Sawchaill's life had been the cost.

Had the payment been worth the result? Would he rather have reversed time, take Lainn's sight away from her again, to have Sawchaill back? Conall didn't know.

How could one balance a life against sight? How did one barter pain for convenience? Sawchaill had been a sentient, living creature. He'd been a beloved friend and companion. What price would he pay for such a life lost?

A horrible, wailing keen drifted through the roundhouse. Ammatán's head flung back as he howled, his eyes closed and his teeth bared. He gripped Sawchaill so tightly, his fingernails pierced the raven's body. With nervous glances to the Fae, Lainn drew him aside. "We should leave him alone for now."

With a glance at his tortured lover, Conall agreed. They stepped outside, and Conall glanced to the thatch where Sawchaill liked to perch.

Eight enormous ravens perched along the edge of the roof with their wings half-furled.

Ammatán's moans rose, ululating like a gale wind whipping through an oak grove. His voice grew rough with anguish. The ravens on the roof all fluffed their wings in unison and added their voices to the *caoin,* making Conall's skin pebble with the unearthly sound.

With the additional bird's voices, crashing sounds from inside the roundhouse began. Thuds and rips, punctuated with a screeching yowl that tore at Conall's sanity.

When Ammatán appeared in the doorway, his feral face held nothing of the kind, loving Fae Conall remembered. Instead, a crazed, wrathful visage glared at them, panting with savage breaths and savage hunger.

His robes hung in shreds and his snow-white skin looked raked with lines of pink blood. Conall took a step forward, his hand out to comfort Ammatán, but the Fae shrieked.

Conall froze as the Fae rushed toward him, his hands outstretched like talons for his face. Lainn yelped and tackled Conall to the ground, out of the Fae's path.

They both scrambled to their feet as Ammatán slowed and turned to find his missing target. No bit of reason or sanity remained in the Fae's black eyes. They glittered with visceral lunacy.

Once more, the Fae lunged for them. Conall still held the bronze knife, but he couldn't bring himself to stab his own dear lover.

His brooch! He'd completely forgotten his own power. With desperate haste, he drew upon his will, pulling it through the earth and into his hands. He wrestled the power out just as Ammatán attacked him again, shoving the Fae into the pond.

Conall dragged Lainn into the roundhouse, praying he'd be able to get his brooch in time. Then he stuffed several loaves of bread, fruit, nuts, and the last of the dried fish into his sack, grabbed his sister's hand, and rushed out of the roundhouse.

One last glance at Sawchaill's broken body brought a surge of grief to his heart, but he pushed it away. He had no time for tears.

Ammatán dragged himself out of the water, his eyes still glowing with madness over the dark ripples. With another magical thrust, Conall knocked him back into the pond while he and Lainn ran along the path. They ran with ragged breath and frantic speed around the water. They passed the first trail, the one to the Queen's palace, and raced to the second one.

Down the reed-lined track they fled, as Conall glanced over his shoulder several times, waiting for Ammatán to appear. After a frantic search, they found the black stones.

Ammatán had told them to walk three times around the stones, opposite the sun's path. Instead of walking, they ran, almost tripping over their own feet. Conall gripped Lainn's hand as they reached the end of the third circuit, and together, they placed their hand on the interior face of the northernmost stone.

The stone radiated warmth which spread through his arms and down his body until it connected to the earth. A sound behind him made him glance up in time to see Ammatán, fraught with rage, march into the glade just as the vision of Faerie faded from their sight.

Chapter Sixteen

Birds chirped in Conall's ear. The sound reminded him of Sawchaill's death, and he lost control over his grief. After giving in to sobs, he wiped the tears away with his right hand and opened his eyes to see a bee buzzing lazily above him. A hawk swooped down and ate the bee. Conall shuddered.

He still held Lainn's hand. They were sitting in a summer-sweet stone circle he didn't recognize. Trailing vines wrapped around each stone, and a canopy of flowering trees ringed them, cutting off all landscape from view. "Lainn, wake up. We're back home."

She rubbed her eyes and sat up, looking around. "This doesn't look familiar."

"Not home, home. I mean, the human world."

His sister blinked, as if clearing Faerie from her eyes. "Ah. Have you any idea where we are, then? In relation to our real home?"

He shook his head, breathing in the rich, humid day. Meadowsweet and honeysuckle cloyed the air, along with sun-warmed stone and recent rain. Sunlight streamed through the trees, dappling the ground in dancing shapes.

Faerie had been heart-breakingly beautiful, but the lack of sun and familiar creatures kept it an alien place. Conall felt more at home in this strange part of his world than he ever had, even in Ammatán's arms.

At the thought of his lover, his tears returned with a vengeance. They burst through his dam, ripping his throat raw. He screamed and pounded the ground with his fists until they grew bloody.

He sobbed over the loss of his love, his first love, the only person he'd ever surrendered himself to. The one and only night they shared seared in his memory, both from sheer joy and utter sorrow. His heart was empty now, a shriveled husk.

Lainn put her arms around his shoulder and held him as he cried. "We'll find our way back home, Conall, I promise. Gemmán taught me the stars, and how they appear at home. I'll discover where we are when they emerge tonight."

How could he explain to her the real reason for his tears? He almost wished Ammatán *had* caught them, torn him apart in crazed grief. Conall deserved such a punishment for his failures. And justice demanded Ammatán should deliver the sentence.

With no will left to move on his own, he let Lainn draw him to his feet. Neither of them wished to remain near the stones in case Ammatán followed. Neither of them spoke of their fears.

For several days, they traveled south, toward the land they once called home. Around bogs, along rivers, and past *túatha*, they walked in silence.

Occasionally they stopped to work for food, fish in the river, or snare a rabbit. Such living off the land came much more easily in the height of lush summer than in the depth of cruel winter.

Each night, after Lainn fell asleep, Conall remembered Ammatán and cried himself to exhaustion.

As the landscape began to look familiar, the *túatha* looked larger, more populous, than when they left. Eventually, they found the entrance to the oak grove, but the arched trees grew wild and unkempt.

Lainn furrowed her brow, concerned at such neglect. "Something isn't right, Conall. I need to find out what happened."

Conall scowled, glancing down the path toward home. "We need to find Mother, Lainn. Gemmán can wait."

"No, we have to do this first."

Still harboring his guilt over all his poor decisions, Conall wouldn't deny her.

Lainn hurried through the tree tunnel and Conall rushed after her. The blessed sunlight disappeared, creating chilly gloom and mysteries in every shadow. Branches reached for him to scratch his skin. Conall's heart sped as they moved through the passage to the oak grove.

He sighed in relief as they emerged to the other side, but the glade looked different. Where tall oaks had ringed the circle, with several paths leading into the cheery forest, now only two paths remained. Fewer oaks stood, while several appeared dead or dying, their rotten trunks split by lightning or fire.

Lainn gasped and covered her mouth, tears glistening in her eyes. "They can't all have gone, Conall. Where would they go? Why would they leave? This is a sacred space, the land consecrated for seven generations. The Dagda blessed this grove."

Conall searched for any sign of life, but even the bees had disappeared. "Perhaps they found a better grove? We might find a c-clue down one of the remaining paths."

Her eyes darted between the two choices and pointed to the left. "Gemmán used to live in his hut down this path. I'm sure this is the right one. It must be. He can't have just disappeared."

The rising desperation and panic in her voice concerned Conall. He set his jaw as they walked down the wild path, pushing aside undergrowth and bracken with each step. A raven cawed, and both halted, searching the leaves for the bird as it fluttered away. Conall held a kernel of hope that it was Sawchaill, but it couldn't be their friend. The wake of silence as the bird flew away grew heavy upon both their shoulders.

As one, they continued as the path widened and they approached the second clearing. A small, round stone hut stood in the center, surrounded by modest gardens and a lone beehive.

With a small yip of delight, Lainn ran to the door. She rapped on the frame several times, but no one came.

She looked around. "This is Gemmán's home. His garden looks recently weeded. He must still be here."

"Not at the moment, it seems. Let's go home, Lainn. We can come b-back later when he's home."

His sister shook her head, her eyes once again darting around. "I need to check the other path. That's where the Christian chapel stood. He might be visiting the monk."

After backtracking, they turned down the other path. This one seemed wider, more traveled, than the path to Gemmán's hut. This clearing held not a small chapel, but the active construction of a large church.

Conall didn't remember such a large building so near to his home. He'd never been in a Christian church, but this would have been a sight for any mason to marvel at. The foundation seemed a full *forrach* long, enough to fit three of Sétna's large roundhouses inside with plenty of room to spare. Tall walls were almost complete and scaffolding for the roof had been erected. The foundations for several side buildings lay prepared and awaiting stones. Conall took in the details with wonder and confusion.

Several workmen stopped to watch them as they approached.

Lainn glanced at Conall, a glimmer of fear in her eyes. "How long were we gone, brother? This was a simple, wattle-and-daub church the day before we left."

"I don't know, Lainn. Masonry like this takes years. We left in winter, and now it's mid-summer, so we must have been gone at least six months."

She nodded with great reluctance, then narrowed her eyes at a man digging a trench for an outer wall. "Conall, he looks familiar. Who is he?"

Squinting his eyes, Conall noted the burly shoulders, solid barrel chest, and even white teeth. He shook his head in disbelief. "But… but T-Tomas should be my age. That man is at least twenty seasons older than me. Maybe that's his father? I thought his father had died years ago."

Lainn whispered in his ear, her eyes darting between the man that looked like Tomas and the workers staring at them. "We should leave, Conall. I'm uncomfortable in this place. We don't belong here."

"Shh. I mean to discover information."

A pleasant male voice caught their attention. "How may I help you, children? You're welcome to *Cluain Eraird*. Do excuse the noise."

They turned to see an older man, perhaps around sixty seasons, with a round belly and a fringe of white around his head. His smile grew wide below sparkling blue eyes.

Conall bowed to the Christian priest. "Thank you for your welcome, priest. May I ask how long this construction has been working? I apprenticed to a mason, you see, and am curious about the time such an impressive project takes."

"Do call me Father Finnian, lad." The man gazed into the sky, rubbing his white-stubbled chin with an audible rasp. "Hmm. Let me see. We drew up the plans in the Year of Our Lord 535. Then we got approval from the Archbishop the following summer. We had a great deal of trouble finding the right stone, as the nearby quarry was already mined out. I believe construction began two summers ago. We should be finished in another two summers, if God blesses our progress."

"I'm so sorry, Father. We've lived in the hills for a long time, and I don't remember how your Christian years work. How do your numbers compare to the reign of our chief, Muircheartach Mór Mac Earca?"

The old man scowled. "Muircheartach? Why, he's been dead these last fifteen years, killed in the twenty-fourth year of his reign. Tuathal Maelgarbh ruled for eleven years after him, and now Diarmaid mac Cearbhaill has ruled for four more. You aren't old enough to have remembered Muircheartach, my son. You're barely eighteen years old yourself, and the young lady here might be sixteen, at the most. Where, precisely, have you been living?"

Conall did a quick calculation in his mind, knowing Muircheartach had been in the eighteenth year of his reign when they escaped into Faerie.

With growing dread, he glanced to where the man who looked like Tomas leaned on his shovel, watching Lainn with speculation.

He grabbed Lainn's hand and his words tumbled out. "I am so sorry to have interrupted your work, Father. Thank you for your time. We must be going!"

They ran down the path, ignoring the priest's startled protest. When they exited the tree tunnel, they both stopped to catch their breath.

Conall turned to his sister as he panted. "Did you figure out how long we've been gone?"

She stared at the path behind them. "Over twenty winters. That must have been Tomas, after all."

A female voice spoke behind them. "Tomas? What about my Tomas?"

Conall and Lainn both turned to find a tall, stout woman carrying a large basket on her ample hip. With a momentary shift of perspective and a moment of disorientation, Conall recognized her.

Before he blurted her name, Lainn came to the rescue. "We're searching for cousins of ours, a brother and sister. We're told their mother might still live nearby. Perhaps you know them? Their names are Lainn and Conall. The mother is Ligach."

Several expressions flickered across Aoife's face, from frustration, disappointment, and finally, resignation. "You do look remarkably like your cousins. Yes, I remember them both. They disappeared one night,

216

and no one's heard a whisper since. Ligach and Sétna both still live in their old homestead."

She glanced over her shoulder and wrinkled her nose. "If you go down along that path about three leagues, you'll find it. It's near the old, worked-out quarry."

Lainn thanked her and Aoife stared at them as they passed. Conall felt her eyes boring into his back. Just before they'd walked out of sight, he glanced back. She still watched, a pensive expression on her face.

Lainn giggled. "I can't believe that was Aoife! She looks so old and fat!"

Conall shoved her shoulder. "Lainn! That's not nice. If she's married to that lout Tomas, she can't have had an easy life."

Lainn stopped smiling. "Fair enough. I suppose once you disappeared, she had to settle for what she could get."

He glanced back again, but the path had curved too much for him to catch sight of Aoife. "I wonder if I would have settled for her if I'd stayed."

"I thought you didn't like her?"

"You're right, I didn't. I still don't. But…" His throat closed as he thought of Ammatán and what he'd had and then lost with the Fae.

"Gemmán always told me not to worry about *what ifs*. He said we had the will to choose our paths, even if we don't always choose the best one. Every path, wise or not, can teach us something important."

What had his choice of Ammatán taught him? That he could love? How idiotic he'd been to love a Fae? More likely, how stupid he'd been to trust Bodach.

Lainn stopped. "Conall? What if something's happened to Gemmán? If it's been twenty winters, he might have fallen ill, or injured, or too old…"

Her expression turned so bleak, he drew her in for a tight hug. "We'll find him, Lainn, right after we find Mother. We have to find her, right? She's our mother. We have a duty to her."

Lainn stared at the forest floor. "Aoife said both Ligach and Sétna lived there. I suppose it was too much to hope Sétna died or left, isn't it?"

With a wry chuckle, he nodded. "Too much, indeed. Still, twenty winters is a long time for an adult. He'll be weaker and older. I've been hauling stone around, and I've grown in muscle and strength in Faerie, even if it's only been a little while. I'll protect you, Lainn."

Her answering smile turned half sad and half sardonic. "You'd better, big brother. That's your duty, too."

Conall draped his arm around her shoulder, and they headed to their old home in a much brighter mood.

Chapter Seventeen

As they approached their mother's home, both siblings' moods grew somber. They held hands and turned the bend.

They barely recognized the roundhouse they'd lived in just a few months before. Vines sprouted from the thatch in some places and showed black rot in others. Moss clung to the kerbstones and weeds choked the path and garden. Conall could just glimpse the quarry, but a pool of standing water in the center had grown green with algae and cattails.

Conall didn't know what he'd expected, but this wasn't it. His mother had never been particularly vicious with cleaning, but she'd never have allowed such a slovenly state.

Even Sétna, as much as Conall detested him, had a basic sense of neatness and order which he found difficult to fault. What had happened to allow their home to descend into such a state?

They exchanged a worried glance. As one, they walked to the door. Conall hesitated and then rapped on the doorframe.

Nothing stirred inside, so he knocked again.

Something crashed, shattering the silence and making both of them jump. With another glance at Lainn, Conall pushed his shoulder against the wooden door.

It took several tries, as the door stuck, but it finally flew open with a bang. A putrid stench assaulted them, and both staggered back.

Another crash came from inside the gloom. Conall covered his nose with his hand and forced himself into the roundhouse.

Previously a central table had been ringed by neat alcoves and shelves. Now, a mélange of broken pottery, ripped fabric, and rotting food lay on every conceivable surface and the flagstone floor.

Searching the shadows for anything that moved, Conall went from space to space, stepping carefully. After a while, he stealthily drew upon his power and swept aside the broken pottery to avoid injury, forming a circular path around the edge.

When he finally reached his mother's alcove at the far side of the roundhouse, a figure on the cot moaned. He recognized her voice and knelt beside her. He dug under several layers of sweat-stained cloth and matted furs to find a wasted shadow of his mother.

Lainn knelt on the other side of the cot, taking their mother's hand. "Conall? What's wrong with her?"

Conall stared into her mad, unfocused eyes, her drooling lips, and her dirty face. "I'm no healer, Lainn. You'd have more training than I do, from Gemmán. What do you think?"

She examined her mother's mouth, face, and hands, but shook her head. "I don't know, either. We need help."

With a crazed screech, their mother snatched at their hands, pulling them in to her chest and wailing. "He's coming! He'll come for me, and he'll come for you! The branches, the trees, they'll come for us all! You cannot run, you cannot hide! The vines will rip you and bind you and tear you apart!"

With growing horror, Conall searched his mother's gaze for any shred of sanity but found none. Her haggard face and prominent bones made her look halfway to death, but the crazed eyes removed all vestiges of his mother's familiar face. She'd become a stranger.

A roar behind him made him spin, ready to face this new threat. The wasted form of his stepfather had lifted a shattered stick of furniture with both hands over his head. The same madness that haunted his mother's eyes shone in Sétna's.

And he was about to kill Conall with his makeshift club.

Conall had no time to think as his stepfather swung the weapon at his head. He yanked on his magic and shoved Sétna away, and he crashed into the darkness. A strange shimmer covered everything and popped, like a bubble, until something restricting his heart eased.

Conall grabbed his mother's left hand, wrestling it down to her side.

Lainn stood, her eyes wide. "Conall? What happened to him? How did you do that?"

As he tried to catch the other hand, he glared at his sister. "It doesn't matter now. Help me with mother."

She crossed her arms. "What do you imagine we can do, Conall? If you can't tell, she's gone mad. Holding her down won't help. She needs healing. Neither of us is a healer."

After taking a deep breath, Conall had to admit that Lainn had a point. "Fine. At least grab her other hand, so she doesn't hurt herself."

Lainn held their mother's hand while she twisted and wiggled, trying to get free of her captors. She spat out curses to them both, though it was clear she didn't recognize either of her children. Eventually, she wore herself out and drifted into a troubled sleep.

Conall swallowed and looked up at his sister. "Will you stay with her? I'll go find Adhna. He might be able to help."

"Adhna? He must be long dead by now. He'd already been old twenty winters ago."

Conall sighed. "I have to try, Lainn. Don't you see? This is all my fault. I took us away and left Mother to Sétna's care. I should never have abandoned her."

Lainn glanced back down at their mother's haggard face. "Go find Adhna. I'll wait here."

With a brief flash of gratitude in his smile, Conall put their mother's other hand into Lainn's.

"Be quick, Conall. I won't be able to hold her if she wakes again. And when things have calmed, we're going to talk about what you did to Sétna."

At the mention of his name, Conall remembered to check on his stepfather. He'd crashed into the large wooden block table. He'd hit it with the middle of his back. Conall caught his breath at his stepfather's blank, staring eyes before he allowed himself to breathe again.

Emotions warred within him. Relief at being free from his stepfather's rage and abuse, either for him, Lainn, or Mother. Guilt at killing someone, anyone, even such a horrible person. Shame for such a cretinous action, using magic to kill.

Inaction paralyzed him until Lainn yelled at him. "Conall, just go! He only got what he deserved."

After swallowing his shame, he threw one last glance over his shoulder. Lainn held their mother's hands to her chest, speaking to her in low, soothing tones while caressing her head. He sprinted out the roundhouse door and along the river toward Adhna's cottage.

Twice, he took a wrong turn, expecting trees where none existed or where the bend in the river had shifted. Once he came close to Aoife's old homestead and veered away. She must live with Tomas now, but he still had no wish to deal with an encounter.

When the cottage finally came into view through the summer leaves, Conall gasped. The place hadn't changed in the slightest in over twenty winters. The same ivy-ridden thatch topped the same crumbling kerbstones. Even the trees around the cottage looked the same age.

He slowed his pace as he approached, marveling at the oddity. When he finally rapped on the doorframe, he did so hesitantly, not expecting an answer.

A querulous voice came from behind the oaken door. "What do you want? Go away."

"Adhna? Adhna, is that you?"

The door flung open to reveal the old man, exactly as Conall had left him.

"Conall? Conall is that really you? By the Dagda, you've returned! My boy, my boy, you have no idea how good it is to see you safe and sound."

The old man's arms engulfed Conall as Adhna buffeted and hugged him to within an inch of his life. His hair smelled of honey and moss. When Adhna finally released him, his grin looked fit to crack his face. "You are a sight for an old man's eyes. Is Lainn with you?"

He peered over Conall's shoulder, searching for a sign of his sister, but Conall shook his head. "She's at our roundhouse. Well, our p-parents' roundhouse. It's Mother… she needs healing, Adhna. She's gone quite mad. Can you help?"

The smile faded as he stared into Conall's eyes. "Your mother? Oh, my dear boy, I'm afraid I can't help. I don't have such power. I've seen her now and then, and your stepfather as well."

Something must have shown in Conall's expression, for Adhna asked, "What, Conall? Did Sétna do something?"

After casting his gaze down, Conall said, "I did something. I… I think I k-k-killed him, Adhna." He looked up, hoping for forgiveness. "I didn't mean to, truly! He tried to hit me with a piece of wood, and I didn't *think*. I just took p-power from the brooch and flung it at him. I pushed him away, and he hit his back on the table, and…"

Relief settled the lines of Adhna's face, and he hugged Conall again. "Be at ease, lad. It's all you could have done. You must defend yourself, and I'm glad to know you will when you must. It's all Sétna deserved, after all he's done."

He pulled himself from Adhna's arms. "What's he done, Adhna? What do you know?"

The older man shook his head, the beads in his beard braids rattling in a staccato rhythm. "That's not my tale to tell, lad. Suffice to say no one will mourn the man. Now, about your mother. I can't heal her myself, but with your help and Lainn's, I might know a place where we can ask for help."

Conall narrowed his gaze. "What place?"

Adhna studied the young man for several moments. "You have learned caution, my lad. This is a good thing, though a sad necessity. This place has its dangers, but it's the only way I can think of getting true help. Are you willing to trust me?"

Conall had no way to heal his mother, and no way to find another healer. Even if he'd known one before, twenty winters later, people move away or die. Adhna's offer remained his only choice. He nodded.

"Grand. Now, let me get a few supplies. I'll be out forthwith."

After scrambling back into his cottage, Adhna shut the door. Bumps, scrapes, a few muffled curses, and one crash of broken pottery emerged before the bearded man returned with a small sack and his walking staff.

"Come now, it's not too far. Wait, have you eaten aught today, child? You look as if I could knock you over with a feather."

Conall tried to remember the last time he'd had anything to eat. His puzzled expression gave Adhna all the answer he needed. The older man pressed a chunk of white goat cheese in his hand along with a small loaf of rye bread. "Eat this, then, for strength. You know I must care for you if I give you my cheese, lad!"

With a chuckle, he stalked off, using his walking stick as they climbed a little-used path leading from the back of his cottage. Conall followed, breaking the bread in two, inserting the cheese, and taking a bite. He took a moment to savor the rich, sweet cheese and the rich bread. Adhna must have flavored the cheese with honey to get that flavor.

Chapter Eighteen

As they crested the top of the hill at dusk, Conall beheld a vista before him. Misty valleys lay like gray pools across the landscape, with hills rising like islands from the sea.

Purple twilight enfolded each hill in a velvet embrace, and Conall sighed for the wonder of the human world. Day and night, sun, moon, and stars. How he'd missed the simple pleasures of the cycle of life.

When he glanced at the hilltop itself, his blood grew cold. Three small standing stones were arranged in a tight circle. They shot sharp and thin against the deepening sky, an ominous harbinger of danger.

"Adhna? Where is this p-place? I've never seen it before, in all the years I've lived here."

"Oh, you wouldn't find it unless you knew the road, child. It's hidden from most humans." Adhna pulled several items from his sack, including a bowl, a waterskin, honey, and a small wheel of cheese.

In his past life, these words would have intrigued him. Now, with his skin prickling, Conall backed up. "I d-don't think this is a good idea, Adhna.

"Patience, Conall. This will all come clear soon. Now, do be a good lad, and sit down right there, will you? I'll be ready in just a moment."

With increasing anxiety, Conall watched while Adhna set up a ritual offering in the center of the circle. The three thin stones stood close together with barely enough room for one person to stand, much less two.

Grateful that he must stay on the edge, Conall clenched his fists and prayed Ammatán wouldn't be the one to answer this call for help. Even if the Fae no longer burned with insane rage, seeing his erstwhile lover might drive Conall himself over the edge. In his heart, he hoped Ammatán had found some solace and peace.

"Now just a few more moments, Conall." Adhna walked around the circle three times, chanting in an ancient language. Conall understood only a few words. He heard *pain* and *help*, but the rest was a fluid tumult of syllables.

A low hum tickled the edge of his mind, and Conall gritted his teeth in anticipation. The music swept over the hill, making his skin pebble grow icy. He'd felt this power before and realized before the white light appeared who was answering Adhna's call.

When the furious mind-scream ripped through his skull, Conall flung himself to the ground and covered his head and ears, trying to keep out the pain and madness.

The Faerie Queen, resplendent in a shimmering robe of translucent nothing, stepped from an invisible dais to greet Adhna. "Why do you call me, old one? For what emergency do you presume to ask my aid? Have you not yet learned your lesson? Or must I increase your sentence?"

Adhna bowed low and stayed there, his back bent almost double. "My Queen, I do beg your pardon for this request. But you possess a particular talent with the insanity that plagues humans, and I have seen traces of one of your own agents in this area. Did you perchance send Bodach to haunt someone in my *túath*? Such an action seems against our agreement, but I tasted his scent several times in recent seasons."

When Adhna mentioned Bodach, Conall risked a glance up. The Faerie Queen tapped her lip, considering Adhna's question. "Yes, he is one of mine, but no, I did not send him on any missions in this… this place." Her delicate nose crinkled in disgust. "I will never understand how you live in this squalor."

With no inflection, Adhna replied with a bow. "I do so at your command, my Queen."

"Hmm. Just so. If Bodach has taken it into his head to interfere with your time here, I shall deal with him." She raised her hands to clap, but Adhna forestalled her.

"Please! Before you go, may I ask a boon? His actions caused the mother of a dear friend to lose her sanity. I would ask for healing."

"A dear friend? Is it that creature cowering outside the stones? A human? What have you come to, Adhna? Indebting yourself for such creatures?"

Conall gulped and buried his face again, hoping to keep his identity from the Queen. But she approached him, and her gaze forced him to stand. He tried to fight against the compulsion, but she was much too strong, even in the human world.

She put one shining finger beneath his chin, turning his face back and forth. "I recognize this human. He did a service for me once." Then she held his face still, her gaze burned into his soul, making him scream in silent pain. Her control was so strong, he couldn't even move his mouth. "However, since then, he has deprived me of one of my trusted courtiers. This act I cannot condone nor forgive!"

Adhna leapt from the circle and inserted himself between Conall and the Queen. Conall collapsed, still unable to move. He rolled to the side, his shoulder burning with the sharp pain of impact.

Adhna's voice held a tone of desperate entreaty. "My Queen! Please, he is but a puny mortal. Certainly, such a base creature is not worth your direct punishment. Allow your courtier to do the honors when he is able, I beg you!"

The distraction caused her to turn aside from Conall and regard Adhna directly. "I do not take advice from lesser Fae, Adhna! Have a care I don't increase your own sentence for this impudence."

Conall tried to move his toe, and almost cheered when it wiggled. His fingers finally obeyed him. With slow movements, he gained control over his limbs and quietly crawled away, inch by inch.

Adhna placated the Queen while he reached the relative safety of the tree line. He carefully rose to his feet and crept further away, hoping to escape the sphere of the Queen's immediate influence.

Obviously, the old man had dealt with the Queen before this night. He might even be working out a punishment by living with humans. As much as Conall carried the guilt of leaving Adhna to her tender mercies, the old man should be able to deal with her anger much more easily if Conall wasn't nearby to protect.

He'd get no help healing his mother from the Faerie Queen. The disastrous break with Ammatán had ruined everything in his life, from his own first love to his mother's life and health.

Conall stumbled downhill through the dark forest. If he found the river, he could find his way back to the house. His mother wake again soon, and Lainn would need his help.

He also needed to deal with Sétna's body. Part of him wanted to dump the awful man unceremoniously in the scummy pond next to the quarry, but another, more humane part, needed to honor the other human with decency and dignity.

Shadows leapt for him, but he kept pushing his way down the hill. Some wore Sétna's face, and others wore Ammatán's. Sometimes the Faerie Queen tried to grasp his clothing, pulling him into an abyss of despair. Each time, he pictured his mother's worn face, aged and helpless, with Lainn holding her hand against her heart.

Something slid under his feet as he lost his balance and tumbled toward the riverbank. He ignored a crashing sound behind him as he clutched at a tree stump, dragged himself to his feet, and stumbled upstream.

Step by step he trudged through the dark woods. The further he got from Adhna and the Faerie Queen, the easier he could breathe. An eternity later, he found the familiar quarry. Male voices came from within his old home.

A crash, similar to the one at the stone circle, rang out across the dim clearing. With no regard now for his own safety, he flung the door open and rushed inside.

The dim glow of the peat fire showed only shadows. He glanced at the spot Sétna had fallen, but he couldn't discern a body.

Four figures stood in the red light. Two struggled near where his stepfather had fallen, and two more were near his mother's alcove. He focused on the two struggling and recognized Lainn's braids swinging as she tried to escape from Tomas' grip. The thunderous look on his face and a growing dark spot on his cheek spoke of her resistance.

Another man, his blond hair shining in the low firelight, stood behind his mother, a spear point against her neck. She lay limp, her eyes closed, and Conall prayed she was still alive.

"Let them both g-go!"

Tomas' laugh rang harshly in his ears. "Let them g-g-g-g-go? What are you going to do, stutter us to death? I don't know how Lainn stayed so fresh and young for so long, but I've a mind to find out. She's far more tasty-looking than Aoife's become. You remember Aoife, don't you, C-C-C-Conall? She still calls your name in her dreams. Perhaps we should trade."

Lainn scratched at his eyes, but he pulled his face back out of her reach. "None of that, hellcat. I'll teach you some manners, I swear it."

The blond let out an exasperated groan. "Leave some for me, Tomas. You promised!"

Tomas waved a hand toward his cohort. "Take the old woman if you want. I'm having this one first."

"I don't want anything about this mad crone. She stinks. Teaching *that one* a lesson is the whole reason I went along with your mad plan!"

Another crash yanked his attention away from his mother. Lainn had kicked something over and Tomas growled, pulling his fist back to slam her in the face. She shoved at him, and he stumbled back with a cry and a thump. He rose quickly, rage glowing in the pinched lines of his face.

After pulling his will through the magical brooch, the power surged through Conall's feet and into his hands. He shoved with all his might, and even though he stood across the room from Tomas, the bigger man fell backward over Sétna's still-slumped form. Lainn shouted in triumph and kicked savagely between his legs several times.

"Lainn! Stop that and run!"

She glanced down at Tomas's form as he shouted in pain, struggling to shield his privates. "But—"

"For once in your life, don't argue! Run to safety!"

With a parting savage kick to Tomas' knee, she fled outside, her red braids flying behind her.

Now Conall had to face the two bullies left and extract his mother from their power. He set his mouth into a grim line as Tomas tried to crawl to his knees. "You have t-t-two choices. Leave now, and you'll hear no more from me, provided no harm has come to either woman. Or you can stay and fight."

He glanced at Tomas, who moaned, doubled over himself. The blond man's glance darted to his fellow, uncertain of the balance of power.

In light of their hesitation, Conall decided they needed another demonstration. He no longer cared if someone witnessed his magic. He just needed to save his mother. Conall shoved at the blond man, causing the spear to fly out of his hand and into the shadows with a clatter. The man fell back, but so did Conall's mother.

Tomas cried out, "Ernán! Don't get up! He'll just get you again."

Conall squinted his eyes at the blond, trying to reconcile his older features with the young acolyte who'd witnessed his sister's final trial, a lifetime ago.

Ernán ignored Tomas' advice and struggled back to his feet. "Why did you let the girl go? She's the whole reason we came here, you idiot!"

"The whole reason *you* came here, you mean. I have a score to settle with the boy."

Instead of using his magic as a shoving force, Conall applied a steady pressure over Tomas' chest, holding him down. He had to admit, he enjoyed watching him squirm, flailing his arms like a turtle trying to flip itself. "A score to settle? With me? You d-don't even know me. Maybe you remember my cousin, but I'm not him."

Tomas spat to the side, contempt clear in his eyes. "You're Conall, no doubt. Stone-boy! Don't think I don't remember you! You and that st-st-st-stupid st-t-t-tutter!"

While he cursed this obvious identification, Conall kept his false confidence up. "Brave words from a man pinned to the ground."

Warned by the shift in Tomas' gaze, Conall ducked, the breeze of Ernán's swing whooshing over his head. He shoved with his brooch's power into the blond man's gut, and he gave a grunt of surprise.

Conall grabbed a few turnips from the shelf, hefting them to gauge their usefulness. He juggled the two to demonstrate his ability, speeding them up with his magic to an almost comical speed. "Both of you, heed me. Leave this place and do not t-trouble any of us again. Do you understand?"

The older man's eyes widened as he watched the turnips speed in circles in Conall's hands. Conall finally let up on his pressure and both men scrambled to their feet.

Ernán grabbed his spear and, with one last look over their shoulders, they both ran. He hoped he'd given Lainn enough time to get clear and find a place of safety.

Conall ran to his mother's side, thankful against all hope to find her heart still beat strongly. She only slept, thank all the gods.

Her eyes fluttered open, and she focused on his face, her brow furrowed. "Fíngin? Is that you? It's been so long. Did you go with *her* again? You said you'd never leave me again. Did you bring yet another child of hers?"

Her words made no sense to him, except for the fact she mistook him for his father. "Shh, mother. It's Conall. You're fine. The evil men ran away. I'm here to help you."

Remembering Sétna, he glanced into the corner where his stepfather had fallen. The shadows covered all sins. Conall didn't want to know if he'd really killed Sétna. Regardless, he needed to make sure Lainn had escaped.

Would she run to Adhna's cottage? No, probably Gemmán's, despite the cottage looking ruined. Conall hoped Gemmán still lived there. Would Conall be able to find it in the dark?

His mother clutched at his hand. "Mother? Have you eaten? Can I get you water?"

"No, Fíngin. But, I ache for you, it's been so long. Come lie with me." She reached out for him, trying to drag him to the cot with her. Disgusted, Conall pulled back, shaking his head. "I'm not Father, I'm Conall! Mother, Father's long gone."

She pouted, curling herself under the blanket, and turned her back to him. "Fine. Go back to your faerie woman, then. I'll have none of you."

Conall closed his eyes and prayed for patience. He begged her again to take some food, but she refused to speak. He considered returning for Adhna, to see if he'd found something to help her, or if he'd even escaped the wrath of the Queen.

Guilt at abandoning his old friend stabbed him, but he didn't have time for guilt right now. He must find Lainn to make certain she was safe. After all, he'd promised his father to do so, always.

He took a deep breath and walked outside. Bright moonlight shone upon the clearing, gleaming from the quarry face. No trace remained of either Ernán or Tomas, so he walked the old familiar path through the woods to the druid grove.

Chapter Nineteen

Conall marveled once again at how much the trees had changed. Bushes cleared into new glades, ancient oaks had fallen, and insects had eaten the rotten wood. The path shifted into unfamiliar bends, and at one point, the river had changed course to cut away at the land.

Dawn broke as he walked, filling the forest with the song of summer birds. The wash of bright colors flooded his vision, disorienting him so much he imagined he was back in Faerie. With growing trepidation, Conall found the druid's glade where he'd taken his sister so many mornings, a lifetime ago, now so overgrown.

No one was at the entrance to the oak grove, but shouts rang out in the distance, down the tunnel of trees that had frightened him so long ago. Conall ran headlong through the shadowy space.

He made it to the first glade, then darted down the path toward the druid's cottage. The voices were coming from there.

Pine needles and fallen bracken crunched under his feet, masking the voices, but when he burst into the glade, a tense tableau lay before him.

Two men stood near the humble cottage. One, he recognized as an older version of Gemmán, but the other, younger man, was a stranger. Tomas and Ernán stood on the other end of the clearing. The blond man held his spear poised at Lainn, who took a few slow, backward steps toward to the cottage.

Turning to the bullies, Conall shouted, "I t-told you to leave her alone!"

Tomas sneered. "I don't know what sort of trick you pulled at the quarry, stoneb-b-b-boy, but we don't take orders from the likes of you!"

Just as Conall drew upon his power and shoved Tomas back, Ernán let loose his spear, Lainn screamed and ran to escape the path of the weapon, but she wasn't fast enough.

He should have saved his power to shield her, but he acted too slowly. It took a moment to draw more power, a moment he didn't have.

Gemmán and his companion rushed forward to keep Lainn from falling to the ground, but the spear had pierced her side. The deep red stained Conall's heart as anger clouded his vision.

Now his power surged up again, and he pulled as much as he could from the brooch, channeling it through the earth and his arms. He shot it forward into the two bullies, but Gemmán stepped in the way as his companion cradled Lainn.

The older druid held his hand up, blocking Conall's magic. "Stop! Conall, this is not the way. You must not harm them with your magic."

But Conall had no thought to listening to Gemmán. He wanted to punish Ernán and Tomas for harming his sister.

The older man held up his staff to the sky, and the carved and painted swirling designs glowing in the slanted sunlight. Conall's blast of power deflected against that staff and upwards, away from the bullies.

Then, Gemmán sang.

With disbelief, Conall stared at the druid. Now wasn't the time for song. Now was the time for fighting back, for taking back what had been stolen. Now was the time for standing up for themselves and refusing to be bullied into submission.

Still, Gemmán sang. Glowing lines on his staff danced, making the colors swirl in the sunbeams like an eddying rainbow. His voice caressed the trees and the bees flying into spirals around each human. A sweet perfume of wildflowers surrounded Conall with comfort and memory. The stranger picked up the tune, singing in descant against Gemmán's melody, entwining and complementing the older man's voice.

Conall tried to move and failed. Both Ernán and Tomas stiffened and then collapsed, closing their eyes. A glow surrounded each of them from the dancing lights from Gemmán's staff.

Lainn glowed as well. Her eyes had shut as dark red blood seeped into the green summer grass, just as his vision faded to gray. Before he lost consciousness, Conall realized he hadn't protected his sister. Not in this world or the Faerie realm. He'd failed in everything his father had entrusted to him.

Chapter Twenty

Conall's arm throbbed.

To be fair, his entire body ached. He tried to curl his hand and sparks of pain shot up his hand. At first, he thought he was blind because he saw nothing when he opened his eyes. And he considered it just punishment for his failure to protect his sister.

However, the dim glow from the moon grew as a cloud blew away, shining in through a small window.

A window to where? Conall had no memory of a building or how he came to be sleeping in one.

He tried to move his arm, but it wouldn't shift. He wiggled his fingers and toes, but his limbs were tied down. Not like when the Queen's magic held him; that force had kept even his muscles from clenching. This felt more like ropes or belts holding his arms and legs to the cot. The shapes of several other slumbering figures circled the room, but no other details.

Another cloud occluded the moonlight, and the world returned to inky darkness.

Conall needed to relieve himself, and his throat felt parched. He might cry out for help but hated the thought of being helpless. Had someone taken him prisoner?

Memories of Bodach's cruel smile made his heart race with fear and the Fae's mad laughter haunted his mind. He remembered the sweet smell of summer wildflowers. And blood. He remembered blood.

Images flooded his mind. Lainn, lying on the grass with her life's blood flowing from a spear injury. Her eyes staring up into the blue sky as bees buzzed around them in ordered spirals, then closing. The song Gemmán and his friend sang as they all passed into a deep slumber.

The darkness enfolded him and he returned to that slumber.

Conall woke again to the morning sun shining warmly on his face. When he opened his eyes this time, two bright green eyes blinked and startled back.

A pleasant tenor voice said, "Oho! Our young man is awake, Gemmán!"

In answer, the druid came into sight. "So, I see! Conall, can you speak? Do you know where you are?"

His throat rasped raw as if he'd slept with it open to the night air. He coughed a few times before Gemmán offered a waterskin. Conall tried to sit up to drink, but the restraints kept him in place.

The stranger apologized and untied his hands, helping him sit up and drink. After a few swallows of cool, clear water, Conall found his voice. "I d-d-don't know where I am."

With a patronizing smile, the stranger said, "You're in my chapel! Well, the chapel I help run. At the moment, it's more of a crumbling hospice." He frowned and glanced around at several other cots. The walls showed spots of crumbling ruin and a few patches of thatch needed repair, but the cots themselves looked strong and comfortable.

Conall spied his sister's limp form in the next cot, and he struggled to be by her side. "Lainn!"

Gemmán clutched his arm. "Crimthann! Get his other arm. Conall, hold still. You're not fit to move yet. Lainn's fine, she's just sleeping."

Conall fought against his healers, needing to be next to Lainn. "Let me go!" He reached for his brooch's magic to help him, but even straining to the limits of his connection, the line was faint and tenuous. He must be far from the brooch. He couldn't even remember where the brooch was at the moment.

Finally, Conall stopped struggling and glared at Gemmán. "You swear she's just sleeping? She'll be fine?"

The druid nodded, sage comfort in his eyes.

Conall frowned, looking at the other man. "Where are we, though? Who is this?"

Gemmán glanced at the other man. "Crimthann is one of my students. He's Christian, but he's studying with me for a few seasons to gain musical wisdom. He came from the north to study with Finnian, the priest building that grand church in the next glade."

Crimthann meant 'fox,' and Conall didn't trust someone named for the crafty animal to care for his dear sister. His mid-brown curls were cut much shorter than most warriors, not even reaching his shoulders, with his forehead shaved in a half-circle. The odd hair style and his simple brown robes made him look foreign to Conall, a stranger in his land.

With narrowed eyes, he addressed the Christian. "From the north? How north?"

Crimthann cocked his head. "My family's in Dunaghmore, near the shores of Lough Neagh, some thirty leagues to the north of here. My great-grandfather was Niall of the Nine Hostages, and I've been a deacon in Laighean for these past two winters. I assure you, I've cared for many invalids and seekers in my time, young man. You and your sister have gotten my best care these last weeks."

Panic gripped Conall as his mind reeled. "Weeks? We've been here weeks? My mother! I left her alone in her roundhouse!"

Gemmán placed a strong hand on his chest, holding him in place. "Shh. The old hermit is caring for her. Adhna? Is that his name? He came here the day of the attack."

Conall took a deep breath, calming his nerves and his fright. Adhna lived. His mother lived. Lainn lived, but she wouldn't wake. He didn't quite relax, but at least the frenzy dissipated.

Crimthann brought him a bowl. "Here, drink your broth. You need to build up your strength to walk again."

Conall accepted it with grudging grace but didn't take the spoon. He relished the warmth of the broth through the bowl, though. "You said I've b-b-been here weeks. How long?"

With a glance to Gemmán, the younger man pressed his lips into a thin line. "Almost two moons now. We worried about your chances of waking, but you stirred in your sleep, so that gave us hope."

Conall glanced at Lainn, and the deacon surmised his worry. "Yes, she's also stirring. She should wake soon."

"What happened? My memory is jumbled."

Crimthann sat on a stool beside Conall's cot and folded his arms, his expression determined. "I'll tell you after you finish your broth."

Conall scowled at the obvious manipulation but found no sensible argument against it. He took a hesitant spoonful, and then another. The hot, salty broth tasted delicious, trickling down his parched throat. His stomach chose this moment to growl so loudly, Gemmán glanced over with a fierce frown.

Giving the druid a sheepish grin, Conall took another spoonful, grateful for the warmth. Crimthann nodded with approval. "When Lainn ran into our glade, Gemmán had been in the middle of a lesson. As soon as she burst into the clearing, those two ruffians came hot on her trail. The blond man, once Gemmán's student, held the spear as a threat and commanded her to be still.

"She froze while Gemmán tried to talk reason to him." Crimthann shook his head. "The man wouldn't listen to his words. Later, Gemmán told me how Lainn had succeeded in something the lad had failed at years before. He must have been harboring that envy ever since. Gemmán could do nothing to soothe his pain."

Conall clenched his fist hard around the spoon until he realized Crimthann had stopped his tale, staring pointedly at the broth. Conall took another sip so the deacon would continue.

"When you arrived, Gemmán had just about given up on the lad and spoke to his companion, urging him to be the voice of reason. I begged him to at least use his staff to good purpose, but Gemmán isn't a violent man, and decided talking would be a far better solution." Crimthann stopped with a frown. "What do you remember of the rest?"

Conall's head ached as he tried to capture the details. "I remember the spear hitting Lainn, and Gemmán and you singing. Then I remember nothing."

"You collapsed, as did Lainn and both of her assailants."

Conall peered at the other cots for the first time, looking for Ernán and Tomas. None of the other three men looked familiar.

"No, they didn't survive the song. The magic, you see, pulls evil from a person's soul. It pulled on you both a little, as you have, I'm sure, some small evils in your past. However, the other men had a much greater past of evil acts. The song pulled too much of their soul."

Conall swallowed. "They both d-died? He killed them?"

Crimthann nodded, his expression grim. "Gemmán regretted their deaths but counted them as unavoidable. He is not a man of violence."

"And you are?"

Crimthann pressed his lips together in a grim line. "When necessary."

"What song d-did you sing?"

Crimthann's scowl returned. "It's druidic magic. Not something I can speak of to a layman."

Conall narrowed his eyes. "I thought you were a deacon? Isn't that a Christian t-title? Why are you learning druidic magic?"

The other man glanced at Gemmán with a wistful expression. "The song. It's all about the song. I'm drawn to the music in ways my heart cannot explain to my own God. In truth, I'm not supposed to be here. I should be in Finnian's school, learning from him. He teaches students from all over the land. And yet, when I came to his school, I was drawn to the music of the bee-glade."

Conall swallowed at a memory. "Lainn has sung songs to the bees, the test Ernán failed, the one that made him seethe for twenty winters in jealousy."

Crimthann nodded. "I thought as much. You see, the music's in her voice. I had to help Gemmán save her. It cost us both, but it was worth it."

"Cost? How did it cost you to sing?"

Crimthann shook his head. "Unless you have the magic, you'd never understand. Suffice to say, all magic comes at a price, no matter what type of magic it is. Druidic or Christian, nothing comes free."

Conall understood the truth of that too well. He glanced at Lainn. "How long did you say we'd been here?"

With a half-smile, Crimthann nodded. "Yes, even healing comes at a price. But we can talk of that later when you and Lainn are both stronger."

Conall took the last few sips of broth and wished for more. After staring at the bottom of the bowl for several moments, he looked into Crimthann's green eyes. "If I can do some work to fix your c-chapel, would that pay for my and Lainn's healing? Might it also p-pay for healing for my mother?"

Chapter Twenty-One

Between Crimthann's care and medicine, Conall's bumbling help, and Gemmán's singing, Lainn healed more quickly than Conall would have imagined. Granted, they'd both slept for two moons, but he almost had to learn how to walk again after sleeping for so long, so he figured she'd have to do the same.

But Lainn defied all expectations. She ran and laughed amongst the rolling hills within days, while Conall still tripped or stumbled, despite having woken a full three days earlier than she had. As soon as they could, they returned to their mother's roundhouse to care for her.

His mother, however, remained very ill. As weeks passed, Crimthann brought tinctures and prayers. Gemmán brought songs, and Lainn joined him in singing. But their mother raved and struck out at friend and foe alike.

Some days, she simply slept, sullenly pouting over their strictures. Other days, she tried to pull any man she saw into the cot with her, young or old, related or stranger.

In the darkest part of the night, her screams woke Conall, and he rushed to her side. She ranted about the trees coming to take her, and he wondered if Bodach was tormenting her. It sounded like something he would enjoy.

The days she raved like a *bean sídhe* were the worst. Her screeching wails cut across the woods and chilled the heart of all who heard. The scratches she inflicted on them tended to fester.

Some days, Conall could do nothing but cry over her sleeping form, his father's brooch in his hand, begging whatever magic infused the piece of jewelry to help him heal his mother. It never worked, but he kept the brooch close at all times. He didn't want to risk being too far from it.

When Crimthann came with his latest noxious potion, the odor impregnated the room with disgusting fumes. Conall almost gagged and didn't relish trying to get his mother to drink it. She'd barely eat the stew he cooked, and he knew darn well the stew tasted better than anything she'd ever made.

Crimthann wore a hopeful look that made Conall give a rueful chuckle. "If you expect her to d-drink that, you'd better administer it. She'll just bite my hand if I try."

The priest's mouth pressed into a grim line. He knelt by his mother's cot, but she ignored him. First, he prayed, his hands folded near his stomach, praising his God and asking for patience, luck, and healing for this good woman.

Next, he poured some of his potion into a mug. The stink permeated the room. Conall breathed through his mouth to avoid vomiting.

Then, the deacon spoke in a soft voice. "Ligach, I've brought something to make you feel better. Will you do me great honor as your guest and drink some? I would be most grateful for your help."

For a moment, Conall thought his clever words might work. His mother sat up and took notice of the mug he offered and blinked several times as if trying to focus.

With a snarl and a hiss, her hand snaked out and knocked the mug from Crimthann's hands, crashing it against the wall support. This made the stench worse, if that was possible, and Conall rushed outside. Crimthann followed upon his heels.

244

Conall paced outside, frustrated at this latest fiasco. Everything they'd tried over the last few weeks jumbled in his mind, each one a failure. He halted and rounded on the priest. "None of your healing works with her. I've d-done all the repairs on your cottage and built a well besides, and still, your healing is useless!"

The deacon retreated, his brow furrowing. "But I'm bringing the best medicines I know of, Conall! I can't think of anything else to do!"

Conall growled and resumed pacing. He wished Lainn were here, but she'd resumed her lessons with Gemmán and spent most of her time at the oak grove, leaving Conall to the house. He resented that she left him to care for their mother almost exclusively. She certainly never hurried back home after lessons. "It's not helping. If anything, she's g-getting worse."

"I wish I could offer more. Truly, I do, Conall. You must believe me."

"I don't. I don't believe anything anymore. Christian potions, D-Druidic magic, it's all nonsense. None of it *works!*"

Someone cleared their throat, and he spun to see Adhna behind him. He'd survived the Faerie Queen's wrath that night but refused to speak of the details to Conall. He'd been tirelessly working to help Conall's mother to recovery, along with both Gemmán and Crimthann. Everyone but Lainn, really. Still, nothing had worked.

Conall scowled at Adhna. "And what do you want, old man?"

The visitor blinked several times, glanced at Crimthann and his empty bottle, and offered Conall a reassuring smile. "I'm simply here to offer what comfort I can, Conall. To you or to your mother, whoever needs it most."

"Comfort! What use is c-comfort? I need healing. You promised to heal her with help from Faerie, and that obviously didn't work. Crimthann here tries p-potions and t-tinctures and prayers, and nothing made a bit of difference. They only make the place stink like pig shit. Gemmán sang to her, and his songs fall flat."

Gemmán and Lainn appeared at the other end of the yard, shock plain on both their faces.

Conall decided he'd had enough of them all. He waved his hands like he was clearing a field of chattering crows. "All of you, just get out! I don't want help from Faerie, or from the old gods, or from your d-dead God. None of the help is worth a thing! G-go away and don't come back."

Gemmán held out a hand as he approached, but Crimthann stopped him with some murmured words. The druid frowned and asked a question, but Crimthann shook his head. Conall glared at Lainn, daring her to say something, anything.

Gemmán's voice rose. "Why would you try that? No one's ever reported that to work, Crimthann."

Trying to keep his voice low, Crimthann mumbled some defense of his actions, but Gemmán furrowed his brow. "That makes no sense! Come, I think you need some another lesson in herblore before you attempt more healing. People are not for experimentation with every wild notion that comes to your head."

"We need to do something, Gemmán! That woman in there is dying, and we might be able to save her!"

The older man crossed his arms, frowning. "So, you want to give her every concoction you can think of? You might kill her before you cure her!"

Crimthann threw his potion bottle on the ground, and it bounced on the soft grass. "At least I'm trying something other than chanting nonsense songs to dead gods over her every day!"

Gemmán gripped his staff with both hands. "Oho! The truth comes out! Why did you seek my teaching, then, if you disdain the old gods so much? Go pray to your hanged God for salvation and see how far that gets you!"

Conall shouted a primal scream, the echoes of his voice reverberating through the woods. "Pox and boils! Enough, b-b-both of you! My mother is not a b-battlefield for your religion!"

Lainn placed her hand on Gemmán's shoulder, but he shrugged it away. "Sorry, lad. This needs to be settled, and I want an answer now. Crimthann, did you come to me in good faith to learn my path, or are you simply trying to find your enemies' weaknesses to further your own God?"

Crimthann smiled, his teeth gleaming white. "What would you give to know the truth, old man?" It wasn't a kind smile.

Thunder clouded Gemmán's eyes which would put any storm to shame. He began to chant while holding his staff horizontally across his body, gripped with both hands, and sparks flew from the wood. They crackled and danced as he sang, and the swirling carved symbols on his staff glowed, bathing his opponent in blue light.

The first time Conall had heard the old druid sing was with Lainn before they'd gone to Faerie. Then, his voice had been light and sweet, a soft caress on a warm, summer day.

Today, he didn't sing a pleasant, bucolic song of bees and butterflies. Today's tune was a martial song of strident phrases and strong refrain. His voice boomed across the clearing and soared into the air, to rustle the green, summer leaves.

The sun grew dim as the storm in his eyes formed above them with swirling clouds and dark thunderheads, creating a maelstrom. A chilly wind ripped through the surrounding woods, whipping leaves into eddies full of dancing green. Conall rubbed his eyes as the dust flew past him.

Conall tried to understand the words, but the druid's language felt ancient and primal. Some names poked through the jumble of syllables, such as the Dagda and Cerridwen, but the rest swirled in a dangerous soup of anger and retribution.

Thunder rumbled down through the trees and into the very earth, and the ground trembled beneath their feet.

Crimthann glanced up at the storm, but determination flashed across his face as he chanted back in Latin, the language of the Christian priests. Conall had no idea what he said, but it sounded ponderous and momentous, filled with compelling rhythm and robust language.

With another anxious glance at the sky, the Christian priest switched to their own language, his booming voice now resounding across the glade.

> *Christ has our host surrounded*
> *With clouds of martyrs bright,*
> *Who wave their palms in triumph*
> *And fire us for the fight.*
> *This Christ the cross ascended*
> *To save a world undone,*
> *And, suff'ring for the sinful,*
> *Our full redemption won.*

His tone didn't change, the force of the song was in the long syllables and harsh consonants. The storm began to scatter.

For a moment, Conall thought he'd dispel the druid's weather-working and stolen it for himself. However, Gemmán renewed his song and his clouds re-coalesced. Sparks of lightning danced across the sky, and the metallic scent of a summer storm swept the glade.

Soon, two thunderheads opposed each other above them, arches of heat lightning darting between each. As Gemmán increased his volume, one cloud grew.

Crimthann shouted his chants and the opposite cloud expanded until the entire sky had darkened to an ominous gray, flashing with almost constant flares of lightning. The metallic odor of ozone and burning leaves tickled his nose.

Lainn jumped between them, her hands out. "Stop it! This is ridiculous! Both of you are grown men, and this petty jealousy becomes neither of you!"

Crimthann's gaze was locked with Gemmán's as he shoved her out of the way, never pausing in his monotone chant. The priest reached into his robe and pulled out a golden cross, a symbol of his God's sacrifice. The cross glowed brightly in the dim light.

Gemmán paused as his eyes flickered to his young acolyte, but he sang louder after an apologetic shrug. The ground shook again as Conall leapt to grab Lainn from danger.

Before he reached his sister, Adhna cried out and fell into a crumpled heap as a shining star flashed next to him. The light grew so bright, Conall had to close his eyes from the pain.

He knew that pain. He recognized that light. The scent of wood ash and lavender permeated the clearing.

The brightness resolved into a voluptuous female form, taller than anyone in the yard. She was dressed for battle in shining bronze armor and a wicked-looking spear in her hand.

The Faerie Queen glared at each human, with a dismissive glance at Adhna at her feet. The older Fae moaned and crawled out of reach. Conall wanted to make certain he wasn't injured, but he could no longer move.

Both the priest and the druid had stopped singing. Conall didn't know if their actions were voluntary or if the Queen had forced them to stop. He suspected the latter.

"What transpires here? I sensed the workings of great magic in this place, and I do not tolerate such workings in my domain without permission."

Two shadows flickered behind the Queen. He squinted, trying to make out who accompanied her to the human realm. Eventually, the gnarled skin of Bodach came clear. His mother's ravings suggested that Bodach haunted her, bedeviling her with visions and fears.

Next to him, the white skin and ink-black hair of Ammatán made him catch his breath. Conall searched his ex-lover's eyes for any trace of affection or love. He found nothing but the raving rage he'd last seen as they escaped Faerie. He squeezed his eyes shut, wishing himself and Lainn anywhere but here, in this impossible place.

A crash behind him made him spin to see his mother, her mouth wide in a silent scream. She'd fallen on the threshold of the roundhouse, her arm stretched up to the Queen in supplication. She was frozen in place, unable to move or speak. Conall couldn't even go help her.

Lainn hummed.

It was low at first, but her hum grew louder and changed in tone as she slowly moved first her hand and then her arm. Her foot moved next, and she took an agonizingly sluggish step toward their mother. Conall watched in horrified fascination as her song cut through the Faerie Queen's magic.

Step by agonizing step, Lainn got closer to their mother. Their mother's eyes flick to both him and Lainn and back to the Queen. She seemed aware of her surroundings but unable to do anything about it. Conall mentally urged Lainn faster, cheering silently for her success.

The Queen screeched in a pitch so high, Conall barely heard it. The sound sliced into his mind, splitting into several tones. She pointed at Lainn, and her screech grew louder.

Conall ached to hold his hands over his ears and felt a trickle of something—Blood? Sweat—down the side of his neck. Red lights engulfed both Lainn and his mother, and Lainn collapsed, her still form not moving. Their mother sprawled on the ground, her eyes wide open and staring at the swirling stormy sky.

Conall knew, deep within his heart, his mother was dead. Part of him, an ungrateful, horrid part, felt relief at her passing. She'd be at peace now, no longer plagued by her waking nightmares. No longer haunted by Bodach. More selfishly, he realized he no longer needed to tend to her, no longer had the duty of a child to an uncaring parent.

Lainn moaned, and the other part of Conall's heart, already beginning to mourn both his mother and his sister, soared with hope and triumph. The Queen hadn't killed her!

Conall begged her silently to stay still, to keep the Queen from hurting her more. He tried to speak, to attract the Queen's attention away from his sister. It came out a creaking gasp.

The Queen's head swiveled to him, her terrifying regard now completely upon him. If he'd had any control over his muscles, he'd be shivering in horror.

Bodach stepped forward, bowing low to the Queen. "My Queen, may I beg your indulgence for a moment?"

Conall wanted to scream *no*. He knew Bodach meant no good for any humans, and to allow the Queen to listen to his idea would surely be to the detriment of all he held dear.

Ammatán also stepped forward, his mad eyes darting to each figure in the yard. Conall felt his heart break at the Fae's first words. "May I play with the humans, my Queen? I have many plans for each of them. None will be gentle, I assure you."

A moan from Adhna drew her attention instead. In a rasping, labored voice, the old Fae said, "My Queen, I have an idea that may also please you."

The Queen stared at each Fae in turn, obviously considering each. She nodded first to Adhna, evidently lifting the blanket of force from him. He struggled to his feet, but then immediately prostrated himself to her. She smiled. "Rise, Adhna. Have you a worthy suggestion for my treatment of these insects?"

He clasped his hands. "The children were not the cause of this battle. The druid and the priest cast the magic, as they were arguing about their relative power of healing. With the death of the patient, their battle has been rendered moot, and any punishment you wish to grant should be directed toward them. However, they do have the protection and regard of powerful gods. If you prefer, I may offer myself in exchange for their punishment."

Conall ached to stop Adhna, to tell him all about his own time in Faerie, his work for the Queen, and his night with Ammatán. Time gave him no chance. Time was a horrible master.

The Queen gave Adhna a counter-offer, but Conall couldn't pay attention, as Lainn moaned and reached a hand toward him. He inched nearer, and while Adhna and the Queen conversed, he clutched her hand so hard she squeaked. He tried to swallow past the lump in his throat but failed.

She whispered, "Mother's dead, Conall, and I'm dying. I can feel it."

"No, no, no! You'll be healed! I'll d-d-do everything I can to make things better, I promise."

She shook her head. "No, even Gemmán's magic won't heal this. I know just enough healing to realize the truth, Conall."

His father's words about keeping the brooch secret flitted through his mind, but he didn't care anymore. "I'll… I'll give you the brooch! That might work! Its magic may help."

"Brooch? You mean the one Da gave you?"

"Wait, you know about it?"

Her wan smile made his heart break. "I've always known about it, Conall. How could you think I didn't? We've lived together all our lives, silly. You could never keep a true secret from me."

He struggled against the Queen's magic to pluck the brooch from his pocket. When he unwrapped the white cloth, blood-red stones gleamed in the dim light, pulsing like a heartbeat within his palm. The brooch felt warm, despite the chilled wind that still flowed through the trees. Lainn's eyes grew wide, and she reached out.

When her fingers touched the entwined metallic animals, the brooch sparked and sizzled, like flint striking granite. She yelped and yanked her hand back in pain and surprise.

Her cry caught the attention of the still-arguing Fae. The glade grew heavy with silence as Bodach and Ammatán stalked toward him.

The Queen's voice cut through the awkward hush. "What have we here? More human magic? I thought you said the adult humans were the source of the magic, Adhna. You have lied to me!"

Her hair rose as if teased by the wind, forming a green halo of terrible beauty, the light behind her growing with drama and intensity. She looked even taller as her expression turned to rage. She bared her pointed teeth and opened her mouth as if to scream again.

Adhna held up his hand. "No, not in the slightest, my Queen! This magic, it's old Fae magic, I promise you. Nothing active, just a latent enchantment. The boy has had it all this time, hidden and harmless."

She mulled over his explanation, glancing again at Crimthann and Gemmán, still held immobile by her force.

Bodach and Ammatán both reached Conall, hands out to take the brooch. Bodach smiles so wide, Conall's blood grew cold. "Oh, this is a delightful artifact. Let me touch it, human child. Let me caress its delicious magic. It tastes familiar. Doesn't it taste familiar, Ammatán?"

The dark-haired Fae drew in a long breath, closing his eyes. He licked his lips in a sensual gesture, smiling as if he had just tasted the most luxurious of treats. "It smells delightful. I'm certain I've seen such a thing before, in another lifetime. I...I can't remember..."

His eyes darted to Conall and back to the brooch, a flicker of sanity flashing in his eyes. For a moment, he frowned and blinked, looking into Conall's eyes. A trace of affection shimmered within. "I... I know you... I think..."

Lainn gasped as Bodach touched her cheek with a gnarled finger. "This one is leaking life, my Queen. Do you wish her to live? Or may I feast upon her life-force? She has a juicy aroma. I would be delighted to devour her."

Ammatán's attention shifted to his sister. The madness returned in the Fae's eyes, and his smile grew, more horrifying than Bodach's. All trace of lucidity disappeared from Ammatán's eyes as his feral laughter tore through Conall's heart.

Lainn moaned and took a few quick breaths. Adhna leapt to her side. "My Queen! Take me to Faerie for punishment but allow this girl to come with me. She is dying as a human, but we can transform her into Faerie form and save her life. She has Fae blood, and I can train her as a loyal servant to you as Faerie, I promise!"

The Queen put a finger to her lips in a surprisingly human gesture. Conall whispered angrily to Adhna, "You would t-t-take Lainn away from me?"

The Fae whispered in urgent tones. "She's dying, you fool. Can't you see that? This is the only chance she has."

Conall shook his head. "As Fae? She won't be Lainn any longer."

"But she will live! She'll remember you. She can protect herself *and* you from Ammatán and Bodach. It's the only way, Conall."

"Why? Why would you d-do this? Aren't you offering yourself up for punishment for all this?"

"I promised your father long ago to watch after you, Conall. You and Lainn, both. If I can't remain here, I can at least watch after Lainn in Faerie."

Conall glanced at the Queen, but she was speaking with Ammatán about something and paid them no mind. "On one condition."

Adhna raised his eyebrows.

"Tell me if my father is alive."

Adhna let out a deep sigh. "For the sake of your sister, and keeping my vow for her, I must break another. Know that I cannot do this lightly, Conall. You've put me in a difficult situation."

Conall gestured toward the Queen. "More difficult than what she'll put you in?"

Letting out a short bark of laughter, Adhna shrugged. "Fair enough. As far as I know, your father is alive. I don't know where. Somewhere in Faerie or one of the Otherlands. He didn't wish to be found, as there are others who search for him. He'd be in great danger if they find him. If you *do* seek him, it may expose him to great peril. Keep that in mind, Conall."

Hope surging in Conall's heart. *Father lived!* Lainn wheezed, and he glanced to his sister, the to Adhna, and gave the Fae a single nod.

The Queen evidently completed her consultation with the Fae and took two steps toward them. "I have made my decision, Adhna. I shall accept your proposal, and this human shall become my attendant. You may train her as the rest of your punishment."

Ammatán spoke up. "But she will be mine! You promised!"

"Yours to claim kinship with, but not to train."

Conall frowned. "Kinship?"

The Queen scowled at him, censure at his interruption apparent. "Because she has Fae blood, he has claimed her as a sister."

Conall felt ready to cry in frustration. "I don't understand!"

Adhna placed a hand on his shoulder. "I'll explain in a moment."

That tiny spark of sympathy glimmered once again in Ammatán's eyes before getting lost in the madness. Was that the Fae's way of reassuring Conall that he'd watch over Lainn? That he'd keep Bodach from harming her? But that may have simply been Conall's over-active imagination and hopeless optimism.

The Queen and Bodach vanished in a clap of thunder and a flash of green light. Everyone in the yard could move again. Both the priest and the druid gasped and bent over, coughing and spitting. Ammatán sat against a tree, gripping his knees together with both hands.

Conall turned to Adhna. "Explain, Adhna!"

The old Fae knelt beside Lainn, her breathing more difficult now. "Her mother was Fae. And yours, in truth."

"What? What are you t-talking about? Our mother was human! You knew her. She just died! How could she be Fae?"

Adhna shook his head. "Fae can die, but it's more difficult. That woman in there, Ligach, the woman who raised you as her own? That's not your mother, Conall."

Lainn gasped and coughed. "What?"

"Your true mother, Ellbrig, had been a Fae woman of uncommon beauty and grace, and a dear friend of mine. She did die, many years ago, when your father knew her. She died giving birth to her second human child, a lovely girl with the sunrise in her eyes." He smiled down at Lainn who tried to smile back.

Conall couldn't even think about what that meant now. He scowled at the Fae. "What else aren't you t-t-telling me?"

"Patience, Conall. When she left him with two children and no wife, Fíngin found a human wife willing to take his children as her own."

"Why does Ammatán claim Lainn is his sister?"

Adhna closed his eyes for a long moment, gripping his staff. "Because Ammatán is distantly related to Ellbrig, your real mother."

Cold gripped Conall's stomach. "Ammatán is related to us?"

"He's really more like a distant cousin, but such relations among Faerie are fluid."

"And our mother? I mean, Ligach? Why did she n-never say anything?"

"She vowed never to tell you, though I knew. That's one reason she never liked you visiting me. When Fíngin had to leave, he charged me with your care."

"B-but you said he is still alive somewhere?"

Lainn gasped again, which turned into another cough.

Conall had to make a decision now, a decision that would change his life and Lainn's forever. He'd made many poor decisions in his past, both for himself and for others. But he couldn't risk letting that happen again. He must do what he must to help Lainn live. She deserved that much, at the very least.

He took Lainn's hand. "We haven't t-t-time to discuss this now. Lainn needs your help. Keep her safe, Adhna. I trust you, over all others."

"I vow to do so, Conall. For now, and unto seven generations, I shall watch over your family."

The air shimmered and crackled as the earth accepted the powerful vow. Adhna took Lainn's hands and stared into her eyes. Hers grew wide as the power crackled along his arms to hers, blue and green sparks glowing in the dusk. "Do you accept this transformation of your own free will, human child? Will you become a true Fae? You must take on a new name, a new appearance. Your skin may change. You may grow taller or shorter. Your personality may change."

Lainn nodded with another cough before she whispered, "I do accept this transformation."

Gemmán drew closer and gripped Conall's shoulder as they watched. He'd almost forgotten about the druid.

Blue-green light resolved into dancing sparks. Lainn and Adhna both shut their eyes and threw their heads back as the very woods around them thrummed with power.

Lights swirled into complex entwined patterns, similar to the markings on Gemmán's staff. This glowed as well, and Gemmán held it out to offer any help he could to the magic. Behind them, Crimthann spit and cursed, but didn't interfere.

The two floated a handspan above the ground, turning in a slow circle as the lights grew brighter, enveloping them in a mass of glowing embers. The thrum turned into a hum that sounded both joyful and dangerous.

When the lights finally dimmed, Adhna stood before him as a much younger man, hair dark brown rather than shot with gray. His beard had shortened by at least an arms' length.

Instead of his sister standing next to the old Fae, a tall, slim young woman with skin the shade of a robin's egg and dark hair stood, examining her arms with wide eyes. She held out her long fingers, wiggling them in experimentation, and looked at the ends of her hair. "I won't miss the red hair, that's for certain!"

Her labored breathing had eased, and she seemed perfectly healthy, if alien. Conall took a tentative step forward. "Lainn?"

She shook her head. "Adhna said I should have a new name. I think…" She glanced around for inspiration and smiled. "Flidasinn. It sounds musical."

A single bee buzzed around her head as she and Adhna both faded from sight in a shower of sparks.

Chapter Twenty-Two

Conall shouldered his sack and glanced up at Gemmán. The old druid had reluctantly agreed to introduce him to this set of druids, but he didn't approve of Conall's purpose.

"You know more than most how dangerous such a venture would be, son. You have a home, a trade, and a future. Why would you squander it away on such a mad quest?"

Conall shook his head. "I appreciate your counsel, but how can I *not* search for my f-father? I've buried Ligach and Sétna and properly honored their memory as tradition dictates. I've given you the roundhouse so you might continue your school. I've taken care of all my duties. That part of my life is finished."

"Your father evidently doesn't wish to be found. Perhaps you should respect his wishes. Besides, Aoife would like you to stay. Her husband is dead, and her children need a father."

"Adhna said he doesn't want his enemies to find him. But I'm not an enemy, I'm his son! Besides, I should let him know of Ligach's death. And of Lainn's... change. As for Aoife," Conall shook his head, "she's attractive enough to find any number of husbands who would be far more interested in her charms than I would ever be."

Gemmán nodded, but the unhappiness stayed in his eyes. "I miss Lainn and mourn the loss of such a promising student. Still, she'll likely live a much longer and richer life than as a human. I wish her well. If you should see her, please pass on my love."

Conall nodded. "I will. Are you certain the d-druids at Uisneach will allow me to use the Old Way into Faerie?"

"If you had approached them on your own, most certainly not. But I shall vouch for both your worth and discretion. Keep in mind this might not be a valid passage back to the human realm. While the Old Ways remain open on this side, they change in Faerie. Or it may become dangerous to return this way. Those two that accompanied the Queen didn't look like they were the welcoming sort."

Conall shoved down the memory of his erstwhile lover and Ligach's tormenter. "The white-skinned Fae had been our friend before a tragedy turned him to madness. It's possible he will recover. If I find my father, I may return to see if I can help with that."

Unexpectedly, Gemmán drew him in for a fierce embrace. "I wish you luck with that, lad. You have a great store of patience, despite your frustration with your mother's healing, and a strong faith in people. I hope your faith is rewarded."

Gemmán's expression grew dour, likely recalling his faith in his most recent student.

Conall took a few steps and then turned back. "Did you find out what happened to Crimthann? After the incident at our house, I mean?"

The druid gave a scowl. "Crimthann didn't come back to be taught, of course. He decided the Christian faith was the only one of any worth, and became rather vociferous against my *interference,* as he termed it. The last I heard, he'd moved to some island in Alba to start his own enclave of priests. He even changed his name. He's calling himself 'the Dove of the Church,' if you can believe that."

"Him? A d-d-dove?" Conall couldn't stop the laughter bubbling into his voice.

Gemmán cracked a smile. "Aye, a dove. Fox suited him much more clearly. But he's adopted the name *Columba* and hopes to make a name for himself. He's got the education and the ambition. Perhaps he might even do some good along the way. We can only hope so."

The entrance to the druid's grove came into view, and they fell silent.

Gemmán wasn't personally known by most of the druids. As a solitary teacher, he wasn't part of the grove. Yet, all teachers of the lore were highly respected, and he'd achieved a high rank amongst them.

He made formal introductions and when he finally parted from Conall, they embraced again. "Keep yourself safe, young man. You've grown much in the time I've known you, but you have even more potential if you don't squander it with foolishness."

Conall gave him a knowing half-smile. "I'll try to think what you might do in my place, or Adhna."

"For a Fae, he was a good man. There are many worse examples to emulate."

With a final clap on the shoulder, Gemmán left him in the care of Dianaim, an older druid. With a silent nod, she led him to the stone circle within the grove.

Dianaim handed him a plain wooden staff. "Take this gift with our blessing, young quester. Gemmán explained some of your purpose. We shall welcome you back to the human realm if you return this route."

"I th-thank you."

She gave a curt nod. "Walk around the stones three times, sunwise, chanting the words Gemmán taught you. Then enter through the eastern gap, here. When you do so, the world should change. You have been to Faerie before, is that correct?"

Conall nodded, his stomach doing flips. He shouldered his sack, complete with traveling food, the bronze knife, and his brooch.

"This portal has led to a peaceful spot in Faerie in the past, but they shift. I cannot guarantee your arrival place, but if it hasn't changed, a small *túath* of friendly Fae lay not too far away. They can help you begin your search."

With more confidence than he felt, Conall began the circuit around the stones. The first resulted in no effect, but the second made the air shimmer and sparkle. By the third circuit, the air grew thick, as if he was pushing through water.

The last few steps were a hard slog through thick honey. The light dimmed to darkness, and he had to work to push forward.

When he finally broke through the other side, the familiar non-light of Faerie greeted him, with rolling soft blue hills and several festiwings. He watched them flitter by with a bittersweet memory of Lainn's fascination with them.

Perhaps, if he found his father, he could tell him about Lainn and her love of the festiwings. Even if he daren't seek her out while she was in the Queen's service, he could keep her alive in his memory.

He picked a direction, shifted the sack across his shoulders, and began his new quest.

A barely remembered childhood. A search for a mystical treasure. Can a gentle man fill in his past and be reunited with his birthright?

Ireland, 500. Fingin lives from hand to mouth. And though his mind is as clear as any, the shy fisherman avoids others for fear his terrible stutter will make him look mad. But the day he rescues a dog from drowning, his special ability to speak to animals leads to an unbreakable bond.

Can Fingin survive brutal thugs, treacherous crossings, and faery magic to fulfill his destiny?

Buy *Age of Secrets* to step beyond the veil today!

https://www.amazon.com/gp/product/B0B6D9CGLS

Thank You!

Thank you so much for enjoying Age of Saints. If you've enjoyed the story, please consider leaving a review so other readers can discover Conall and Lainn's adventures!

If you would like to get updates, sneak previews, sales, and contests, please sign up for my newsletter.

https://greendragonartist.com/about/newsletter-2/

Other Books by This Author

**See all the books available
through Green Dragon Publishing at**
http://www.greendragonartist.com/books

Pronunciation Guide

People
Adhna—/Eye-na/
Áine—/Aw-nye/
Ammatán—/Om-ah-tawn/
Aoibheall—/Ee-vul/
Bodach—/Bud-ukh/
Conchobhair- /Kruh-khoor/
Crimthann- /Krih-hin/
Cú Chulainn—/Koo Khu-lun/
Deichtire—/Jeh-chir-eh/
Dianaim—/Jeen-em/
Flidaisínn—/Flee-sheen/
Gréine de Leicne Bán—/Gray-nye jeh Lek-neh Bawn/
Rawninn —/Raw-nin/
Oonagh—/Oo-na/
Sawchaill—/Saw-khil/
Sencha—/Sen-uh-kha/
Setanta—/Se-tan-ta/

Places
An Mhi/ Mide—Meath /on Vee/ /Mee/
Cnoc an Dúin—Hill of Down /Kruk on Doo-in/
An Bhóinn—The Boyne River /On Voh-in/
Maelblatha—Mullingar /Mayl-blah-ha/
Cnoc Uisneach—Hill of Uisneach /Kruk Ish-nukh/
an Mhumhain—Munster /On Woo-in/
an Chláir—Clare /On Khlaw-ir/
Tiobraid Árann—Tipperary /Tib-red Aw-ren/
Sliabh Fuaid—/Shleev Foo-id/
Tír na nÓg—Land of the Ever Young /Cheer nah Nohg/
Cluain Eraird—Clonard /Kloo-in Er-erd/
Fir Rois—Airgialla /Fihr Rish/

Other

Alban Eilir—Spring Equinox /Ol-bon El-ir/

Bean sídhe—Banshee, a female spirit who presaged death by wailing /Ban-shee/

Caoin—to wail in grief (keen)

Fochlac—Druid rank, 2ⁿᵈ year /Fukh-luk/

Forrach—About 40 yards /Fur-rukh/

Géis—A curse or requirement /gesh/

Iníon fuirmedh—Druid rank, 3ʳᵈ year (female) /In-yeen foor-may/

Léine/léinte—A long belted tunic (singular/plural) /Lay-na/ /Layn-tah/

Túath—Medieval extended household /Too-ah/

Dedication

Many thanks to the wonderful folks in my authors' group, who continue to offer valuable feedback and encouragement of course, as well as my fantastic beta and ARC readers.

Siobhán of Bitesize Irish has been delightful in her help with proper Irish pronunciations for my increasing list of Irish words.

I also thank Walker Metalsmiths of New York for the use of their wonderful brooch for inspiration for the cover art.

Author Note

The 6th century in Ireland was a time of great change. The Christian religion had only recently gained a foothold upon its emerald shores, and the change amongst its people grew slowly. Even today, strong elements of the pagan past shine through Celtic Christianity. St. Columba, born Crimthann, is but one of three patron saints of Ireland, along with St. Patrick and St. Brigid. He took Christianity from Ireland to Alba's shores. Still, the details of the new religion hadn't yet filtered down into the small *túatha* of rural Ireland.

As a nation, Ireland wasn't called such until later in history. At this time, the people were Milesians or Éirish and called their land Éire.

About the Author

Christy Nicholas writes under several pen names, including Rowan Dillon, CN Jackson, and Emeline Rhys. She's an author, artist, and accountant. After she failed to become an airline pilot, she quit her ceaseless pursuit of careers that begin with the letter 'A' and decided to concentrate on her writing. Since she has Project Completion Compulsion, she is one of the few authors with no unfinished novels.

Christy has her hands in many crafts, including digital art, beaded jewelry, writing, and photography. In real life, she's a CPA, but having grown up with art all around her (her mother, grandmother, and great-grandmother are/were all artists), it sort of infected her, as it were. She wants to expose the incredible beauty in this world, hidden beneath the everyday grime of familiarity and habit, and share it with others. She uses characters out of time and places infused with magic and myth, writing magical realism stories in both historical fantasy and time travel flavors.

Social Media Links:
Blog: www.GreenDragonArtist.net
Website: www.GreenDragonArtist.com
Facebook: www.facebook.com/greendragonauthor
Instagram: www.instagram.com/greendragonartist9
TikTok: www.tiktok.com/@greendragonauthor